The Honeymoon

THE HONEYMOON

JANE E. JAMES

JOFFE BOOKS

Joffe Books, London
www.joffebooks.com

First published in Great Britain in 2025

Cover art by Nick Castle

ISBN: 978-1-83526-975-6

For Karen and Graham

PROLOGUE: THE SURVIVOR

The sights and sounds of Bali are the first and last memories I have of my honeymoon and rather short-lived marriage. The island's natural beauty and the gentle smiles of its people are beyond words. From the moment we arrived at our five-star luxury resort in Indonesia, we were shielded from the outside world by a privileged tranquillity. I held on to that feeling tightly, as if I was entitled to it. All of us did.

We had been promised white beaches, azure skies and warm waters so there was a palpable sense of excitement in the air. We were the latest honeymooners to arrive on the private island, which could only be reached by speedboat, along with two other couples. The fact that the locals referred to our resort as "Black Magic Island" was unknown to us at the time.

Our charming concierge Putu made sure we were waited on like kings and queens. All of us newlyweds clicked right away. Given that we were young, rich and in love, why wouldn't we when we had so much in common? More than we could ever have imagined as it turned out.

Back then none of us realised our pasts had already collided without our knowledge, and that this would cause a disastrous ripple effect that would ultimately destroy us all.

Just how we were all connected was quite the mystery at first, but all would be revealed gradually over time. That is how the island works. The pace and way of life is slow.

But let's go back to those first magical moments in paradise, when I still believed that dreams could come true but discovered instead that it was a place where one could easily fall out of love.

As a group, we did everything together, racing mopeds through the dusty mango groves, visiting the sacred monkey forest and roaming the rice terraces. After an arduous trek up an active volcano, during which one of us nearly lost our life, we watched the spectacular sunrise from Mount Batur. Looking back, that near-death experience was an omen of things to come . . . Nobody can forget the tragic conclusion to our trip to Tegenungan waterfall where everything began to unravel. We weren't to know that even greater dangers lurked in the shadows. Like who was trying to kill who, or were we all trying to kill each another?

I will always cherish the memories of visiting the bustling local spice markets, exploring the vibrant temples and bathing in the lurid-green holy waters, but the truth is my husband and I should never have married. I knew that even before we exchanged rings. Both of us had lied about our pasts and continued to keep dark secrets from one another. Our marriage was doomed from the moment we set foot on the island.

People are meant to survive tsunamis, avalanches and wars, not honeymoons. Nevertheless, that's what I have done. I am the sole survivor.

We were promised fourteen days and nights of paradise, but it didn't take that long for our secrets to surface, like something dead in the water . . . like the bodies discovered on days three, five, seven, nine and eleven.

CHAPTER 1: SAMANTHA

'You sigh too much,' Nathan comments a little too nonchalantly, considering there's a warning tightness in his jawline that makes me uneasy.

'Says who?' I force a smile onto my face, not wishing to start a fight on our honeymoon, but even so, I can feel his discontent smouldering away like the raging active volcano we are intending to climb before daybreak tomorrow. I've been told that it's a three-hour hike in the dark, and I'm not looking forward to it. It's not exactly my idea of a honeymoon activity.

'Way too much, actually,' he sulks, fumbling with the buttons on his linen shirt, which he will only roll up to the elbow once he's outside because although it's barely nine o'clock it's already thirty-one degrees.

Now that my new husband is finally out of the ensuite, I intend to take a shower myself, so I grab a moist towel off the floor because it appears he's used them all, and I'm about to enter the massive marble his and hers bathroom when he points an accusing finger at me and complains, 'They'll be wanting to know what you've got to sigh about being married to me.'

Ah, so that's what this is about. His ego. Nothing to do with me at all then. But why should that surprise me? Haven't I always known that Nathan's needs take precedence over mine? He's built that way and he's not afraid to admit it nor go after what he wants. Just as he did with me. I foolishly believed it to be love, but looking back I see that his passion for me was more like an obsession. And, since he has sacrificed so much to be with me, as he likes to remind me daily, I feel obligated to stay with him. Where else would I go anyway? It's not as though I have any other family.

'By *they*, do you mean the other married couples? Timothy and Jonah and Angelika and Bartosz?'

'If you say so,' Nathan mumbles as if names are unimportant to him. As indeed they are. Unless they come with a CEO title.

My husband's hidden bald patch, like our age gap of fifteen years, is a sensitive topic for him, and it's only visible to me because I'm five inches taller than he is — *another sore spot* — fortunately, he has an abundance of floppy blond hair at the front of his head to distract eyes away from his thinning pate. Although he works out at the gym, he's in danger of being considered chubby if he puts on any more weight. Part of me is riddled with guilt as I think this. God forbid I should mention that to him even though he sometimes criticises my flaws in public. He boasts that I'm "a work in progress" as if he's moulding me into the wife he's always wanted and feels he deserves after spending so much money on the last two. This is nothing new. It's not like he ever kept any of his personality traits hidden. He takes pride in being a straight-talking businessman and is the first to admit, even to strangers, that he can be brutally honest, to the point of being hurtful. Except, in my opinion, that level of candour is rarely asked for, embraced or needed.

'You don't usually care what other people think,' I observe with a frown as I take off my silky dressing gown, allowing it to float to the floor at my feet. Nathan's blue-eyed gaze wanders to my long limbs, flat stomach, and small but perfectly formed breasts with all the eagerness of a second-hand car salesman. I don't get worked up about nudity as some women do. It's one of the rare things Nathan appreciates about me, even though he'd prefer that I smile more, exercise more, tan more. Be more . . .

With my waist-long flame-red hair, copper freckles and white, almost translucent complexion, I would much rather sit in the shade with a book in my hand and an oversized straw hat on my head than spend an entire day in the sun like the other couples on the island do. I also don't drink, unlike the majority of holidaymakers here. Since it's an all-inclusive resort, I worry Nathan might be tempted to drink more than is good for him. *Us.*

He gives up trying to button the shirt, flapping his hands impatiently and appearing a little helpless as he admits, 'I just don't want the others to think I don't satisfy you, that's all.'

At that, I arch an eyebrow, almost amused. *Almost.* Because since when was satisfying me a priority. But then I remember that he once told me sarcasm doesn't look good on me, although red lacey underwear does apparently. Am I just a body to him, I wonder? Were we ever in love?

A flicker of annoyance passes over his handsome-and-he-knows-it face as he turns away with a wounded look, but I'm distracted by the enviable balcony view of the pool and the beach. Nathan had to have both. One was simply not an option. Or enough. Like the multiple wives and children he's already abandoned. I can make out the palm trees swaying on the beachfront, beckoning us to join them on the powder-soft sand. The scent of coconut permeates the air, while the sun-loving flowers of the frangipani plants fall to the balcony floor like confetti, a reminder of why we are here.

Yet the idea of a full English breakfast moves my husband far more than this slice of paradise. He may be able to conceal his receding hairline from the rest of our party, but he is unable to cover up the rumblings of hunger coming from his

5

stomach. I find myself sighing again, more heavily this time, when I see the room key clenched in his sweaty palm and I realise that he isn't going to wait for me so we can go down to breakfast together.

It's on the tip of my tongue to snap, 'So much for romance,' but I catch myself just in time. Because if I were to ask him how he felt about me he would say something like, 'Well, I married you, didn't I?' as if I could never ask for anything more. Neither he nor I listen to each other and seem unable to get past this situation. Nathan believes he has the perfect solution. He thinks having a baby will fix us. And by that he means *me*.

What I can't tell him is that I'm already a mother and therefore beyond fixable — because I gave up my child for adoption when I was twenty-one, single and broke. My son, who I think about every day, was born with the same red hair as me and would now be four years old. I never dared hope I would see him again, not before he was eighteen anyway . . . should he decide to come looking for me.

Imagine how I felt when I arrived on the island and met Timothy and Jonah's adopted child Connor, who is travelling with them on their honeymoon, and instantly recognised him as my own.

CHAPTER 2: TIMOTHY

I'm in the resort's main restaurant eating nasi goreng, an Indonesian meal made of fried rice with chicken and vegetables, and kolak pisang, a dish of boiled banana and coconut milk, which is all unexpectedly delicious . . . when I unintentionally glance at the man with the perspiring underarms who is sitting at the opposite table. It's the same man who introduced himself yesterday as "Price, Nathan Price" like he was James Bond. His forceful, confident handshake made me take an instant dislike to the *man's man*, as I labelled him in my head. Unfair, I know, but there was something about the arrogant manner in which he approached us, as though he were in some way superior to everyone else, that put my back up.

I see that he is tucking into a large plateful of fried bacon, sausages and eggs instead of any of the local Balinese dishes. A typical Brit abroad, then, which leads me to suspect that you get what you see with this guy and there aren't likely to be any surprises. He was just as predictable with his misogynistic remarks at the bar last night which had my new husband, Jonah, in stitches. He and I couldn't be more dissimilar; hence why he took a shine to Price, whereas I would have been content to ignore him for the duration of our stay. Compared to me, Jonah is a lot easier to get along with. He comes across as bitchy but he's actually too nice for his own good. It tends to get him in trouble. However, I suppose he wouldn't be with me if he wasn't kind, as there's a lot to put up with and even more to forgive. God knows I try to be the perfect friend, lover, husband and father but it doesn't come naturally to me as it does Jonah. He genuinely is a sweetie.

Of course, we both adore our son Connor. We jumped through enough hoops as part of the adoption process to get him and felt like the luckiest people alive when we finally brought him home with us when he was nine months old. However, our son can occasionally be a handful. Correction, our son is more often than not a spoiled brat. Sometimes I think setting some firm boundaries and taking a tough stance would be good for him but Jonah, who had a miserable childhood, insists on us raising him using gentle and liberal parenting techniques involving the three c's. That's communication, connection and consistency, for the likes of you and me. Although I'm not always in favour of allowing Connor, who is only four, to make his own decisions, I try to go along with it for Jonah's sake.

I can't help but snigger when I see a blob of alarmingly red ketchup drip from a spoon onto Price's impeccably ironed white linen shirt. As he looks around to see if anyone has spotted his faux pas, I hastily avert my gaze, guessing that he wouldn't welcome being laughed at. I see him angrily shove his plate away and get up to leave, one hand covering the scarlet stain across his heart that gives the impression he has just been stabbed. Serves him right for calling me Tim, even though I introduced myself as "Timothy, not Tim" as I always do. Jonah doesn't see why I get so worked up over people shortening my name, but in my opinion, this is an insult to my mother, may she rest in peace, because that's the one she gave me. Brought up on the toughest, poorest streets of Dublin as a gay Irish catholic who was also a mummy's boy means I've earned the right to take offence if I want to.

Price's wife though, whose name I can't remember just now, seemed lovely. Very graceful and serene with hidden depths, I suspect. God knows what she's doing with a bore like him. With those aqua-blue eyes and milk-white skin, I would love to paint her. Don't get me wrong, I don't think of myself as a professional artist or anything like that, but I do like to dabble from time to time. She has definitely awakened my creative interest. As for that gorgeous titian hair, she looks less like somebody's wife and more like one of those models you see in Renaissance paintings in stately homes.

Now that I think of it, Connor's thick mop of unruly hair is almost the same shade. Everyone says he's a handsome boy, and he used to have such beautiful hair, but since he decided he no longer wants it brushed it's become matted and untidy. There are moments when I feel ashamed to be seen with my son — not just because of his messy hair but also because of his terrible behaviour. Not that I'm allowed to mention it. Jonah would wipe the floor with me if I dared to suggest Connor isn't perfect.

I owe Jonah for tending to Connor this morning and letting me eat breakfast by myself. He's the stay-at-home spouse and our boy's primary carer, except when he's in daycare, so he takes on the lion's share of parental duties. The change came as a surprise to both of us. Who'd have thought the one-time shrewd property developer and entrepreneur would have the patience to be a full-time dad and homemaker? But as it happens, he's a natural at both. I'll return the favour and let Jonah enjoy breakfast by himself tomorrow since eating with Connor can be a nightmare due to the amount of food that gets flung around. However, he's likely to refuse, because as far as he's concerned, *there are three people on this honeymoon.* Jonah did not forgive me for weeks after I suggested we leave our precious boy at home as you only get one honeymoon, but my husband, who can be quite obstinate when he wants to be, wouldn't hear of it.

While I tend to be reserved, Jonah is the life of the party. He is impulsive, whereas I'm risk averse. Touch is his love language, and I dislike public displays of affection. I'm the bad mood he never wakes up with and if I am sometimes distant with Jonah it's because I worry he hasn't truly gotten over his ex. "His one true love" as I once heard him describe Noah (even their names rhymed) died of food poisoning while on a cruise, and poor Jonah was inconsolable for a very long time. I've always felt second best despite knowing how much he loves me. But if he is hiding his true feelings from me, who am I to judge when I have the biggest secret of all?

I made every effort to talk Jonah out of choosing Bali for our honeymoon but was unable to change his mind. No one is aware — not even my new husband — that this is not my first visit to the island. I've been here before, a long time ago, and I'm still haunted by the crime I committed *and* got away with. My greatest fear came true when I stepped off the boat and walked straight into the one person from my past who also knew my secret.

And now that he's entered the restaurant, he's grinning at me . . . letting me know that he hasn't forgotten me. He knows exactly who I am.

CHAPTER 3: ANGELIKA

He barely notices us as he pushes past us, seeming intent on exiting the restaurant as fast as he can, yet my eyes linger on him. I recognised him straight away. Of course I did. How could I not? The punter from whom I'd pilfered money all those years ago. I haven't always been a highly sought-after translator, commanding exorbitant hourly rates due to my proficiency in five languages. I was once a sex worker. But my appearance has changed a lot since those days, for the better I might add, because last night at the bar, he didn't seem to recognise me. Then again, he was always self-centred. Also, he didn't used to go by the name of Nathan. He'd clearly given me a fictitious name. But so had I, going by the name of Anzela as it was much sexier than Angelika. Nathan hadn't amassed his wealth at this point either. He was still a struggling businessman. That's why he was furious when he discovered I had stolen a grand out of his wallet after he passed out drunk on the bedroom floor of a cheap two-star hotel.

He informed my coworkers that he had planned to use that money to close a business deal and was screwed without it. I was long gone by the time he woke up, but without that money, I was screwed too, since my ailing mother was living with me at the time so I could help take care of her, and I was being threatened with eviction for rent arrears. I believed that I was in far greater need of that money, so his threats to find me and pay me back for what I had done went unheeded. It appears that he owes me a favour anyway because, from what I understand, the business venture he'd wanted to be a part of had failed spectacularly.

In the end, the money didn't do me any good either because the landlords evicted us anyway, leaving me and my mum homeless. After that, she had to move into a hospice and passed away soon after. For that, I will never be able to forgive those faceless money-grabbing bastards who never had any intention of letting us stay because they realised they could make a killing on the property in our so-called "up and coming" red-light area. They were rich property developers from Bristol, and if I ever run into either of them, I will stab them in the heart.

Bartosz hushes me anytime I use language like this for fear that people will take me at my word and read too much into it, but it's just the way I am. Passionate and fiery. We both grew up in the same rural village in east Poland before migrating to the city of Lublin, where he worked his way up from pot washer to chef and I became a sex worker and made decent money for the first time in my life. I thought I had it made when I went to England and sent for my sick mother. However, because I lacked the necessary credentials, I was forced to work the streets again instead of pursuing my dream career as a translator. Bartosz and I didn't cross paths again until after my mother died. He was a head chef by then, so he paid for me to attend Cardiff University, where I received my degree in translation three years later. Our love was so strong that we made it through those first few challenging years even though Bartosz was gone for a good portion of that time working on cruise ships and travelling the world.

Since Bartosz now owns a successful chain of restaurants in Bath and I'm doing well in my chosen profession as a home-based translator specialising in Polish, Russian, Lithuanian, Latvian and English, we agreed it was the right time for us to get married, although we've decided against having children. Instead, we have our fur babies, Hunter and Chase, a pair of identical Belgian Malinois. I miss the dogs desperately and can't wait to return home to see them again. If it were up to me, I would have stayed in England and taken our honeymoon somewhere where the dogs could go too, but Bartosz wanted me to see some of the world as he's convinced I'm missing out. I should be grateful, and I am, but I'm a homebody, so it doesn't bother me if I don't leave the house for days at a time, except to walk the dogs. I have so much to thank my new husband for. He's a good man. The best. Without him, I would die. That might sound fanciful but it's the truth. When I love, I love passionately. I am nothing if not loyal.

Bartosz is fully aware of my background and, unlike most men, he never brings up my past as a way of punishing me. He is a man in a million. And because we are each other's family, we don't keep secrets from one another. Bartosz was orphaned at a young age and for most of his life, there was only him and his twin brother, but Stanislaw, who had been ill for some time, died five years ago from a heart attack after confronting a road rage driver. Bartosz has never recovered from the loss of his twin, and he continues to blame the other driver for his death. After all, he was the one who started it. He got out of the car first and was the one to poke a finger in his brother's chest. The man couldn't have known that Stanislaw had a heart problem but that didn't make him any less guilty in Bartosz's eyes. But as no blows were exchanged and the man called an ambulance when he realised his opponent was in trouble, he walked free from court.

Quite why I haven't mentioned to my husband that Nathan is a former client of mine, is a mystery to me. Why haven't I? Is it because I sense Bartosz is also, for the first time, keeping something from me? Last night at the bar, he was exceptionally quiet, *he is a man of few words at the best of times, especially among strangers,* but the way he kept staring at the other guests unnerved me as if he too had met one of them before. My husband is not jealous as a rule but having never come face to face with a man who has slept with his wife before, *even if he did have to pay for the privilege,* is not something the majority of men would be comfortable with, so I think on this occasion, seeing as Bartosz seems to be struggling with his own issues, remaining silent might be the best option.

Also, I may have omitted to tell Bartosz about taking the money from Nathan's wallet. Unlike some, I am not ashamed of my lurid past since a girl needs to do what she has to in order to survive. But Bartosz prides himself on being a hard-working, honest, upstanding individual — and although he can forgive me for having slept with hundreds of men because it was "my job" and not through choice — he would be upset to learn that his new bride is nothing but a common thief.

CHAPTER 4: SAMANTHA

I'm relaxing in the shade beneath the canopy of a luxurious beach bed with a cloud of white billowing drapes encircling it. As I lean against a stack of silk cushions, I use a straw to sip my coconut water, served in a whole young coconut. People watching through my shades is a favourite pastime of mine, but it makes me realise how very plain my black swimsuit is in comparison to the revealing tropical-print bikinis the other women are wearing.

The only other bride who wears anything even halfway as modest as me is Angelika who we had drinks with last night, along with her husband. When I say *had drinks* with, what I really mean is that I had a polite mocktail or two before retiring to bed at 9 p.m. After twenty-four hours of travelling, I was exhausted. I cannot fall asleep on aeroplanes, unlike Nathan, who crashes anywhere. Although he tried to persuade me otherwise, flying business class didn't make any difference. I assume it was the unlimited booze that caused him to nod off for almost the entire flight. I have no idea what time Nathan crawled back to our room last night, only that he was there when I woke up, with his familiar red-blooded male gaze. Sex was on his mind as usual. You could argue this was to be expected. It is, after all, our honeymoon. He's always in the mood, though. Unlike me.

On that thought, I sigh deeply, knowing I can because Nathan isn't sitting next to me. Never one to stay still for too long, he's out there swimming in the gorgeous blue water right now. Knowing how much he needs to be admired, I wave to him every time his head comes up out of the sea, like a small child, to let him know that I'm still watching him. Although he can't see my expression from all the way out there, my face passes through the same admiring nods and smiles expected of it. It's as though I'm cheering him on every time he dives, floats, backstrokes and crawls through the water. Again, like a small boy. As if I were his mother!

Sadly, the boy I'm convinced is my actual son isn't at the beach today. I haven't seen anything of his adopted parents Timothy or Jonah either, which is a shame, as I'm only out here at all in the hope of being allowed to help Connor build sandcastles in the sand. Usually, I'd find a nice shadowy corner and hide myself away from everyone else. Disappointed, I set down my drink after one last noisy suck on the squashed end of my straw and restlessly take up my romance novel.

I give up all pretence at trying to read it when a small black shadow appears over me. Glancing up, I see that it is Angelika and she's grinning playfully at me.

'Samantha, isn't it?'

'Yes. Hi.'

'I'm going to grab some lunch. Would you like to join me?'

Taken aback by her offer, I'm still thinking about how to respond when she entices me with—

'Don't be shy. And please don't say no.'

'What makes you think I'm shy or that I'd say no?' I ask a little huffily because she's right, my plan was to politely decline. Make up an excuse. Because there's only one person on this island that I want to make friends with. My son. *I swear it's him, but I need to know more. And there's only one way of finding out . . . by getting to know him and his parents better.*

'I like your costume. It's Boden, isn't it?'

16

I nod, surprised, because she looks more like a Dolce and Gabbana customer to me. She's petite in every way and absolutely gorgeous.

'I have one just like it,' she explains, gazing longingly towards the beachfront restaurant that sits on the pristine white sand and has panoramic views of the sea. 'So, are you coming?' she prompts.

Sighing under my breath, I stand up and force a tight smile as I slip a black and gold sarong around my waist. As I go to knot it, Angelika swats my hands away, complaining, 'You're doing it all wrong. Here, let me.'

When she's done, she stands back to admire her work and gives an appreciative nod. 'That's better.'

'You're a bossy little thing, aren't you?' I chuckle, deciding that I like her and that it wouldn't hurt to have lunch with her, just this once.

'You know me already, which means we are going to be great friends,' she teases, slipping a possessive arm through mine and tugging me towards the restaurant. I resist though, as I search distractedly for signs of Nathan in the ocean. But he's nowhere to be seen.

He's a strong swimmer so I'm not concerned. He probably got out of the water further along the beach and is most likely talking to someone. That's Nathan for you. But still if I'm not here when he returns . . .

In a panic, I tell her, 'I must find my husband first and let him know where I've gone,' as if afraid she's going to whisk me away against my will.

Amusement in her eyes, Angelika asks, 'Why?'

As we stand side by side under a melting orange sun, I'm aware that her child-sized skull barely reaches my shoulder. Despite being physically much bigger and stronger than her, I lack her bravery.

'Why indeed?' I murmur to myself because Nathan often disappears without telling me where he is going. *What does he get up to?*

'Let him find you. It does them good to keep them on their toes,' Angelika says with a careless shrug, and I'm envious of her self-assurance.

'Let's do it,' I declare boldly, failing miserably at sounding as confident as she does.

As we enter the open-air restaurant together, people glance over at us appreciatively. Our concierge, Putu, breaks away from talking to one of the waiting staff and comes over, beaming. Before saying anything, he places his hands over his heart in a prayer position and gives a small bow.

Angelika and I echo his greeting. She does it with ease and self-confidence as one would expect, but I feel awkward and self-conscious.

'My two most cherished and stunning brides,' he exclaims, beckoning us to a table by the sea for two. He is small and slim with black hair and brown eyes, like most Balinese people. But in contrast to most of the hotel employees, he wears a distinctive linen suit and exudes importance.

'I bet he says that to all the brides,' Angelika smirks, waiting for him to pull out her chair. Unused to such chivalry, I've already seated myself.

CHAPTER 5: TIMOTHY

'My favourite newlywed on the whole island,' Putu taunts softly, while bowing in a typical Balinese style greeting. He's smiling but there's a meanness to his eyes that he doesn't show to anyone on this island but me. We both know why. Narrowing my gaze, I lean back in my chair to observe him more closely.

'And where is *Mr* Timothy today?' Putu simpers.

I cough into my hand and mutter, 'Jonah is feeling unwell so he's staying in his room.'

'A case of Bali belly?' Putu suggests knowingly.

I stare at my uneaten dish of spicy chicken, wishing he would disappear. *If only Jonah hadn't insisted that we spend our honeymoon in Bali.* 'You could be right,' I respond grudgingly, not wanting to engage with him.

Amusement in his dark eyes, he asks, 'And what of the child?'

Sensing the menace behind his seemingly harmless words I stew in silence, wishing I could wipe the smug look off his face. I could too. I'm six-foot-two to his five-foot-six. But we both know where that would lead — to me getting arrested. Again. My secret would be revealed then, and everyone who knows me would shun me. Including my new husband!

'The same. Connor's unwell too,' I snap, without intending to. Because if he sees that he's getting to me, it will only increase the power he thinks he has over me. Who am I kidding? There's no *think* about it. He has all the power a man can have. *What is it he wants from me?* I guess only time will tell, but in the meantime, he seems intent on tormenting me.

'That's unfortunate, I'm sorry to hear that,' Putu puts on a phoney pitying expression, before declaring, 'Children are very precious. We must do all we can to protect them. Isn't that right . . . TIM?'

At that, I scrape my chair back and spring somewhat guiltily to my feet. Jaw clenched, I feel the heat flare on my neck and cheeks as I grind out, 'If you'll excuse me, I must get back to them.'

I avert my eyes from his stare and briefly focus on the two women sitting on the other side of the room. Samantha. That's Price's wife's name. I remember now. She's with the Polish woman that I haven't yet been introduced to. Both women are exceptionally attractive, but Samantha (I will not shorten her name to Sam, even in my head, knowing how much I detest people doing it to me) has the edge. I've known since I was seven years old that I was gay and have never been attracted to women, although I can, and do, appreciate their beauty. That's how I know there's something special about her. And that Price doesn't deserve her.

The two women are staring over at us. Samantha has a worried look on her face as if she fears that I will cause a scene, and her friend's eyes are full of mischief as if she hopes that I will create one . . . something they can talk about later, although to be fair, Samantha doesn't seem like the gossiping type. I'm trying to stay calm, but my body language must give me away. Or maybe the Polish woman is simply more astute than most. I acknowledge them with a curt nod before turning my attention back to the ever-smiling, eager-to-please, dutiful concierge, who is just as much of an imposter as I am.

I start to back away, mumbling an apologetic, 'I need to make sure my family are okay,' but Putu blocks my path cutting off my escape. It's a very subtle move. One that only I would pick up on.

'Ah yes, family,' he nods agreeably, 'The most important thing in the world, don't you think? I know I would die for mine.'

Looking into his crinkled-from-too-much-smiling eyes, I think I can capture sorrow, grief, hatred and a desire for revenge all at once. I know something of this man's suffering, *God knows I wish I didn't*, but even so, I feel no compassion for him. Selfish as it might seem, because he is now threatening *my* happiness, and *my* family, as I once did his — when I was a cruel, selfish young man — I hate him almost as intensely as he does me.

Fixing him with a warning stare, I growl menacingly, in a low voice, 'As I would mine.' Simultaneously, I ask myself, *after what I did, who the hell am I to threaten him?* It works. He shuffles out of my way, his head slouching onto his chest in defeat. As I grab my phone from the table, I think I detect a look of cowardice in his shrunken gaze, *perhaps now he'll leave me alone*, but I realise I'm mistaken when his head bounces up and he objects, in a voice that carries, 'But, Sir, you haven't finished your lunch. And we wouldn't want you wasting away, would we?'

I wave my hand dismissively and continue walking without looking back. I think a better description of my hasty exit from the restaurant would be running away with my tail between my legs, with my cheeks on fire no doubt — given my history of blushing. Although I'm considered buff and muscular from working out in the gym, I was once a fat kid so taunts like that still have the desired effect. Unlike Putu's backwards joke, which seemed to suggest there was no danger of me wasting away due to my sheer size, there is some truth to what I said back there. I *am* worried about Jonah and Connor who both have diarrhoea and high temperatures. I made sure they had plenty of bottled water, snacks and medicine before heading down to the beach for lunch. I also placed the TV remote control in Jonah's hand, so he couldn't complain about not being able to find it, but I still felt horrible about leaving them alone.

Little does my new husband know that I would give anything to be the one shut up in my room, away from the ever-watchful gaze of the man I hoped never to see again. Putu! Even his name sounds like an insult on the tongue. A swear word even. Especially when I say it. Yet here he is on the same damn resort as me. To think, I came here voluntarily, knowing there was a chance we could cross paths. I'll grant you the likelihood of it happening was remote, but it was enough to guarantee I would never return to this part of the world again. Until now, that is. I absolutely detest Bali. It might be paradise to some, but to me it's hell.

CHAPTER 6: ANGELIKA

'He might be gorgeous, but I don't think you're his type,' I tease the lovely Samantha who doesn't seem to realise how stunning she is. She's incredibly humble and seems to enjoy putting herself down. "No need for that", I want to tell her, when she's married to a knobhead like Nathan Price. *Whatever was she thinking?* Unless she's a gold digger, but I don't get that impression. He's partly why I chose to befriend her — out of curiosity — but only somewhat, because I liked her immediately and, if I'm honest, I don't like that many women. I find most of them are two-faced and bitchy.

'I wasn't . . . I didn't,' Sam stutters, sounding and appearing shocked that I've caught her admiring a man who isn't her husband.

I arch my eyebrows and nod towards the attractive man with the fit gym body who is hurrying out of the restaurant like he's on a mission. 'It's okay, Sam. Just because you're married doesn't mean you can't look.'

Sam's slender white fingers flutter to her mouth, 'I swear I wasn't.'

I start giggling at that point and choke on my pineapple crush cocktail. Sam frowns comically, and I can tell she's afraid I'm about to choke to death. I reassure her, 'Relax, I'll live.'

'What are you laughing at anyway?' she grumbles, passing me a napkin to wipe my mouth on.

'You,' I tell her, continuing to laugh.

'Me?' Samantha scolds and folds her arms.

'You're so funny,' I chuckle some more, purely to irritate her, but only for fun. As I've said before, I like her.

'I've never been called that by anyone before. Usually, I'm accused of being too serious,' she replies softly, but oh so seriously.

'Oh, Sam,' I sigh fondly, 'What am I going to do with you?'

Her eyes sparkle. 'That's simple. Did you not promise to feed me?'

'I did indeed,' I agree, gesturing for the waiter to come and take our order. When he's gone, Sam whispers conspiratorially, 'I'm always hungry. Nathan says he wishes I had the same appetite for sex.' Seeming content now that she's revealed something intimate and girlie with me as if it were expected of her, she flicks out her magnificent red hair and beams.

This one gesture transforms her from being stunning to truly beautiful. She has a smile like Julia Roberts, the actress. Honestly, I'm in awe of her. She could be a famous model. So why a nanny? Things I have discovered about my new friend in the last twenty minutes: 1. She's afraid of dogs (remind me never to invite her to my house); 2. She's miserable because she married a jerk (something I already knew) and 3. She has a secret. Don't ask me how I know this. I just do. It takes a guarded person to know one. I'm just relieved she doesn't know mine (i.e. that I've slept with her husband multiple times). She'll never hear that from me though, as I'm not a backstabbing bitch.

She's chattier once our food arrives and is tucking into her meat skewers, nibbling the charcoaled flesh off each stick. She really wasn't kidding when she boasted of having a massive

24

appetite. There's no way I could put away what she does. I won't finish half my avocado salad.

'In any case, what made you think I wasn't his type?' she poses idly.

I frown. 'Who?'

'Timothy.'

'I'm still no wiser,' I shrug.

'The hot guy who was in here earlier,' she fakes impatience.

'Are we still discussing him?' I widen my eyes. 'I haven't had the pleasure of meeting him yet, but regardless of how gorgeous you are, he wouldn't be into you because he is quite obviously gay.'

She winces as if it pains her to be called gorgeous. 'How can you tell he's gay if you haven't met him yet?' She's obviously intrigued, but she's also gazing around as if worried someone might overhear our conversation.

So what if they do, is what I say to that. I've got nothing to hide. Except, I do . . . That stolen grand for one thing. What would happen if Nathan suddenly remembered me? What an absolute horror of a honeymoon that would turn out to be. Not to mention how ashamed and humiliated Bartosz would feel if he found out I was once a thief. I would never consider doing anything like that today, of course. It's easy to avoid stealing when you have plenty of money. Don't I know it.

'I have a gaydar. I can spot them a mile off,' I eventually say.

Sam pauses chewing to steal another look around, before turning to me and cautioning, 'I'm not sure that's a very PC thing to say.'

'Probably not,' I concede, not taking it personally.

Sam purposefully switches the subject by asking, 'Are you doing the walk up the volcano tonight to see the sunrise?'

I can't contain my excitement as I reply, 'I wouldn't miss it for the world! How about you?'

Sam bites her lip worriedly, appearing disappointed by my response. 'I'm not at all outdoorsy but Nathan wants me to go,' she finally admits.

Keen to help, I suggest, 'What would you prefer to do instead? Is there any way we could arrange something else for another time?'

'That's the thing — I don't know.'

Puzzled, I ask, 'What don't you know?'

Finding my drink empty once again, *oops*, I signal at the waiter, and mouth the words "same again, please". Like everything else on this island, it arrives in a matter of seconds. Let's hope that's not the case with tsunamis.

Sam picks up where she left off, 'Well, I don't have hobbies like other people. It drives Nathan mad because he's into everything. Golf. Running. All kinds of sports really. I don't go to the gym or have spa days with friends. I'm quite boring,' she sighs defeatedly.

'But you like to read. I saw you earlier with a book in your hand.'

'That's true,' she exclaims gratefully, latching on to this.

'What else do you love?' I probe, remembering to add, 'Apart from Nathan, of course.'

A tear slides down Sam's cheek as she murmurs forlornly, 'My son.'

CHAPTER 7: SAMANTHA

The words fell out of my mouth. I'm not sure why when I've kept my son a secret for years. Then, for some reason, the first chance I get I blab everything to a stranger. What if Angelika mentions this to Nathan? He would never forgive me for keeping something like that from him although I'm sure he hides plenty of "stuff" from me. I wouldn't blame him if he wanted to get a divorce. He thinks I'm having trouble becoming pregnant when I've already given birth and am therefore as fertile as any of his previous wives. If he knew he was being duped, he would be furious.

Angelika thinks I was lustfully gazing at Timothy because I fancied him, but she's wrong. I'm keeping a close eye on Timothy because I want to know what he's like. Jonah too. More importantly, what they're like as parents to my son.

'I never knew you had a son, but then again, why would I when we've only just met,' Angelika exclaims, while carefully chewing on her salad, which, quite frankly, doesn't look like it would satisfy a child, much less an adult. But then again, she is incredibly tiny. A petite little thing really with glossy auburn hair and muddy-brown eyes. She appears harsh until she smiles, and I've noticed that she always smiles for her husband.

I feel a pang of envy when I recall how Bartosz looked at her last night. He's always touching her. A soft guiding hand on her back. Or a gentle caress of her arm. Being with them last night made me feel a little awkward since it seemed like I was witnessing real intimacy for the first time. It makes me realise just how distant Nathan and I have become.

On that thought, I extend my hand to grab Angelika's and lay mine on top of hers, causing her eyes to widen in surprise.

'You mustn't tell Nathan,' I plead. 'He doesn't know.'

Frowning, she insists, 'Doesn't know what?'

As I explain, 'About the child or that I had him adopted,' my heart is thumping hard against my chest.

'You poor thing,' she sympathises, setting down her knife and fork. She's obviously finished eating even though she's barely touched her food.

In a rush to get my words out, I stammer, 'I was young and foolish. The father wasn't around and I didn't have a job, anywhere decent to live or any family to help me. So, I—'

She cuts me off, 'Hey, you don't have to justify yourself to me. Or to anyone else. You did what you felt was best. That's all that's important. And what business is it of mine to repeat it to anyone else?'

Upon hearing this, I feel my shoulders visibly relax. 'Thank you, Angelika. I really appreciate it.'

'No problem. Now, who do I have to screw around here to get another drink?' she laughs dirtily while staring into her empty glass. Like Nathan, she drinks excessively, not that it's any of my business. I've noticed that most of the honeymooners on this island drink like fish.

'I think about my son every day. All the time,' I confess, feeling tears in my eyes once more.

'Of course you do. That's only natural,' Angelika mumbles, but I sense she's growing bored. She is obviously not into kids, and I'm not brave enough to ask if she's planning to have any. So, I leave well alone. As she orders another drink and a top-up of water for me, I watch her closely. She has a set of neat white teeth that are small and dainty, just like her. Her hair is worn at shoulder level, and she has flawless olive skin, two shades darker than anyone else's. I bet she tans easily, unlike me. I'm as pink as a lobster after five minutes in the sun. Nathan says it's not an attractive look, but I'm more concerned about skin cancer, which my mum died of.

Angelika's husband is the opposite of mine. In that, he is quiet and reserved. He considers his words carefully before speaking and is extremely courteous. To Angelika's five-feet-two, he must be at least six feet tall. Nathan was very careful not to stand next to him at the bar last night. He is not exactly short at five-feet-seven, but at five-ten I am taller than him. I know better than to wear heels. Fortunately, unlike his previous two wives, I'm not into them. I'm not glamorous at all; preferring comfy trainers and wide-legged jeans to body-con dresses and stilettos.

I glance at my watch. It's almost 2 p.m. By now Nathan must be wondering where I am. The thought puts me on edge, but I'm not sure how to make a quick getaway without seeming rude or Angelika guessing what I'm up to. It would amuse her to know that I go out of my way to please my husband. Scaredy cat that I am.

In another thirteen hours, we're going to be picked up outside the hotel and taken by boat and then car to the base of Mount Batur, where we'll walk for three hours to reach the summit and witness the sunrise. It's one of Bali's "must do's" yet I'm dreading it. Why? Due to my asthma, climbing isn't good for me and I'm afraid of heights. But Nathan brushed off all my concerns with his typical, 'Stop overthinking things, Sam. Everything is going to be fine. You'll be with me.'

He makes it sound like I could easily perish without him. He couldn't imagine me being brave enough to take driving lessons without his knowledge or permission (Nathan reckons I'm too anxious to be a driver) but I have. My instructor (a woman) says I'm doing well. Nathan enjoys being needed.

And I do need him. Or did. But I feel like I'm losing myself in this marriage and I'm at a loss as to what to do about it. There are moments when I don't think Nathan and I will make it. And that would be a shame because, let's face it, I did a very selfish thing by marrying him. It saddens me that I'm not the nice person Angelika thinks I am.

Whenever anyone asks how Nathan and I met, and people do that all the time when you're on honeymoon, we feel obliged to make something up. Out running (chance would be a fine thing), bumping into each other at a coffee shop when Nathan accidentally spilled a vanilla latte on my top or at the library (Nathan is not a reader — he's a doer). What we can't admit to, because people would undoubtedly judge us for it, is that we met when I was working for his second wife, as a nanny for their children.

CHAPTER 8: TIMOTHY

Connor is feeling better, but Jonah continues to have a fever. I joked that he'd never looked uglier than when he was sweating profusely in bed. He laughed and threw a pillow at me, chirping "You love me anyway" which I obviously do. Without Jonah, I'd be lost. He and Connor are everything to me. Although we didn't need a child to make us whole, Jonah was desperate to become a father. And to deny him the opportunity to become a parent would have been unfair, even cruel, because he is so naturally gifted at it. So Jonah can rest, I've brought Connor to the beach where we're building sandcastles. But despite the powder-soft sand, clear blue sky and the rustling of palm leaves, I would still rather be anywhere else in the world than here.

Jonah had to go over my parental responsibilities at least three times before I was allowed to leave our suite. I have a full set of instructions. Remember to keep applying sunblock to Connor's skin. Being a redhead, he will burn otherwise. Make sure he drinks enough water and monitor his temperature in case he starts feeling ill again. Remind him to wash his hands thoroughly after using the toilet. Jonah is a neat freak, so our house is always spotless. And full of cushions. "Who doesn't love cushions" Jonah insists whenever I complain that we don't need any more. The truth is I would buy him a thousand cushions if it made him happy. I think we both thought that having Connor would take away his sadness, but it's still visible on his face. I know he's still grieving for *the love of his life*, even if he tries not to show it. We don't discuss Noah anymore. It hurts too much.

I watch our son playing in the sand. His tiny pink tongue is poking out of the corner of his mouth with determination. He does this whenever he's concentrating hard, and it makes me wonder — not for the first time — if he has any undiagnosed behavioural problems. He has trouble focusing most of the time. "Away with the fairies" my wee mum would have said. God bless her. Connor's skin is white and scratchy from the sand and his blue eyes are almost as dazzling as the sea. But our boy is nervous of the water, even if it is calm and clear. Jonah tells me not to worry. Connor will learn to swim when he's good and ready. Wet sand gets under my fingernails as I dig out a moat with a plastic toy spade. This part of the beach is deserted. We have it all to ourselves. No sign of Putu, thank Christ.

'Connor, are you hungry? Would you like to go and get a sandwich or some chips?' I ask, placing a hand on his arm, so he can't ignore me.

He pulls a face and moves away, complaining, 'We have to put the flag on the top of the castle first.'

I laugh at his disgust. He addresses us both as though we were simpletons. And perhaps we are. Because what other parents would let a four-year-old do whatever he pleases? I'm tempted to brush those knots out of his matted red hair, whether he likes it or not, but Jonah would be upset if I did that. "He has to have autonomy over his body, Timothy" he's fond of telling me. I don't argue since Jonah has told me about his childhood sexual abuse at the hands of his stepfather. I would kill that man for what he did to Jonah if he weren't already dead.

Connor and I are quite similar in that we shy away from showing affection, but I find it troubling that he seldom asks his parents for cuddles or to sit on either of our laps. Earlier, when I refused to let him eat a third bag of sweets (as if) he threw an extremely loud tantrum, screaming at the top of his lungs and lashing out at Jonah. Being the more authoritative parent, Connor never usually strikes me. He takes his temper out on Jonah instead, who always finds an explanation for our son's actions. This afternoon, his excuse was that Connor was still not fully recovered. "It's because he's ill" he protested tearfully. Every time Connor has a meltdown, Jonah gets emotional. "Is it?" I had demanded sceptically, hoping to bring up the subject of ADHD right there and then, but I backed down when Jonah burst into tears. He always cries. He's the sentimental one. I wouldn't have him any other way. As I said, we complete each other.

When I turn to face my son again, I notice that he is no longer interested in building sandcastles and is instead gathering seashells. 'Connor, don't you want to finish the sandcastle?' I sigh.

He doesn't respond. Doesn't even look at me. He simply keeps collecting his shells and piling them into mounds. He becomes disinterested easily. He climbs on things when instructed not to do so. Is aggressive to other children and wary of strangers as a rule. And he's constantly restless. I've read that all of these are symptoms of ADHD. The idea that my son could be suffering from an undiagnosed mental health disorder pains me deeply. Jonah angrily disputes any suggestion of this, claiming that Connor's extreme sensitivity and intelligence is what makes him different to other kids his age. When you combine this with a healthy dose of typical toddler behaviour, Jonah is inclined to believe there is nothing wrong with our son.

I remove my Ray-Ban shades, give them a quick clean to get rid of any sand, and put them back on my head. I look ridiculous when I go on vacation since Jonah insists on buying us all matching clothing. I'm wearing beach shorts and a Hawaiian shirt, as is Connor. I was already tanned before I got on the plane because I'm no stranger to a sunbed. After a few hours in the sun, my skin will have taken on the colour of mahogany. Remembering Jonah's advice to *slip, slop, slap*, I sit up straight and grab the high factor SPF50 organic sunscreen out of the beach bag Jonah packed for us, even though I am more than capable of doing it myself, and I'm about to apply it to Connor's body, when—

'Look. Look!' Connor shrieks excitedly, jumping up and down.

Before I get a chance to see what he's pointing at, he bolts, heading for the ocean. Panicking, I leap to my feet and take after him, but I trip over the pile of shells and fall face down in the sand. I'm immediately on my feet again, tearing after him. God, if anything should happen to our boy. Jonah would never forgive me. I'd never forgive myself come to that.

'Stop, Connor! Wait. Come back.'

He's now just a few feet away from the sea. If he falls in, will the lapping seawater take him under? What if he drowns? I knew coming to Bali was a terrible idea. Truly frightened now, I find myself screaming at the top of my lungs, 'Stay away from the water!'

CHAPTER 9: ANGELIKA

I hear the flush of the toilet from the ensuite, a throat clearing and a meant-to-be-silent fart, followed by an apologetic "Pardon" before Bartosz returns to the bedroom. I'm in bed naked, with only a plain white sheet draped loosely about my body.

'I smell of sex,' I complain to my husband, pulling a disgusted face.

'*Pyszny*,' he laughs, getting back into bed.

'Not yummy at all,' I tell him, flipping over to face him.

I've always been fascinated by his beautiful body. Unlike Timothy from the restaurant, who is beefy and muscular, Bartosz is slim and athletic, and I like it that way. Although I am considerably smaller than him, smaller than everyone I know, we could be mistaken for brother and sister because we are very similar. We share the same brown eyes, hair and skin tone. We even have the same pointed chin. We joke around that it's kind of like having sex with oneself. But there's nothing like sex with Bartosz. He is an amazing lover. I should know as I've had more sex than most people. I'm often shocked that my libido stays as high as it does, given my history. One of my favourite things is having sex in the afternoon and, fortunately, I have a young, virile husband who is happy to oblige me.

As I stroke his chest and playfully tease his nipples, he doesn't react as he usually would. Now that I come to think about it, he has been quieter and more withdrawn than normal. I noticed this change in him when we first arrived on the island, and it's clear that whatever is bothering him hasn't gone away. He usually tells me how much he loves me and likes to cuddle and hold my hand after sex, but now he doesn't do any of those things. Instead, he is grimacing as he looks up at the ceiling.

'Is something wrong, Bartosz?'

'What could be wrong?' he asks. 'We're on our honeymoon.'

I protest, 'You didn't answer my question.'

He assures me, 'Nothing's wrong, Ange,' but his eyes reveal otherwise. He's lying. And that's something he never usually does.

'Are you having second thoughts about marrying me?' I ask him as I sit up in bed and meet his gaze.

He widens his eyes. I believe I've shocked him. It's his turn to sit up straight in bed now. And just as I wanted him to do a few minutes ago, he's now holding my hand. 'No. How could you possibly think that?'

'You seem a little off. Quieter than normal.'

He runs a hand through his short crew-cut hair and rustles up a weak smile for me. He even kisses the back of my hand. 'If I am, Mrs Dabrowski, it has nothing to do with being married to you.'

'I love it when you call me that,' I swoon, leaning back against the exquisite white Egyptian cotton pillowcases.

'Mrs Dabrowski, Mrs Dabrowski,' he repeats seductively in my ear, as though he's hoping it will get me in the mood again.

'You can expect less sex now that I'm a married woman,' I playfully tell him as I push him away.

Nuzzling my neck, knowing full well that this turns me on, he whispers, 'You wouldn't be able to hold out. You find me too irresistible.'

'You're probably right,' I agree, but I realise that he's using sex as a distraction because he doesn't want to talk about what's really on his mind.

He jokingly tells me to, 'Stop talking woman, and start kissing,' tickling my ribs in the process, which makes me laugh out loud. I can taste myself on his tongue as we begin to kiss. We pause for a second, and I spoil everything by asking, 'Do you think the other couples are having sex in their rooms, or is it just us?'

He rolls off me then, sighing, 'Who knows. Who cares.'

My brow wrinkles as I stare at the twitching muscles on his back. Again, this isn't who he is. We usually discuss anything and everything. Since when did he become so dismissive? He loves to gossip almost as much as I do.

I try again, 'Today, while you were at your Balinese cooking class I had lunch with Samantha Price.' Is it just my imagination, or does her name make his back tense even more? He couldn't be attracted to her, could he? Is that what's making him moody and withdrawn? I know she's beautiful, but Bartosz loves me, so he wouldn't . . . In my mind, I hear my mother's sharp warning, "All men are the same. Mark my words."

He takes a while to respond. 'Oh, and where was her husband?'

'Swimming, I think. For newlyweds, they don't seem very happy.'

His head snaps around as he poses the question, 'No?'

Why should that matter to him? Unless my suspicions are correct, and he *is* attracted to Sam. Maybe he wants to rescue her from the awful Nathan, who I could tell Bartosz took an instant dislike to.

My voice is tight as I say, 'Do you think she's beautiful?'

'She's too good for Price if that's what you mean.'

It wasn't. Nor am I the jealous kind. Unlike Sam, I'm aware of my value as a woman and have never been short of confidence — just height.

I'm intrigued though. 'What makes you say that?'

He shrugs. 'It's just a feeling, nothing more.'

Let's hope that's all there is to it. I'm a sensible woman and my marriage is strong enough to survive an infatuation or two, as long as it doesn't result in anything more. Those who break their vows and commit adultery, in my opinion, are the lowest of humans. Scum.

'They're also going on the climb first thing.'

Bartosz rubs his chin, appearing thoughtful. 'Is that so?'

'If she pushes him off the summit of Mount Batur for making her go up there, it wouldn't surprise me. He can be such a bully.'

'How do you know that?' Bartosz is glaring suspiciously at me, making me wonder whether I have said too much.

I smile disarmingly, 'It's just a feeling.'

Despite my outward composure, I'm afraid he's figured out my secret. Has he worked out that I knew Nathan from before? That he was one of my clients. But how could he? Unless Nathan has told him. Maybe Price did recognise me, after all, and is playing some sort of game. I wouldn't put it past him.

CHAPTER 10: SAMANTHA

My son races barefoot across the sand towards me under a melting orange sun and I feel the promise of more days like this stretching out in front of us as he throws himself into my arms, excitement in his eyes as he gazes up at me. Our reunion is everything I could have wished for. He must have instinctively recognised me as his own flesh and blood. As I did him.

'You're the Little Mermaid,' he announces, with a serious expression.

I laugh at that because I can barely swim. Just when I think I have him all to myself, Timothy rushes towards us, appearing anxious and panting heavily. A trickle of perspiration runs down his forehead. His handsome face is peppered with sand, and he has a cut lip.

'Oh, thank God, you caught him.' He lets out a long, shuddering exhale.

'I think it was the other way around,' I chuckle as I swing Connor up onto my hip, where he belongs. *This is like a dream come true.*

'He ran off before I could stop him,' Timothy frets, dabbing perspiration from his brow and peering down at his son with worried eyes. 'Are you all right, Connor? You're not hurt at all, are you?'

Even though I know he's itching to get his hands on the child, I stubbornly resist, saying brightly, 'He's fine. Aren't you, Connor?'

'Yes, Ariel,' he nods obediently, putting a soft, gentle hand on my cheek. I feel so moved by his touch that it's almost my undoing.

'Ariel? I thought your name was Samantha.' Timothy gives a bewildered shake of his head. I'm guessing Connor can be a bit of a handful judging by how out of control he is. If I had custody of him, I wouldn't take my eyes off him for a second. Timothy seems like an irresponsible parent, letting Connor wander off like that. He should be more careful.

'It is Samantha, Sam actually. But Connor thinks I'm the Little Mermaid, you know from the Disney movie.'

'Ah yes,' he nods patiently, 'I see the resemblance now.'

'It's the long red hair and blue eyes that do it,' I acknowledge.

Somewhat awkwardly he replies, 'Thank you again, Sam, for stopping him from going into the water. I dread to think what—'

Timothy doesn't seem to think it wise to finish his sentence in front of Connor, so with the intention of removing him from me, he extends his arms, but the child wriggles out of reach, protesting, 'No.'

Timothy chastises, 'Connor, you're too big a boy to be carried.'

'He's not,' I protest, wrapping my octopus arms around him even tighter because I don't want to let him go. Ever. Nevertheless, knowing I will eventually have to put him down, I entice Connor, 'How about I put you down, and we can walk hand in hand, if you like, to get an ice cream?'

'Okay,' he agrees without hesitation, surprising both myself and Timothy, who I suspect was anticipating a battle on his hands.

'You've obviously got the magic touch,' Timothy enthuses, impressed, as I put Connor back down on the sand. His eyes widen further when Connor slips his hand in mine and gently tugs, saying, 'Come on, Ariel.'

After Timothy pauses to pick up a beach bag and a towel, we head back to the resort to get an ice cream from the beach house gelato.

Holding Connor's hand tenderly, I confide, 'I'm going to have mango and apricot in a cone.'

His blue eyes sparkle. 'Strawberry and chocolate for me.'

'With sprinkles?' I laugh.

'As well as blue syrup.'

Timothy, who I keep forgetting is walking right beside us, comes out with, 'I bagsy the pistachio and mint.'

Connor and I both look at him as if he were crazy and simultaneously groan, 'Ugh.' The fact that we both dislike nuts is more proof that he is my son. If that sounds irrational, I don't care.

Timothy hoots with laughter at our disgusted expressions, and we continue on our way, but this time he refuses to be left out of the conversation and asks me, 'How come you were at the beach on your own when you're on your honeymoon?'

'I could ask you the same thing,' is my response.

'I'm not exactly on my own.' He points out reasonably, nodding to Connor. He may not have intended to, but he's just made me feel more alone and isolated than I ever thought possible.

As if sensing he has somehow offended me, he hastily adds, 'Not that there's anything wrong with being on your own.'

'Nathan went snorkelling,' I reply bluntly.

He turns to face me, 'And you didn't want to go with him?'

I shrug as if I hadn't purposefully planned to run across Timothy and Jonah with their child this afternoon. 'I'm not great in the water at the best of times but the thought of swimming anywhere near those giant stingrays . . .' I shudder for effect, making Connor giggle. He has a gorgeous smile.

41

'Jonah is suffering from Bali belly,' Timothy explains.

'Oh, no, how awful,' and I truly do sympathise as I've heard there's nothing worse. But I'm not above using this information to my advantage, by slyly suggesting, 'If you and Connor want company, while your husband is incapacitated, you know where to find me.'

'On a deserted beach waiting to save lives,' Timothy grins. He has a nice smile too. Despite the bad parenting, I believe he is a good man.

'On a deserted beach waiting to save lives,' I echo. Then, reluctant to take credit for something I haven't done, I continue, 'Not that I saved anyone's life today. Connor was quite safe and had no intention of going into the water,' I say with complete conviction as if I already know my child.

'Well, if not Connor's life, then you saved mine. Jonah would have killed me if I had taken him back to our hotel room drenched and dishevelled.'

Timothy comes to a sudden halt, but we haven't reached the gelato yet. 'What is it?' I ask, wondering why he's staring at me so intently.

'Your eyes,' he gestures to my face, 'Surely they're too blue to be real.'

I smile. 'They're not contact lenses if that's what you're thinking. Don't worry, I get asked that all the time.'

Frowning, he looks from his son to me. 'They're just like Connor's.'

CHAPTER 11: TIMOTHY

A light breeze scurries across the sea, like a fish on its way somewhere, and I notice that Connor and Samantha look as if they belong together. Observing the two of them giggling as they stick their tongues in their ice creams, I feel fortunate to have made a new friend on this godforsaken island. Not only is Samantha a perfect flame-haired beauty, who may have saved my son's life — despite her humble denials to the contrary — she appears to adore Connor. She is different from most of the others on this island, who make a point of avoiding us rather than having to deal with a demanding and unruly four-year-old. *I can't say I blame them.*

I knew when I first met Samantha that she was special. Didn't I say as much to Jonah, who merely rolled his eyes and looked bored, because, unlike Samantha's husband, she is reserved and unopinionated? Price on the other hand had Jonah in stitches all night with his sarcastic and very dry humour. Like I said, Jonah and I are very different. "Opposites attract" as the saying goes, which makes our relationship work — most of the time.

'Your son is amazing. You're very lucky to have him,' Samantha is saying to me now, with a wistful expression on her face.

It crosses my mind that she may not be able to have children. If that's true it's a real shame because she was born to be a mother. She's a natural.

'Yes, I know,' I acknowledge, flinching at the sudden burst of self-inflicted pain brought on by the ice cream on my sensitive-as-hell teeth.

Am I the only one who doesn't recognise the goodness in my child? First Jonah and now Samantha. Both are blind to his flaws. I start to doubt my love for Connor because of this. I wonder, is it different when they're your own? And by that, I mean, if he were my biological son, would I feel prouder of him? However, Jonah doesn't feel that way, which just makes me feel even more of a rubbish parent.

'Can we take Ariel to see Dad?' Connor asks, eyes full of mischief.

'Her name's Samantha and I'm afraid she's not really the Little Mermaid,' I explain logically, because we have taken the decision, or rather, Jonah has, to raise Connor not to believe in fairy tales. He isn't meant to believe in Father Christmas either, but Connor, as usual, has other ideas.

Connor's bottom lip quivers, not wanting Samantha to be anything other than a Disney princess, as indeed she is to all intents and purposes. But then she whispers something in his ear which makes him grin.

'If I call her Sam, can we take her back to meet my other dad?'

Cheeky little bugger. He's bright all right. Too intelligent for his own good. But even as I think this, I'm chuckling, 'Only if you're a good boy.'

'I can't imagine him being anything other than a delight,' Samantha remarks to me, reaching out a hand for Connor to take, which he accepts.

I scoff, 'That's because you're not his mother.'

Samantha's face darkens, and her smile disappears, so the joke backfires on me. I feel guilty because I'm certain now that she's unable to have children but desperately wants them. I rescue the situation by adding, 'You seem to be doing a better job at parenting him than me though.'

Looking almost tearful, she admits, 'I love children,' while bending to knot Connor's shoelace. I don't ask her why she's so emotional on her honeymoon, because I sense it will only make her feel worse. It's evident that she doesn't want to discuss her problems. Since Connor doesn't usually stay still long enough for me to tie his shoelaces, or button up his shirts, I generally have to chase him all around the house. But with Samantha, he's docile and obedient. This has me questioning whether depriving him of a mother was the right decision on our part. Maybe we should have allowed him to live with a husband-and-wife couple so that he could grow up with a mother *and* a father figure. Connor must find it confusing to have two fathers. He refers to both Jonah and me as "Dad", so half the time we have no idea who he is talking about.

I'm genuinely shocked when Samantha smooths back Connor's hair with her long, white fingers and he doesn't attempt to wriggle out of her way.

'This way,' I say, gesturing to the Aphrodite wing that is made up of six luxurious ground-floor suites that have direct access to the beach. Each has a veranda with rattan outdoor furniture and a plunge pool.

When I reach the screen door, I notice that the white linen blinds are still drawn, so I tap on the door before entering, calling gently, 'Jonah, are you decent? I've brought someone to see you.'

Knowing Jonah loves company, I'm not surprised to hear an answering murmur, followed by the sound of running water and a flushing toilet. Samantha and I exchange knowing glances and laugh at the same time, 'Bali belly.'

'Come in,' Jonah cries, sounding more alert.

I'm excited for Jonah to get to know Samantha better as I sense that she'll be good for us, especially Connor. She seems to have a positive influence over him, and in my view, that can only be advantageous. I'm daring to think he might let her comb the knots out of his hair. I push open the door and we proceed inside, with me opening the blinds around the room, letting bright sunlight in. Typically, Jonah's position in bed is a dramatic one, with one arm draped across his glistening forehead, as though close to death.

'How are you feeling?' I ask, but before he can describe his most disgusting bowel movement to our guest, I say, 'I've brought Samantha to see you.'

Jonah looks a little disappointed as he sits up in bed. Who did he think I had brought along? A celebrity?

'You're Nathan's wife,' Jonah lets out a long sigh, unable to disguise his weariness. He then motions for Connor to join him on the bed. But Connor remains where he is, clinging to Samantha's hand.

'That's right,' Samantha replies, appearing a little shy now that she's here. But she wasn't like that on the beach when it was just the two of us.

'She's a real-life Disney princess!' Connor exclaims enthusiastically.

Jonah's mouth tightens. I know the look. He thinks of himself as the biggest princess of all, so this is the last thing he wants to hear. Furthermore, because Connor appears to temporarily prefer Samantha, he perceives her as a threat. It is beyond me how someone could believe that of a lovely, shy and humble creature like Samantha who really does look and act like a Disney princess.

CHAPTER 12: ANGELIKA

When the alarm went off at two in the morning, I immediately got up and showered. I suspect Bartosz may not have gone to sleep at all, but remained awake all night, staring moodily at the ceiling. I wish I knew for sure what's bothering him, but I know better than to keep asking. He'll tell me when he's good and ready. Or he won't. We've been warned it can be chilly on the summit of Mount Batur, so I'm dressed in jeans, trainers and a hoodie. I'm really looking forward to the three-hour trek up the steep and rocky terrain. Like Bartosz, I enjoy working out, running, weightlifting and spin class. Exercise gives me a high that is comparable to sex.

When I return to the bedroom, I notice with a grimace that Bartosz has not changed. If we want to see the sunrise, we have to leave in fifteen minutes. Rather than hurrying to get ready, he's lying on the bed staring at his iPad. When I approach, he closes the lid, but not before I see a picture of Sam Price and her husband on the screen. My heart sinks. He's really infatuated with her then. Alternatively, he might simply be curious to know more about our new friends. However, I wouldn't class Nathan as a friend. More like the enemy. Especially if he *is* playing mind games with me. Nathan loves nothing more than wielding power over others. Tonight, I intend to find out for certain if he knows who I am or not. I won't be able to unwind or enjoy this honeymoon till then.

'You need to get a move on,' I warn Bartosz, but he just gives me a wry look and starts taking clothing out of his side of the wardrobe. Bartosz, like me, prefers to dress in dark colours. We mostly wear black. All designer brands of course. It's our signature thing, if you like.

'Who else is coming tonight . . . I mean today,' Bartosz aims for casual, but he doesn't fool me. He wants to know if Sam is going.

'I already told you once,' it's not like me to snap, so I explain, more softly, 'Timothy's coming on his own since his partner is ill, Putu said, and then there's Nathan and Sam.'

'She's still coming then?'

He doesn't look at me when he says this but his words confirm my suspicions. All he's interested in is her. Not the other people in our group.

'Why wouldn't she be?' I grumble, angrily shoving a bottle of water into my backpack.

'You mentioned that she's scared of heights and has asthma. I'm surprised her husband is letting her go at all.'

'He's the one insisting on it, remember?' I say flatly, trying to ignore the unpleasant recollection of finding Nathan Price passed out drunk on the floor of a cheap hotel room, while I rifled through his wallet.

'What an arsehole,' he mumbles under the folds of his black jersey top as he pulls it over his face.

'Exactly,' I reply, throwing my backpack over my shoulders. 'Are you almost ready?'

'Two more minutes. I just need to give my teeth a quick brush.'

Sighing heavily, I sit down on the bed. Bartosz is particular about brushing his beautiful white teeth and I know those two minutes will probably end up being five. When I hear water flowing, I move his iPad to my side of the bed, and open it up, all the while keeping one eye on the bathroom door. The picture I saw a moment ago of Sam and Nathan Price is still there. When I realise it's an interview about Nathan's business success, I'm interested to learn more. By all accounts, he's a multi-millionaire now, no surprise there, but according to this article, Sam isn't his first wife. He has two prior marriages under his belt, the second of which produced three children. *What a catch.* Of course, I'm being sarcastic.

I'm surprised to discover that the Prices are from Poole in Dorset, given that Bartosz used to live and work there. That was around five years ago when Bartosz's brother was still alive. It was before we got together and before he succeeded as a restaurant owner. I was living in Brighton with my mother at the time, before I got evicted and things went horribly wrong. Fortunately, Bartosz and I got together not long after she passed away, and when Bartosz was still grieving over the loss of his brother. Wouldn't it be strange if he and Sam had already crossed paths without either of them realising it? Maybe he has seen her before somewhere — passed her in the street even — so he recognises her on some unconscious level. That could account for his fascination with her.

Perhaps they had drinks in the same bar. They may even have exchanged glances across a crowded room. Imagine if he'd met her first, before me and they'd dated! How funny would that be? Not! Alternatively, she might have eaten the food he'd prepared in the kitchen while out for a meal with her friends. But wait, she must have been pregnant around that time, if only a few weeks along, and she claimed to be broke and without a decent place to live, so it stands to reason that she was not dining out in restaurants. Poor Sam. What a terrible choice she was forced to make in giving up her child. The fact that the scumbag of a father didn't stay around couldn't have helped either. I wonder if he was aware of the adoption. Most likely he didn't give a shit. Even though I'm not the maternal type, I know that when the time comes to say goodbye to my fur babies Hunter and Chase, I will be devastated. So, I can sympathise with Sam.

Except for a heading beneath the photo that reads, *Nathan Price with fiancé Samantha aboard his 79-foot yacht "The Goddess"* Sam isn't referenced again in the article. Not even once. Everything revolves around Nathan. That was always the case. And it's obvious that it still is. Sam might as well be invisible. I wonder if that's how she feels. And although I suspect my husband of having a crush on her, I feel sorry for the girl who has everything but the one thing she truly wants. The son she gave up.

When the tap water suddenly stops running, I hastily close the iPad's cover and move it back to Bartosz's side of the bed, feeling like the sly pickpocket I am for spying on my husband.

'Are you ready?' he wants to know.

'Ready as I'll ever be,' I joke as I stand up, thinking that Nathan Price had best watch out if he intends to play tricks on me. Otherwise, I will be the one to push him off the top of the volcano. Not Sam.

CHAPTER 13: SAMANTHA

I'm struggling to keep up, as I knew I would. The others have gone on ahead with our guide, leaving Nathan and me straggling behind. Because of his competitive nature, he hates it. He's a winner. A finisher. Not a quitter like me. The first half of the volcano climb wasn't too steep, and I was fooled into thinking "I can do this" but I was forced to take back my words when we reached the halfway point, because everyone, including Nathan, struggled once the path became steeper and more slippery. My calf muscles burn and there's nothing to grab hold of, except weak branches on either side of the path. Behind and in front of me are hundreds of bright lights, each symbolising a human being with a head torch. I didn't think it would be this hectic. Although the sunrise hike is meant to be a profound, spiritual experience, it feels too commercialised to me.

The moon is behind us in the darkness and the cold has embraced us with its icy grip. No one talks and the only sounds I can hear are the soft chirping of crickets, people's footsteps on the dirt track and my laboured breathing. As I pause to take my reliever out of my pocket and inhale a much-needed dose of Ventolin, I feel Nathan bump into me.

'You need to keep moving. There's a long line of people behind us,' he grumbles. The unforgiving terrain has made him grumpier than usual.

'I told you I would struggle,' I dare to complain, hurt by the injustice of his words. I don't fool myself that he is remaining with me for my benefit. He just doesn't want to come across as uncaring in front of the others.

'Let me go in front so I can help you,' he commands, pushing past me. As I teeter on the edge of the path, arms flailing, I pray that I don't fall. Is it my imagination or did he shove me aside a bit too forcefully?

Panicking, I grab hold of his jacket and scream, 'Nathan, don't let go of me! I think I'm falling.'

'Nonsense,' he hisses softly enough for no one else to hear. 'You're being overly dramatic as usual. I've got you. You're safe.'

And with that, he takes hold of my hand and guides me along the path. Admittedly, I no longer feel in any danger, but just for a moment there I didn't feel safe at all. Though I can't see Nathan's face in the blackness, I can hear his excited voice promising me that 'We're almost there.' However, I can't shake off the fact that my husband almost pushed me off the mountain, leaving me in danger of plummeting to my death. If I had died, everyone would have thought it was an accident. I was clumsy, they'd say. Scared of heights. So, it made sense that I panicked and fell. Only Nathan would have known otherwise.

When we finally reach the summit, I'm still feeling shaky. I'm told that what waits for me here is worth my aching limbs and shortness of breath, but once more, I'm disappointed with how commercialised everything is, especially when I see the wooden huts selling food, blankets and souvenirs. There's even a toilet charging tourists 500,000 rupees to use it. No thanks. I'd rather pee in my pants than use a public toilet in Bali. It's usually little more than a hole in the ground with no toilet paper.

But I forget all the irritations and inconveniences that offend my pampered Westernised ways when I see the sun beginning to break through the thick cloud as if being born for the first time. Naturally, I think of my son then and a smile comes to my face. Next, a dark peak appears out of the white cloud, moving like a giant chess piece on a board, and everyone gasps. It's the next-door mountain, Mount Agung.

People are breathing in the sacred air and meditating with palms facing upwards as they look up at the charcoal sky. It's surreal how many visitors there are. Hundreds. The surrounding forest comes to life as the darkness fades and the temperature rises. As we wait for dawn, some tourists snack on boiled eggs and banana sandwiches that their guides have packed for them. Nathan removes his trainers and empties them of sand and dirt, complaining to our guide, 'If those clouds don't soon clear, I'll be wanting a refund. I haven't come all this way not to see the sunrise.'

Cringing at the way the guide is rolling his eyes and, feeling embarrassed by my husband, I move away, much closer to the precipice than I would normally. But the rock face feels solid beneath my feet, and I am reminded that it has been here for more than 20,000 years. The last time the volcano erupted was only around twenty years ago, but I try not to think about this.

'It's beautiful,' I murmur to myself as I take in the sky's amazing array of colours. Red, violet, orange and grey. Steam billows from the craggy outcrops of volcanic rock and the shadowy black trees cling precariously to the mountainside. Some of the crowd sing along to a Balinese guitarist's rendition of the Beatles "Here Comes the Sun", adding to the atmosphere.

'You're right. It is beautiful,' a quiet voice next to me says. I turn to look at Angelika's husband, who has moved to stand next to me. Meanwhile, Nathan is ordering hot chocolate and pancakes for everyone and is insisting in a loud unmissable voice that he is paying for it.

I can't help but think that Bartosz gazes at me a bit too long and intensely, to the point that I feel a little uncomfortable and look away.

'How was the climb?' He sounds more concerned for me than my own husband did.

'It wasn't too bad,' I shrug, trying to forget the horrifying moment I thought Nathan had deliberately tried to push me off the mountain. But why would he do something like that? What would he stand to gain?

'Worth it for this view, I reckon,' he sighs contentedly, but I realise he's staring into my eyes instead of at the blood-red sky.

I avert my gaze and worriedly chew my lip — Nathan says it's a bad habit of mine — 'I'm with you there, although I can't say I'm looking forward to going back down. Nathan reckons it will be even harder.'

He pulls a face. 'He's probably right.'

'Thanks.' I give a sarcastic snort, and we both laugh.

Out of the corner of my eye, I see Angelika's head jerk up to stare at us and even Nathan has turned to see what we are laughing at. He doesn't like me to have fun without him. I'll be accused of flirting and making a fool of him if I'm not careful. The only one in our group not paying attention to us is Timothy, who showed up for the hike in completely inappropriate attire — a colourful Hawaiian shirt, shorts and open-toed sandals — and is shopping for trinkets like his life depends on it. As a result, he has a wrist full of friendship bracelets already.

When we feel the warm glow of the rising sun on our faces, we turn around to look at it. Everyone around us shuffles forwards then, towards the edge of the crater, to see better. I can feel their bodies pressed against mine . . . their warm breath on the back of my neck. A vein in my temple starts to throb as I realise that I can't turn around and that I am being forced dangerously close to the edge. I look for Bartosz but he's no longer standing next to me. There's no time to ask anyone for help because it's time. It's happening. This is what we were promised — a breathtaking sunrise on Mount Batur. As we wait, a quiet falls over the crowd.

A few minutes pass in complete silence. Not even the monkeys who live on the volcano and the stray dogs that accompanied us on our walk make a sound. At that moment, there is a spine-tingling scream.

CHAPTER 14: TIMOTHY

In the ensuing panic, I didn't see what happened. I just remember hearing someone cry out. That someone turned out to be Nathan Price. There was a commotion to my right and a flailing of arms as Price went down on his hands and knees, clinging to the edge of the crater for dear life. As he was being helped to his feet, he complained loudly, while brushing those well-meaning hands off, 'Somebody pushed me! I could have fallen off the edge and died.' He must have got the wrong end of the stick because there's no way anyone would deliberately try to push him off the mountain. Although I can think of one person who might like to. His wife. It's more likely Price got shoved forward by the surging mob who were desperate to see the sunrise up close. We were crammed in tightly together and it's easy to get caught out like that. At one point, I also felt claustrophobic and thought of trying to escape. Price is lucky he didn't get crushed. He got off lightly.

As Price hobbles off Samantha scurries after him, appearing embarrassed at being the centre of attention. The crowd is now blaming her husband for missing the one moment we had all been waiting for . . . the stunning sunrise. "That's pants, man" I want to tell Price because he seems to be making a huge deal out of something that was just a tumble that has left him with a few scrapes. However, when I realise how shaken he is, I almost feel sorry for him. That doesn't last long, though, because I remember what a jerk he was to Samantha on the ascent.

Rather than comforting his terrified wife and boosting her confidence, he lost his patience and started yelling at her to "hurry up and stop messing about". Poor Samantha looked like she was having trouble breathing, and you could see the tears of frustration in her eyes. I could have punched his lights out at this point and was grateful to the guide who suggested we go on ahead because I didn't want to see Price abuse his wife any longer. He's obviously suffering from small man syndrome and is aware that, when it comes to Samantha, he is punching above his weight. The man is a blustering fool, and I suspect that beneath the bluster there is only more bluster.

How he made his money, I'll never know. But I assume he's the type of businessman who throws lavish lunches for affluent clients in gentlemen's clubs. And for those who want something a little sexier, there'll be endless supplies of cocaine and visits to strip clubs. All expenses paid.

Why I'm still concerning myself with Price when I have my own issues is beyond me. I look around for the other couple who seem nice enough. Angelika and Bartosz. Jonah is bound to adore her because she's a fun person to be around. It's a shame that neither he nor Samantha clicked. This afternoon, they each competed for Connor's attention, and it was painful to watch. Eventually, she gave up and left, with a little prompting from Jonah, who claimed he was tired, but I think he was simply bored. As she walked out of the door, her gaze lingered on Connor.

Despite Jonah's disinterest, I like her just as much as ever. She's like a breath of fresh air and helps me forget about the situation with Putu, which resulted in an ultimatum being issued earlier this evening. I can't say I was all that surprised. In fact, I felt almost relieved when it arrived, since I now know what he wants — a quarter of a million in English money. I need to come up with a plan. *Where the hell am I going to get my hands on that sort of money without Jonah finding out?*

Most of our joint funds are invested in property or other entrepreneurial business ventures. To say that we are cash-rich would be a huge exaggeration. Our joint business account has fifty-thousand pounds in it with an overdraft limit of four times that much. Although it's possible for me to pay Putu off, doing so would bankrupt us. The alternative doesn't bear thinking about. But two signatures are required to release funds from the business account and Jonah would never consent to that without a valid reason. I do have a valid reason, but not one I'm willing to share with my new husband. If he knew what I'd done, he'd never forgive me. As they say, I'd be out on my ear in no time. I might as well pack a case now and leave the island, and him, forever. That would mean saying goodbye to our son too.

To take my mind off the blackmailing concierge, who wants his money *now* and not later, I make my way over to the Polish couple, thinking that Bartosz is a strange sort. I'm still not sure about him. He has unreadable, dark eyes that take in everything, and he stands tall and straight like a statue. My mum would have described him as "the strong, silent type" but he comes across as distant and cold. The only time I detect warmth in his eyes is when he looks at his wife. He is built like an athlete and is the same height as me, but considerably leaner. I would personally prefer not to cross him.

'Is Nathan all right?' Angelika asks impatiently, craning her neck to see.

I shrug and look over at the Prices who are talking animatedly to our guide. Every so often Samantha throws up her hands in surrender, as if trying to calm her husband down. She's losing that battle. 'Seems that way,' I nod.

'A lot of fuss over nothing,' Bartosz scolds, and his trainers come together in a sharp half-salute. I wonder briefly what he does for a living. Maybe the armed services or security?

Although neither of those occupations pays enough to cover extravagant honeymoons like ours.

This is the first time I've heard him say anything besides "Hello" or "Pleased to meet you" and I take back my previous thoughts. If he's a man who, like me, has already concluded Price is no good, then we might have something in common besides our height.

'Did you see it happen?' Angelika asks, wide-eyed as if she can't believe what just occurred. She shoots an anxious glance at her husband but, other than a slight twitch in his cheek, he doesn't move a muscle.

'Not really,' I mumble, 'But I'm sure it was just an accident.' Bartosz nods in agreement but his wife seems unconvinced. She's as tense as barbed wire. Then I recall something that makes my mind spin. My body is on high alert as I turn to face them. 'But the two of you were standing next to Price when it happened. You must have witnessed the whole thing.'

CHAPTER 15: ANGELIKA

As soon as we step inside our honeymoon suite, I lose the phoney smile I've been wearing for the sake of the other guests and hotel employees. The housekeeping staff's sweet gesture of scattering paper hearts and flower petals all over the king-size bed only makes me angrier, so I grab a pillow off the bed, scattering broken hearts everywhere, and hurl it at my husband, yelling. 'Are you going to tell me what the fuck is going on?'

He swallows guiltily, exclaiming, 'I don't know what you're talking about!' and manages to catch the pillow to avoid getting struck in the face.

I jab an irate finger at him. 'Don't lie to me, Bartosz. I'm not stupid. I saw you.'

He clears his throat. 'Saw me what?'

'You tried to push Nathan off the mountain,' I blurt out, shocked by my words. But doubly appalled by what I saw . . . the moment Bartosz covertly slid in next to Nathan in the crowd, he pushed him from behind.

'That's ridiculous. Why would I do something like that?'

I collapse onto the bed and burst into angry tears, 'You tell me.'

59

'You're exhausted from the climb after getting up so early,' he suggests. 'Why don't you get some sleep, and we can discuss this later?'

My head whips up at that, and my dark eyes narrow. Bartosz is not one to insult my intelligence as a rule and he'd better not start now. 'Don't try to gaslight me. I know what I saw.'

He lets out a long, sorrowful sigh and then moves to sit on the bed next to me, but he's fidgety and can't stay still.

Without glancing at me, he finally admits, 'I was going to tell you.'

A jolt of unease touches the base of my spine as I realise that he's about to confess to being infatuated with Sam and, as a result, is jealous of Nathan. I'm not sure I can handle this, so tension crackles in my voice as I cry, 'Oh God, this is because of her, isn't it?'

'Who?' he asks, looking at me with astonished eyes.

'Sam,' I murmur and wipe a tear from my eye.

'Price's wife? What has she got to do with it?'

'You tell me!' I bark.

I glare at him, while he tries to figure it out. I know him so well or thought I did, that I can practically read his mind. 'You think I fancy her, don't you?' he gasps when the realisation dawns on him.

'Don't you?' I mutter, crossing my arms defensively across my chest.

When his guilty eyes drop away and he begins to chew on his lip, I think I have my answer. Seeming conflicted, he hauls himself to his feet and paces the room, dragging a hand over his shorn scalp. 'I can't believe you thought that.' He turns to face me with a pained expression. 'There's only one woman for me. You know that.'

'Why were you trying to kill her husband if not so you and her can be together?'

Bartosz heaves a sigh and bunches his shoulders. 'It's him, Ange.'

'Who?' Now it's my turn to look guilty. Does Bartosz know? Has he somehow guessed? Or has my worst fear come true, and Nathan has taken Bartosz to one side and told him that he'd once screwed his wife and the thieving little whore had stolen his money? Is that what happened on the mountain when no one else was around? If that's the case, my husband would have a motive for wanting to kill Nathan. And I would be to blame.

Bartosz joins me on the bed once more. This time, he takes my hand and gives it a comforting squeeze before opening up. 'Price is the man who killed my brother.'

I gasp 'You mean Stanislaw?'.

He attempts a smile, but it's too fleeting to be genuine. Anger and pain are visible on his face. 'I only had one brother,' he reminds me.

'Are you saying that Nathan was the driver of the other vehicle? The one who started the argument that led to your brother's heart attack?'

Bartosz gives a gloomy nod. 'I saw him at court during the trial but when we arrived on the island, I didn't recognise him at first. I couldn't shake off the feeling, though, that I knew him from somewhere. It was only when I did some research on him that I realised who he was. The same arsehole who was found not guilty of killing Stan and who walked free from court. I can picture him now, not giving a shit and laughing on the steps of the courthouse outside.'

I put my hands on either side of Bartosz's head, kiss his mouth, and mutter, 'Oh, my God, Bartosz,' as his eyes well up with tears.

He raises his distraught gaze and folds his large, powerful hands over mine. 'I always vowed to make him pay for what he did to my brother if I ever saw him again.'

My mind screeches at me to stay calm as I examine his face, my mind humming with questions. His soft, dependable eyes enlarge even more because of my panic when I prompt gently, 'So you did try to kill him?'

Bartosz puffs out his cheeks as if the gravity of what he did has only just dawned on him. *He almost killed a man*, whether he meant to or not. 'I just wanted to scare him,' he admits in a childlike tone.

'Well, you succeeded,' I snap, still furious with him even though I can see why he did what he did. Why didn't he tell me? Even as I think this, I know full well that I am withholding things from him too. Marriage was meant to bring us closer together, we've never had secrets before.

He puts a hand on my shoulder, and I flinch, so he urges, 'I swear I wouldn't really have killed him. I'm not capable of it, you know that.'

His voice is barely audible as if he's afraid of saying the words out loud, but he bravely continues, 'It was just a small shove, to teach him a lesson.'

I hold the air in my lungs until I'm compelled to release it. Bartosz's body is slumped over in defeat. With sobs wracking his chest, he buries his head in my knees and pleads, 'I'm so sorry, Angie. Please forgive me.'

I do as any wife would and stroke his hair, trying to reassure my husband that he is still a good man even though he tried to kill someone. I can't lie, though. I'm feeling overwhelmed by all the things that have happened to us since we came to Bali. Seeing Nathan again and then finding out about his connection to Bartosz. As the English say, *you couldn't make it up.* But *kurwa pieklo*, and that's swearing to it, what a coincidence.

It occurs to me that this would be the perfect moment to confess that I also knew Nathan in the past, but I can't bring myself to do it. Poor Bartosz has already had to face his brother's killer, which can't have been easy. If he finds out that I had sex with the man as well . . . it will push him over the edge. There's no telling what he might do. Once we're home, I'll tell him then. It's not safe to do so here on the island, where a dangerous man like Nathan Price can call you 'Anzela' with a knowing smirk while innocently handing you a cup of hot chocolate on top of a mountain. Of course, it could have been a genuine mistake. Given the similarities between Angela and Anzela, he might have easily mispronounced my name.

Who am I kidding? Bartosz might have needed some time to grasp who the man was, and the same is obviously true of

Nathan, who clearly doesn't have a clue who my husband is but has since recognised me . . . and remembers that I used to go by Anzela. *He knows. Oh God, he knows.* It's anyone's guess how long he'll keep it a secret, but I have a feeling he wouldn't want his new wife to learn about his sleazy past any more than I would want Bartosz to know that I had sex with his twin's killer.

CHAPTER 16: SAMANTHA

This honeymoon is becoming like a never-ending marathon. Originally, I was ecstatic to learn that Nathan and I would be spending our honeymoon in Bali and imagined us enjoying romantic sunset meals on the beach and lazy mornings by the pool. However, in reality, we're constantly on the go. After the early start and strenuous climb up Mount Batur, I had hoped for an afternoon snooze, but instead, we find ourselves at Ubud's sacred monkey forest, which is even busier and more touristy than the volcano.

After his recovery from what he refers to as his "near-death experience" Nathan is enjoying sharing his story of surviving nearly being thrown off an active volcano. You've got to hand it to my husband, who is happy to show off his scraped knees and grazed hands to anyone who shows even the slightest interest, he's a born survivor. Or, at least, a born storyteller. But what about my scare on Mount Batur?

I am unable to suppress the horrifying possibility that my husband tried to murder me. Just because nobody saw it doesn't mean it didn't happen. You wouldn't believe Nathan was capable of harming anyone if you heard him laughing and chatting happily with Timothy and Jonah, who has since recovered completely from Bali belly. I mean, isn't Nathan the life and spirit of any social gathering? In addition, he's generous when it comes to splashing his cash around.

If Connor hadn't wanted to come along this afternoon, I would have stayed at the hotel.

Realising that some of our party are absent, I interrupt Nathan with, 'Where are the other two? You did invite them, didn't you?'

He looks at me in bewilderment, as if to ask 'Who?'

I suck in my breath because he doesn't fool me. For whatever reason, he has developed a sudden and unexpected interest in Angelika, and he can't stop asking questions about her. I'm concerned that she might have told him about me having a child. But I'm almost certain she wouldn't betray me. I may not have known her for very long, but she seems like someone who can keep a secret. Put it this way, I would trust her more than I would my husband. So, I grit my teeth and play along, saying icily, 'Angelika and Bartosz.'

'Oh, I can answer that,' Jonah pipes up from behind me, comical in his over-the-top jungle hat and safari shorts. So far today, he has done everything in his power to keep Connor away from me and I find this upsetting. I must constantly remind myself that Jonah is Connor's legal parent. Not me. It's a difficult pill to swallow *when he has my hair, my eyes, my nose. My blood running through his veins.*

Jonah chuckles dirtily, like a seedy comedian, 'They're spending the day in bed.'

Preoccupied with a monkey who is gruesomely rocking, cradling, and carrying her dead baby around with her — it's too distressing for me to watch — Timothy asks, 'How do you know that?'

'That's what she told me at breakfast,' Jonah gushes clearly tickled. When he adds, 'Proper loved up they are,' I swear he turns to purposefully stare at me. As if to imply that my marriage is somehow lacking in comparison. But how could he know that?

65

What I feel for Nathan is very different to the all-consuming love I experienced when I was younger. Back then, I fell badly. Because he meant the world to me, I made light of my feelings concerning my child's father when I confided in Angelika. Had we been allowed to raise our son together I'm sure we would have been happy. But when I mentioned that he disappeared from my life after learning about the pregnancy, I wasn't lying. I found myself alone, at a very young age, with an important decision to make.

Although I want to love Nathan, I don't have the same passionate feelings for him that I had for my baby's father. What I feel is a sense of gratitude to him for choosing me and wanting to get married because, at the time, I felt I needed to be looked after. There's a tender side to him, though, that occasionally surprises me under all that masculine toxicity. Those are the moments when I adore him.

In the forest, it is humid and dark. The sounds of running water, buzzing insects and the eerie howling of monkeys reverberate in the shadowy trees. We don't belong here, I can't help thinking. This is the world of the monkeys, not ours, and I for one am eager to be out of its shadows. The atmosphere is heavy with the sickly-sweet smell of exotic flowers, making me long for fresh air. Although we've been warned not to approach or stare the monkeys in the eye, especially the bigger, more aggressive males, some visitors think they know best and break the rules. As Nathan is doing. A large monkey has sprung up on his shoulder and is eating a banana from its human perch, but he can't resist making fun of it and touching it. I look away from the primate's massive, crimson testicles that my husband appears so obsessed with.

'How about a photo of you and Connor together?' Timothy appears out of nowhere to beam excitedly at me.

Looking around, I see that Connor has wriggled out of Jonah's vice-like grip. Now that he's free, he places his hand in mine and expectantly grins up at me. "We've found each other again" our glance says.

I respond, 'How can I refuse?' thinking I would give anything to have a picture of my son and me together. 'You will send me a copy on WhatsApp?' I urge.

Timothy nods and says, 'How about over there, on the wall, with the monkeys in the background?'

'All right,' I nod reluctantly. In all honesty, I'm afraid of the monkeys — Nathan reckons I'm scared of my own shadow — and don't want to be that close to them. But I must hide my fear from Connor, or he'll pick up on it. And then he'll be just as frightened. Assuming a cheerfulness I don't feel, I enthuse, 'Come on, Connor,' and pull him over to the wall . . . where a bunch of grey, teeth-bared monkeys are staring at us with interest.

As we snuggle up on the grey stone wall that is surrounded by sacred statues, not to mention the scary monkeys, I understand that when we leave this island, all I will have left of my son is one photograph of us together. The thought is unbearable. As is the grey primate's hand that I can see, out of the corner of my eye, rummaging through my tote bag.

I freeze in terror but wait patiently while Timothy takes picture after picture. As soon as it looks like he's finished, I rush to escape the family of monkeys whose wall we have invaded. But I fail to pay attention, clumsily stepping on a baby monkey's tail. It cries out in protest and its incensed mother immediately launches itself at me, viciously biting my leg. I feel its incisors go in, but I don't scream or make a sound, since I know if I do, the mother will see this as a challenge and become even more enraged. Timothy observes what is, for me, the second physical attack on my body in one day, and comes to my side, looking mortified. He asks, 'Oh, my God, are you all right?' as he protectively picks Connor up and leads me away.

Nodding, I try not to cry, but I panic as my hand flutters to my linen skirt, and it comes away stained with blood. I don't blame the monkey for biting me. I would have done the same in her situation. I too would attack anyone that tried to come between me and my child. And by anyone, I mean even somebody as kind and lovely as Timothy. I allow myself to be guided back to the group by him, trembling from head to foot, and my eyes pull me towards Nathan, who has turned to see what has happened.

Seeing the fear on my ghostly-white face, Nathan unceremoniously shoves Timothy aside and pulls me into a rough hug, asking, 'Are you okay?' which, I suspect, is for the group's benefit. Yet when our eyes meet, I think I see a glimmer of concern in them. But that can't be right, can it? Not when I persuaded myself earlier today that he tried to murder me.

Then, in a strange turn of events, somebody tried to push *him* off the mountain. What are the chances of that occurring twice in a single day? This begs the question . . . if my husband was trying to kill me then who is trying to kill my husband? Or are we all trying to kill one another?

CHAPTER 17: TIMOTHY

In contrast to most UK hospitals, the staff at the Ubud Medical Care Centre wear bright pink uniforms. The facility has a cottage feel and is surrounded by a cluster of randomly parked scooters outside. When we stepped inside, the first thing that greeted us were posters warning of rabies and photographs of monkeys with their teeth bared, which must have freaked Samantha out. Jonah, Connor and I wait in reception while she receives two massive doses of the rabies vaccination. Nathan loudly insisted on accompanying her inside and holding her hand. On the drive here, which was as slow as it gets on Bali's bustling roads, Samantha was obviously shaken even though she put on a brave face. When Nathan requested that the driver go faster, the man rolled his eyes and claimed not to understand.

It must be thirty-five degrees outside at this time of day, so thank God there is air conditioning inside the building. Jonah wears a guarded expression as he sits in a chair across from me. He hasn't said anything to me since we got here, it's obvious that he's pissed off. He expressed reluctance to go with Samantha to the hospital, saying he was worried about Connor being in close contact with someone who might have contracted the rabies virus. He wouldn't listen to me when I told him that rabies was still uncommon in Bali. In his opinion, Samantha has a husband to take care of her, so he didn't understand why everyone else had to tag along.

He's worried about Connor, I know that. But Connor wanted to come, to make sure Samantha was okay. He's really taken to her, and that doesn't happen often with our son. When the door to our left opens and the doctor emerges grinning, I breathe a sigh of relief. Samantha must be okay. Nathan follows him outside and pumps his hand up and down in a too-tight handshake before motioning for us to join him.

'Connor and I are staying here,' Jonah grumbles sulkily, and then hisses in my ear so that only I can hear him, 'I don't want Connor going anywhere near her until we know she's not infected.'

'Okay,' I concede, standing up. However, I feel a pang of regret that he is acting this way with Samantha. It's clear that he is envious of her relationship with Connor, and this is clouding his judgement. Connor has other ideas as usual. He is on his feet and performing an energetic cat-like zoomie around the room as he races towards the door to Samantha's room.

'Not so fast, little guy,' Nathan booms, picking him up and throwing him in the air, which Connor finds hilarious. Based on the look on Jonah's white face, he appears to be about to have a panic attack. Due to his past, he's not a fan of rough play. I understand that he's overreacting to everything because he's afraid. I walk past Nathan, hiding a smile. He seems to get along well with kids, so I wonder if I have misjudged him. When I hear him griping to the doctor about how expensive the one-hundred-and-fifty pounds per shot fee is, I take back my words. Samantha must be cringing behind the door when she hears her husband complaining that everyone in Bali is out to rip off tourists.

Entering the private hospital room, I discover Samantha sitting up in bed, looking pale and exhausted as one would expect following such a harrowing ordeal. She musters a smile for me, but her gaze has already moved on. I quickly realise that Connor, not Nathan, is who she is looking for.

I stutter apologetically, 'Jonah thought it best if Connor didn't get too close,' and pull a sympathetic face, hoping she'll realise I disagree.

She looks down at her shaking hands in her lap, before responding, 'That's okay. I happen to think it's best.'

'You do?' I can't contain my surprise. I'm off the hook and there's no ill-will, even though I blame myself for what happened. If I hadn't asked her to sit on that wall . . . but then again, it could easily have been Connor.

'Although rabies among monkeys is still rare, there's a slim chance that I could contract it, and I wouldn't want to put Connor at risk.'

I nod in agreement. 'How are you feeling?'.

'I'm fine, really I am,' she assures me, but she doesn't look fine. In fact, she looks like she might pass out any moment and her eyes are sparkling with unshed tears. 'I didn't want to make a fuss. But Nathan insisted that we come to the hospital so they could examine me.'

'He was right to insist,' I point out, taking a seat in the chair by her bed. I then smile and say, 'And to make a fuss of you, because you deserve it.'

It's true. She is deserving of attention. When she's with her husband, she takes on the role of his shadow, constantly fetching, carrying and ensuring his life runs smoothly. If she could, she would stop the sun from being too hot for him or the air conditioning from being too noisy. The poor thing deserves a break. I can't help but wish Nathan had been bitten instead of her.

'Oh, I don't know about that,' she murmurs shyly. Humble as ever.

Jonah reckons she's about as interesting as watching paint dry. "Boring magnolia at that", he'd continued in an offended manner because he despises everything beige . . . food, furnishings and people. Earlier, when I was relaying something funny Samantha had said, he'd cruelly snapped at me, "Oh, can't we talk about something else? You're beginning to bore me."

This is what I fear most . . . that Jonah will eventually tire of me and seek out someone new, exciting and adventurous. Like Noah. Let's face it, the reason Samantha and I get along so well is that we are both dull. The colourful Hawaiian shirts Jonah insists on us wearing will never make me seem any less serious or conservative. He can dress me up all he likes but I'm not the action man he wants. I can't lose Jonah, though. Life without him is unimaginable. And what of my other fear? Putu?

'Are you okay?' Samantha probes, watching me.

'Me? Oh yes, of course,' I lie, waving her concern away as if everything in my life were wonderful when nothing could be further from the truth. After that, I avoid making eye contact with her, in case she sees through me. I close my eyes tight for a second, remembering Putu's ultimatum from yesterday, and I want to howl like the monkeys in the forest. I'm to meet him at midnight on the beach. I tense up, shifting in my chair and biting my lip. Because if I don't hand over the money, he'll tell everyone what I did. They'll all know then what a terrible person I am.

A killer no less.

CHAPTER 18: ANGELIKA

After knocking on the door to the "Royal Honeymoon Suite" and announcing myself, I hear a faint, 'Come in'. When I enter, Sam is slumped on the bed, propped up by the plushest of pillows, staring wistfully at her phone. Her face lights up when she sees it's me.

'Oh, I mistook you for the housekeeper.'

'Do I look like a chambermaid?' I scoff good-naturedly, motioning to my black designer off-the-shoulder jumpsuit and quilted Gucci handbag not forgetting the Jimmy Choo heels.

'No,' she chuckles, as she pats the bed and gestures for me to sit down.

I do as I'm bidden but nothing can prevent me from gazing around the room in awe. Palatial in size, it boasts expansive views of the deep-blue ocean and features bi-fold doors that open to a heart-shaped pool with a private rolling lawn, a hot tub and a hammock for two. As for the wine cellar and private bar, I'd be in my element. 'Who did you have to screw to get this room?' I joke, adding, 'It's amazing! Much nicer than ours.'

Sam winces, looking embarrassed to be staying in the most opulent and sought-after suite on the island.

'I'm sure yours is just as nice,' she suggests primly.

'It really isn't,' I assure her

Beside her, the hotel phone rings, and she murmurs, 'I'll just get that.' I observe her cheeks blushing as she exclaims, 'Oh no, that won't be necessary. But thank you so much.'

She places the receiver down and shyly admits, 'That was the butler.'

'You have a butler?'

Sam looks horrified and her hand flutters to her mouth as she says, 'I thought everyone on the island did.'

'You're kidding me, right?'

'To be honest, I find him a little intimidating. He seems very posh,' Sam whispers in confidence.

'And you're not?' I roll my eyes at her. *Duh.*

'No, I'm not.' She heaves a serious sigh, as though exhausted from a lack of sleep. Unlike me, she lacks the energy to even roll her eyes.

'Don't tell me; he called to ask whether you wanted chilled champagne bringing to your room?'

I know I'm right when her cheeks grow a deeper shade of crimson. So, I insist bossily, 'Get him back on the phone and tell him to bring a bottle.'

She nods obediently and grabs the phone again, this time with mischief in her eyes. I've always had the ability, call it my superpower if you like, of bringing out the wild side in others. I listen admiringly, *that's my girl*, as she announces in her poshest voice, 'I have changed my mind. Could you bring a bottle of . . .' her eyes widen in panic as she looks to me for help.

I tell her, 'Laurent Perrier,' without hesitation and she repeats this to the butler before hanging up.

'You're not going to turn into a rabid dog and bite me if I get any closer, are you?' I tease, as I lean in to high-five her.

'I think there's been enough talk of bites for one day,' she gently chastises. In this moment, she reminds me very much of a schoolteacher.

'But you're okay now, aren't you?' I ask, plucking a few grapes from a massive bowl of exotic fruit.

'I'm fine,' she asserts, a little too strongly for her words to be believed. 'In fact, I'm going to be joining you for the cultural dinner tonight.'

'You are? That's great!' I exclaim, popping a grape into my mouth.

She fixes her worn-out gaze on mine and inquires, 'What about you?'

'What about me?'

Sam shrugs. 'You seem a bit down if you don't mind me saying,'

'You said the b-word again.'

She arches an eyebrow in confusion, 'The b-word?'

'*Bit* as in, the monkey bit you on the arse.'

'It was my thigh actually,' she points out primly.

I chew my lip and observe comically, 'You could have taken that bitch.'

'You think?' she bursts out laughing.

I give her a cheeky wink, 'I *know*,' and laugh along with her since it is expected of me, but I'm not sure this is true — especially when I really want to scream at her to "stop being such a mouse and a doormat". From what I've seen of the husband-and-wife duo so far, she's worth more than someone like Nathan Price. Don't get me wrong, I like her, but I wish she would stick up for herself more. As if to prove my point, she catches my critical glare, throws me a flimsy smile and says, 'Nathan has been wonderful. He's looked after me so well.'

She's lying through her teeth, of course. It takes a fibber to know one so I lie right back, 'I wouldn't expect any less of him,' but at the same time, I'm wondering where he's disappeared to *this* time. If he was that wonderful, he'd be with his wife, not tanning himself on the beach gawping at women in their bikinis and sipping pina coladas.

'And where *is* Nathan?' I aim for innocence as I ask this.

She swallows nervously before replying, a little defensively in my opinion, 'He's just popped out for some fresh air. He'll be back any minute.'

Panic cuts through me as I realise that I'm almost out of time because I don't want to be here when he returns, especially after what I'm about to say to his wife. I've thought long and hard about whether to reveal my secret to Sam, but I've made up my mind, so, before I have second thoughts, I blurt out,' Sam, there's something I have to tell you.'

She replies with a shaky, 'Oh?'

I sense her pulling away from me, as though she already knows I'm going to reveal something disturbing about her husband's past.

Changing tack, I approach the subject more subtly, so as not to traumatise her any more than I have to. To be honest, she looks like she's about to faint. She may even have stopped breathing.

'It's about Nathan,' I break it to her gently.

Another, deflated, 'Oh,' and an almost imperceptible shake of her head. Of denial perhaps? Or a desire not to know? Both probably.

I imagine I can see the question behind her startled eyes, "What's he done now" and I despise myself for doing this to her. But she has to know.

CHAPTER 19: SAMANTHA

My eyes hurt from the light streaming through the windows, so I use this as an excuse to briefly close them so I can brace myself for whatever Angelika is going to tell me about my husband. Has she seen him "at it" on the island with another woman? My cheeks burn when I recall that this wouldn't be the first time he has cheated. Not too long ago, I was his mistress, and we carried on behind his wife Cora's back without a care in the world. Even though she was my boss, and a good one at that, all I could think of at the time was that this rich, handsome and generous man had chosen me over his stunning wife, who had given him three equally beautiful children. I still miss Jordan, Will and little Elouise, but they were never a substitute for my own child.

Beneath her fiery exterior, Cora was a pragmatic woman. She was wonderfully cooperative about the affair and the divorce — more than either of us deserved — and we stayed friends, sort of. However, that probably has more to do with our shared secret. If Nathan found out the truth about his second wife, it would destroy him. But her secret is safe with me. After breaking up her family, I owe her that.

I open my eyes again to see Angelika looking at me questioningly. Her deep brown eyes glimmer with compassion. A small voice whispers in my head that she wants to fix me just as much as Nathan does. I'm convinced that getting my son back is the only way that can happen.

'He . . . we . . . found out that Nathan was responsible for the death of Bartosz's brother,' she reveals after pausing to clear her throat.

This is not what I was expecting at all. To say I'm surprised would be an understatement. Rather, I had built myself up to hear that my husband was a cheat. *Once a womaniser always a womaniser*, isn't that how the saying goes? As a result, I stare at her wide-eyed in disbelief, trying to process what she has just told me.

'What? How?' I falter.

'Apparently, Bartosz and his twin were living together in a flat in Poole five years ago at around the same time your husband was there.'

'I'm from there, but that was before Nathan and I got together,' I marvel, relieved to hear that I wasn't on the scene at the time and therefore not involved in any way. 'But tell me about Bartosz's brother. What happened to him and how was Nathan involved?'

'They got into a quarrel due to road rage,' Angelika sighs as she stares down at her hands in her lap, 'It seems that both men got out of their cars over some stupid traffic incident and began pushing each other around.'

I don't say so, out of loyalty to Nathan, but that sounds about right for my husband. He has trouble controlling his temper and can be hot-headed.

'And?' I prompt, overwhelmed with a desire to know more.

'What Nathan couldn't have known is that Stanislaw suffered from a serious cardiac condition. Despite being only in his twenties he'd already experienced two minor heart attacks. He died at the scene and Bartosz has always held the person who started the argument responsible—'

'You mean Nathan?' I finish for her.

78

'I'm sorry,' she commiserates with a consoling pat on my hand. 'I felt that you ought to know.'

'Yes, thank you,' I mumble, blinking away tears. I'm not crying for Nathan, though. But for the poor, unfortunate man who lost his life at such a young age. A bubble of panic rises in my chest then, but I manage to beat it back down as I ask, 'You said his name was Stanislaw?'

She gives me a perplexed look, 'Yes, why?'

'It's an unusual name.'

'Not in Poland,' she shakes her head and grins indulgently at me.

When I don't reply, she stands up and looks in the direction of the door as if she wants to make a move towards it. It seems like she won't be waiting for the champagne to show up after all. I assume by this that she doesn't want to be here when Nathan returns. I don't blame her.

A muscle twitches in her cheek as she runs a hand through her glossy, straightened-to-within-an-inch-of-its-life hair. 'I take it you didn't know, as you seem really shocked.'

'That's because *I am* shocked,' I raise my voice without meaning to. By now, my heart is pounding so hard that I think she can hear it. 'It's not every day you find out your husband is a killer.'

At that moment, the door swings open and Nathan bursts in. He appears astonished to see Angelika standing there but recovers quickly, flashing us a wonky toothpaste-white grin. He then coughs into his hand, before saying, 'I bumped into the butler on the way over.' With that, he raises one hand to point towards the champagne bottle and the other to indicate two flutes. He assesses Angelika with a predatory look, jesting, 'I thought my wife had taken to suddenly drinking in the afternoon. I should have known better because you don't like to have fun, do you, Sam?'

This stings, and I hang my head in shame for a moment, because I don't want to be humiliated in front of Angelika, who I can tell, already finds me meek and compliant. She doesn't know my history though. Or that I'm a home wrecker. If she did, she probably wouldn't want to be my friend.

'If I'd known we had a visitor, I'd have brought another glass,' Nathan dazzles us with his blue-as-the-ocean eyes, and undivided attention, but what he's really doing is dismissing our guest.

Being astute, she doesn't require a second reminder. 'It's all right, I was just about to leave anyway.'

'That's a shame. Are you sure you can't stay for just one?' Nathan treats her to his smug I'm-richer-than-you grin as he grandly offers, 'I could give you a tour of the best honeymoon suite in Bali if you like.'

'Another time,' Angelika tightly replies, without looking at him, which obviously annoys my attention-seeking spouse. She turns to face me instead and her expression softens instantly. 'I'll see you at dinner then.'

'We'll be there, won't we, darling?' Nathan comes over to kiss me on the forehead, and I notice that he already stinks of booze — pina coladas if I'm not mistaken — as he murmurs into my hair, 'I missed you.'

But as soon as he pops the cork and the champagne begins to flow, I am forgotten. Of course, this is all an act, put on for Angelika's benefit. It's her he wants to impress. He'll ignore me once she's gone.

CHAPTER 20: TIMOTHY

Standing next to me poolside, Putu inhales deeply on his cigarette before flicking the smouldering end to the ground. Watching him turn to stare intently at Jonah and Connor, who are splashing around in the swimming pool thirty metres away, makes me uneasy. I only left them for a minute to grab some iced drinks from the bar, but it was long enough for Putu to waylay me. And now I'm feeling cut off from my family, fear knots in my belly as I realise the likelihood of that happening after tonight is all too real.

Putu's voice is thick with menace as he growls, 'Tonight. Don't forget.'

I grind out, 'I've told you. I need more time.'

'You've had years. It's time to pay up now. Or else.'

I feel a flicker of unease as he turns to wave at my family. Connor doesn't see Putu, but Jonah does, and he waves back enthusiastically.

A crushing sadness washes over me when I consider how much I'm going to hurt Jonah if I go through with this. Though, I'm left with just two choices. Pay up and ruin us. Or refuse to pay and be forced to admit my crime. Either way, I'm finished.

'I've told you,' I insist, hoping for understanding — he is human after all — 'I don't have it. Not now, anyway. But I can get it to you later.'

His untrimmed, bushy eyebrows come together in doubt and his eyes say that I need to wise up. His voice is thick with sarcasm as he mutters, 'Once you leave this island, you will forget all about Putu and his family as you did once before.'

He's right. If I had the chance, I would leave this island as soon as I could and never look back. Putu won't let me escape this time, though. He's a man now, no longer the boy I once knew.

As I study his icy gaze, I feel a flicker of anxiety in my chest as I consider what might happen if this man follows through on his threat to reveal my crime to Jonah and the other guests. I can't allow that to happen. So, I try to barter with him like the tourists do vendors on other parts of the island.

'Without Jonah's signature, I can't authorise such a significant payment. However, for the time being, I could transfer one-hundred-thousand pounds tonight. Today even.' I'm as persuasive as I know how to be. Sales is more Jonah's thing. I'm the paper shuffler. The money man . . . if you like. And yet here I am, financially ruining us over a crime I committed years ago. And got away with, I might add . . . because it was deemed an accident.

'Mr Timothy, you are so funny,' Putu chuckles hysterically, as though I've just cracked the greatest joke on Bali. 'You're forgetting that we have internet banking on the island too and I happen to know for a fact that you could make three of those transfers without anyone close to you finding out.' His eyes dart to Jonah and Connor before settling back on me.

He has me there. It *is* possible. I could make three separate transfers to get past the one-hundred-thousand-pound limit on our business account. But do I want to?

Seeing my broken demeanour, he assumes he has won. His eyes flash with greed as he stipulates, 'Midnight on the beach. After the funds are transferred to my account, we part ways. It will be as if I never knew you.'

Pathetically, I demand, 'How do I know you'll keep your word?'

'Because I practise Buddhism and have been taught that a bad deed done on purpose will have consequences in the future. As you now know.'

'But you have to understand, what happened was an accident!' I angrily protest.

'Everything we do shapes the people we become in the future,' he preaches, dismissing me as he puts his palms together in front of his nose, as if in prayer. Then, right before he reverts to his slick, hotel-style manner, he cuts me down with, 'You will receive your karma in the end, Mr Timothy, with no help at all from me. The Gods will take care of it.'

My eyes bore into his shoulders, wanting to burn the skin off his back, as he slips on his fake, submissive mask and walks over to smarmily greet a few hotel guests. My attention then shifts to my family, who appear to be enjoying themselves in the pool. I'm delighted to see that Connor has finally overcome his fear of the water and is jumping up and down in his bright yellow armbands. As I stroll dejectedly over to the pool bar and order a pineapple crush for Jonah, a watermelon juice for Connor and a double whisky on the rocks for me, I study my son's electric-blue eyes, wild red curls and porcelain complexion and feel my heart break. If I go through with this, what about him and Jonah? It will leave us with nothing. We'll be forced to sell the modern, three-storey glass home that we love. And without his sleek, piano-black Land Rover Discovery, Jonah will be bereft.

A switch in my brain flicks on as it occurs to me that there is another more sinister option I haven't yet considered because it would prove that I am no better now than I was eleven years ago when I first arrived on this island. Before starting university, I took a gap year, but my travelling companions decided to stay in Australia because they had met some girls, while I wanted to go to Bali as per our original itinerary. I ended up coming by myself, but I had a tight budget, so I lodged with a local family. Putu's family.

They treated me like I was one of their own. Seven of us were cramped into their traditional three-bedroomed Balinese home . . . Putu's mother and father, who was also called Putu (meaning first born son), plus a younger son, Made, and a married daughter, Dewi, who had a young child. Back then, young Putu was a mere hotel "room boy" and was considered low class because of the family's peasant origins. He's worked hard to get where he is today. When Putu's two-year-old niece, Ni Luh died in tragic circumstances, I was held responsible. Even though the family and the entire village were demanding justice, and baying for my blood, the police had nothing to charge me with. But they kept me locked in a squalid rat-infested cell for three days, before letting me go. After that, I scarpered, catching the first available flight home. There was no way I was doing time in an unsafe, overcrowded prison just because I'd been falsely accused.

I look at my expensive smart watch and see that I have six hours left before my life implodes. I know that whatever happens tonight, nothing will be the same again.

CHAPTER 21: ANGELIKA

The ocean is dark navy in the distance and the air is humid from the absence of rain. Before joining the others for the Balinese cultural dinner, we are having pre-dinner drinks on the balcony of our hotel suite. Tonight, we will be sitting as a group for the first time, and I'm not sure it's a good idea. I fear that Bartosz won't be able to tolerate Nathan's company for even an hour, let alone a whole evening. If Nathan starts showing off, as he did this afternoon, when he bragged about having the best honeymoon suite on the island, I worry my typically quiet and restrained husband will throttle him. In fact, judging by the way he's scowling at me, as he inhales sharply on his cigarette, I think he might want to throttle *me*.

I watch him down his vodka shot in one gulp and immediately refill his glass. His eyes are the coldest I've seen them.

'What's wrong?' I sigh.

As he turns to face me, he snaps, 'Why did you tell her?'

I purse my lips in mild irritation and snap back, 'Not this again. I thought we were done talking about it.'

'I don't understand you.'

'*Ani ja ty*,' I retort angrily, shifting in my seat so I do not have to look at him. It's a childish gesture, but I can't resist.

A beat of silence creeps between us, and for once, he is the first to break it. I can never usually sit through long silences because I'm a fixer.

He warns, 'No Polish, Angelika,' while drumming his fingers on the table.

He typically calls me Ange or Angie, so I know he's still mad at me, but when he demands, 'Stop sulking. It makes you look ugly,' his voice has softened a little, and I can tell he is grinning.

'This face could never look ugly,' I retaliate, tongue-in-cheek, as I turn back to face him. But I too am smiling now. It's time to make up, so I take a deep breath and say, 'I feel bad for her being married to someone like Nathan. Besides, I'd want to know if my husband was responsible for someone's death.'

At that, his head shoots up and his knuckles whiten around the shot glass. If he squeezes any harder, it will disintegrate.

'But would you really?' Bartosz narrows his eyes and leans forward in his chair to give me a fierce look.

The intense look on his face makes my heart still with fear. He's always been the passionate type, but this goes beyond that. 'Is there something you're not telling me?' I ask, stunned, wondering if, like Samantha Price, I don't know my husband at all. What a worrying thought.

'No, of course not. Take no notice of me,' he shifts his attention away from me and gazes out to sea. With a catch in his voice, he bravely continues, 'It's just that I'm having a hard time dealing with him being here, with us, on our honeymoon. It's the last thing I would have wanted.'

Despite being almost certain that he is still withholding something from me, I move over to slide onto the seat next to him and wrap my arms around his dependable shoulders. As I do so, I breathe in his unique scent. He doesn't smell like a chef tonight. There is no trace of garlic, oil, grease or spices. Just the clean, fresh organic smell of flesh and male pheromones.

'*Jestem tu dla ciebie, misiu*,' I whisper into his ear. In response, his shoulders tremble with laughter and he immediately comes back with, 'I've told you not to call me teddy bear, and no Polish, remember? We agreed.'

We did indeed, but I miss speaking in my native tongue and I'm about to tell him so, when a mental picture of Nathan Price lying on top of me, screwing me, hijacks my brain. My mind screeches to a halt at the memory of his boozy-red face leering drunkenly at me.

I push Nathan out of my thoughts and abruptly stand up. I cannot be in my husband's arms when I am thinking about another man, although admittedly not in a pleasant or romantic way. I lean against the balcony for support and breathe in the warm, perfumed island air, praying that the bad memories will fade. But instead, Nathan's back in my head again. This time, I picture him unconscious on the floor. And me, with one watchful eye out, searching through his wallet and ripping out notes. Lots of them.

To rid myself of the unwanted memories, I think of Bartosz instead. This isn't hard, given how handsome he looks in his tight-fitting black shirt. The Balinese sun has already tinted his olive complexion the colour of my favourite coffee. I feel arms encircling my waist as he comes to nuzzle into me, murmuring, '*Tak bardzo cię kocham*.'

'I love you too,' I declare, turning to kiss his vodka-flavoured lips. He has broken his own rule to speak to me in Polish and I adore him all the more for it. When we first got together, Bartosz insisted that we exclusively speak to each other in English, even in private, unless we were with other Polish people. However, he occasionally forgets when we are making love and calls out, "*o Boże. o Boże o Boże*" meaning "Oh God. Oh God. Oh God." After all, sex is the same in any language. I should know.

As I lose myself in his delicious kiss, I feel his hands expertly glide over my body, but dread continues to swirl in my stomach. I am so afraid of losing this man, and that's what

I fear will happen if he finds out about my sexual history with Nathan. He will never forgive me for having slept with the man who killed his twin brother. What man could? Since I suspect Nathan is playing games with me, judging by the smug, all-knowing stares he keeps sending my way, and clearly wants to get even for what I did to him, I feel trapped in a dead end. This cruel trick of the past has blown my mind to a million pieces. Who would have thought that two people could travel more than seven thousand miles around the world, only to encounter the one person they have every reason to despise?

On that thought a burning hatred for the man settles in my heart, weighing me down until I have to hide my face from Bartosz to keep him from seeing me cry. No bride should shed tears on her honeymoon. And no newlywed should be this miserable. Or be formulating in her mind the most heinous, vindicative ideas for revenge . . . For example, what if Nathan Price were to take another — this time fatal — fall from a mountain? He wouldn't be able to hurt any of us again, then, would he? Least of all his lovely, downtrodden wife. She might even thank me for it. The poor thing.

CHAPTER 22: SAMANTHA

'Where is everybody? I thought we were meant to be meeting at eight,' Nathan complains agitatedly, twisting in his seat to stare around the room.

He's wearing his pink striped shirt tonight with all the pride of a rooster. Telling bored listeners that only a real man can pull off a pink shirt or be with a woman so much taller than him is something he likes to do. A lot.

'It's still only ten to,' I point out reasonably, keeping an eye out for Connor, who I believe is also coming tonight. I long to see him but worry that the lateness of the hour won't be good for him because a four-year-old is bound to get tired and irritable. Timothy texted me earlier to let me know that Jonah had a change of heart when Connor flew into a tantrum at being told he couldn't see his new friend (i.e. me) and reluctantly agreed there was no real risk of him contracting rabies from me. Apparently, he sought the opinion of an online doctor just to be on the safe side.

Nathan puffs out his chest, determined to be offended by our friends' tardiness, and then begins to study the menu while we wait for a waiter. He will be dying for a drink by now. I know the signs only too well. The bored sighs, the increased nervous energy levels and the tapping of the foot. Oh God, the tapping of the foot. It drives me mad at times, not that I ever say anything. "Restless Leg Syndrome", he calls it and reckons it's hereditary. More to do with all the booze and red meat he devours, I'd say.

The staff did an amazing job decorating the restaurant for the show. A sea of gold stretches from the floor to the ceiling to create a memorable dining experience. The male-only orchestra has already arrived, warming up while seated on the ground and tinkling with their gongs, chimes, symbols and bells. The menu promises to give guests a unique and captivating insight into Balinese cuisine while enjoying a live dance performance. I want to enjoy this evening but I'm on edge. Time seems to stand still as I chew at a fingernail and wait for the others to join us.

'I am speaking to you. Didn't you hear me?'

Panic flutters in my chest when I realise Nathan is talking to me. Once again, I've been caught not listening. I know it makes him angry. You'd think I'd have learned my lesson by now.

'Sorry,' I mumble apologetically, forcing my gaze to meet his. Being under his scrutiny is like getting some kind of electric shock.

'You're unusually quiet tonight,' he muses, seeming to have given this some thought. He even scoots forward in his seat, as though genuinely interested in what I have to say. However, as soon as I remark, 'I was miles away, thinking, that's all,' he interrupts, asking, 'What about?'

He doesn't take his eyes off me, and I can't stop shivering, feeling as though he's attempting to read my thoughts.

Not knowing what else to say, I shrug, 'Oh, just the usual.'

He scowls. 'I was wondering if you had something to tell me.'

A sense of impending doom makes breathing difficult. *He knows.* Angelika must have betrayed me after all. He is aware that I gave my child away and that I am already a mother. *What else could he be getting at?*

Face softening, he reaches across for my hand and gives it a meant-to-be comforting squeeze. His eyes are alight with hope which makes me think I was wrong before. This is not about Connor. This is about something else.

'You can tell me, you know,' Nathan offers generously, and his cheek lifts into a mischievous, boyish smile.

I can feel the dampness of his flesh on mine, and I want to pull my hand away, but I leave it where it is and gulp nervously, 'Tell you what?'

Seeing my confusion, he appears disillusioned and snatches his hand away. With a nasty hiss he gets to the point, 'I thought you might be late and didn't want to tell me until you were one hundred per cent sure.'

My heart quickens when I realise what he's getting at — he thinks I'm pregnant — *oh, God no.* The fear inside me builds and my hand flutters to my throat as I whimper, 'No,' remembering to add, for his benefit, 'I'm sorry it's not better news but I actually came on this afternoon.'

His nose crinkles in disgust. At me for not being pregnant or because I've started my period, I can't tell. Most likely both.

'Some honeymoon this is turning out to be,' he grumbles, and just as I think he's going to mutter something even more unpleasant, a waiter appears at his shoulder, and I am quickly forgotten. For once I am grateful to be ignored. I'm beginning to feel like I'm taking on the role of the new Mrs de Winter. Before he's finished ordering the best red wine on the menu, we are suddenly showered in air kisses, perfume and aftershave as the others join us. I stand up and extend a warm greeting to both couples, giving Connor an indulgent smile as he clings to Jonah's leg, appearing shy and tongue-tied for once. I then find myself standing awkwardly while the men stoically shake hands — or in Bartosz's case, refrain from doing so. His intense glare as it lands on my husband catches me completely off guard. If looks could kill!

Unaware of the tension in the room, which feels like a dull knife slowly being dragged across my throat, Nathan motions for the waiter to return and then deliberately positions himself next to Angelika rather than myself. That leaves Bartosz and I together. Even though I feel bad for the man, I have very little to say that might interest him. To make matters worse, I can hardly see Connor from where I am because he's at the far end of the table. Realising that this is going to be a long night, I try to attract Nathan's attention in the hope that he will come to my aid. But nope. Not a chance of it. He seems very happy where he is. Next to Angelika.

Not for the first time, I wonder what he is up to where she is concerned. He barely paid attention to her when we first arrived on the island, but now he's all over her, laughing and cracking misjudged jokes. Like me, poor Angelika looks like she would much rather be sitting somewhere else. The expression "Rabbit in the headlights" comes to mind. When Nathan finally does catch my eye and I see the menace in them, blood rushes in my ears and through my veins at the realisation that I am staring into the eyes of a man who is responsible for the death of another — whose brother is sitting right next to me — and has never once thought to tell me about it.

CHAPTER 23: TIMOTHY

'So Bartosz, tell me about your line of work?' I say, feigning an interest I don't feel, as I play with the food on my plate, pushing the meat around with my fork, knowing I won't have the stomach to eat it. My nerves spike at the thought of meeting Putu tonight. Will he keep his word to remain silent if I give him the money? On the other hand, what will I tell Jonah when he finds out I forged his signature, our bank account is empty, and we are £200K in debt?

I can feel Putu's sly, river-brown eyes on me as he roams the room in full host mode, making sure all the guests are happy and enjoying themselves. As I study his frozen smile, I fantasise about stabbing him through the heart with my dinner knife. Admittedly, it probably wouldn't even break his skin, let alone kill him. Despite my size, I'm not a violent man as a rule. In his case, though, I'd make an exception. When I dare to meet his gaze, his chin jerks upwards in a defiant gesture. He taps his watch, taunting me and signalling that time is running out. *Don't I know it?*

I turn to look at Bartosz when I realise he hasn't responded yet, and I recoil at the murderous expression on his face as he glares at Price, who is greedily tucking into a mound of rice and sambal and guzzling copious amounts of red wine while maintaining a constant conversation with Angelika. Her thin, disapproving lips don't move at all, so I assume he's doing all the talking. Why am I not surprised?

Judging by the look on Bartosz's face I can see that I misjudged him. He doesn't just dislike Price, he hates him. It dawns on me that there is a lot of hostility among us despite our luxurious surroundings, where we have everything we could ever want . . . an island paradise with white beaches and electric-blue water as far as the eye can see.

Given that we share certain things in common, you'd think we would have ended up as friends. After all, we are all recently married and landed on the island almost at the same time. Where did it all go wrong, I wonder? Take Price, who is unable to stop nagging his wife whenever he gets the chance . . . and when he thinks no one else is looking. Why did he marry her if he can't stand her? Then there is Samantha herself, who looks so lonely and miserable. Is it because she longs for children but is unable to have any? Or perhaps her husband doesn't want them. That would be too cruel. As for Angelika, she seems to be annoyed with Price as well, evidenced by her persistent frown. Not that the man himself notices. He's too thick-skinned for that. But I'm interested to know her story. Then there's Jonah, who is jealous of Samantha. Finally, there's the man sitting next to me, who I haven't managed to figure out yet.

'Sorry,' Bartosz mumbles, remembering his manners, as his gaze returns to me. 'What were you saying?'

His eyes remain kind but there is gravel in them. As I watch his face go through a slew of emotions, I force a smile, and say, 'I was just wondering what kind of business you're in.'

'I'm a chef,' Bartosz replies in a clipped voice. Then with pride, he adds, 'Actually, I own a chain of restaurants.'

As I fake enthusiasm, even the sound of my own voice is jarring. 'Wow, that's amazing. What sort of food do you serve?'

'A mix of cuisines, but mostly European.'

I reach for my phone, saying, 'What are your restaurants called? I'll look them up. Jonah and I are always looking for new places to eat.'

'They all have the word Galley in them. Galley Bistro, Galley Grill, Galley Brasserie, Galley Steakhouse, Galley Vegan, Galley Kitchen.'

As he speaks, I type in the words "Galley restaurants", and instantly hundreds of five-star ratings and dozens of pictures flash up on my screen. Exterior shots of some of the restaurants. The happy couple themselves are seen in several of the photographs smiling and looking very glamorous.

'How come you called them that?' I enquire, suitably impressed.

'I used to work on ships, in the galley kitchens.'

I try to keep the smile on my face and cast a cautious glance at Jonah, who thankfully doesn't seem to be listening as he's trying to convince Connor to finish his meal. Connor is being particularly difficult tonight because he didn't get to sit next to Samantha. I don't see why Jonah doesn't just let him switch seats.

Turning back to my dinner companion, I sit up straight and feel my body run cold. 'What kind of ships?' I ask, determined not to let my discomfort show.

'Cruise ships mostly,' his words come out strained as his eyes find his wife again. 'I travelled all over the world. Best days of my life until I met Angelika.' He attempts a jokey laugh, but it sounds forced. I cringe at his words, they sound so insincere.

After that, our conversation runs dry, and he turns his attention to Samantha on his other side. I spend the next few minutes stealthily searching the internet for more information on Bartosz Dabrowski, as I find out he is called. Black dots fill my vision as I come across his bio on the "Galley" website and it lists all the places he's worked, including The Pearl Prize.

That was the name of the ship that Noah died on, from anaphylactic shock after eating a meal that contained prawn sauce. I never met Noah, but I am aware that he had a very severe seafood allergy. He and Jonah had received assurances that his dietary requirements would be catered for on board and that they would be seated at a separate table from the other patrons to prevent confusion. Up until the final day of the Mediterranean cruise, everything had gone perfectly until a junior chef made a rookie error that proved to be fatal. He sent the wrong dish to the wrong table.

According to Jonah, the chef was fired immediately but was never prosecuted — a fact that still rankles Jonah to this day — even though the ship's owners were taken to court and fined heavily. Jonah eventually inherited this money, which gave us the startup cash for our property development company. Am I sitting next to — and having dinner with — the same man that accidentally killed Noah? *The love of Jonah's life.* It can't possibly be true. Can it? I mean, what is the likelihood of that happening? And yet . . .

CHAPTER 24: ANGELIKA

'I've told you, it's *Angelika* not Anzela,' I finally snap, putting down my knife and fork a little too forcefully. Enough for concerned heads to turn in our direction, so I smile brightly and take a sip of my white wine when what I really want to do with it is fling it in Nathan's boozy-red face. All evening long, he has been goading me by calling me Anzela and doing so with that ridiculous suggestive twinkle in his eye. I've never heard such outrageous innuendos as the ones he's been firing my way. The whole table must be aware that he is wildly flirting with me, including my husband and his wife. He doesn't appear to care, though. That'll be down to the alcohol. He's already had way too much. Clearly, the man can't hold his drink. I'll be glad when the dancing starts. The distraction will be welcome.

Mirroring me, Nathan sets down his knife and fork and wipes a napkin across his greasy mouth. It seems as if he's about to burp loudly, but instead, he looks down the table shiftily, before muttering, 'That wasn't always the case though, was it, ANZELA?'

I freeze. 'So you do know who I am?'

He chuckles, 'You know, you never did pay me back that money you *borrowed* from me.'

I realise too late that I was mistaken before. He's nowhere near as drunk as I thought he was. He was obviously putting on an act. Hoping I would trip myself up and give away my real identity. It's one thing thinking that he knew who I was but knowing this for sure is quite another. At least now, I know what his game is. Power. And he intends to use this to play tricks on me. I'm proven right when in the next breath he leans in my direction and murmurs, 'You owe me. So, how about one more screw for old times' sake?'

Anger sharpens my voice, raising it a couple of octaves as I narrow my eyes and hiss in his smug, handsome face, 'You bastard.'

He roars with laughter. 'You haven't changed one bit, have you?' and is about to say something else when the music starts up and female dancers make an appearance on the stage in front of us. Nathan twists around in his seat to watch, a clownish grin on his face, giving me a moment to recover from the shock of his surprise proposition.

When he turns back to me, he runs a hand over his stubble before saying, 'Don't look so worried. I was joking before.'

'About the sex,' I ask cautiously.

'God no. I was referring to the money. It's not as if I need it.'

Nothing can prevent me from shooting daggers at him after that. 'If you think I'm going to fuck you, you are very much mistaken.'

Pulling an ugly expression, he shrugs, 'Suit yourself. But don't be surprised if I accidentally blurt out your sordid little secret to the others. What would they think of the newly married, highly respectable Mrs Dabrowski then?'

I swallow the lump in my throat. 'You wouldn't.'

Nodding down the table at Bartosz, he snorts, 'I wonder what Dumbo over there would say if he found out you used to be a sex worker. I take it you *have* retired now that you're married?'

I don't bother explaining that Bartosz knows full well that I was once a prostitute, because I don't think Nathan would believe me. He would never consider that genuine love requires honesty.

'Of all the sperm in the world, how in the world did you choose him? Does he actually speak or only when you tell him to?' He sneers, brow furrowing.

'Bartosz is more of a man than you'll ever be,' I bite back.

He seems bored and slurs, 'Snowflake more like.'

'What would you gain from telling the others? They'd all know then that you had to pay for sex. What would your wife say?'

'Leave her out of it,' he warns angrily, letting me know that I've touched on a sore point.

His desire to keep Sam in the dark about his past serves my interest because it suggests he's not serious about following through on his threat to inform the others. For a split second, I swear I see a twinge of shame in his watery blue eyes. Or am I imagining it? Maybe, after all, he does have feelings for Sam. I take back my words when he places a sweaty hand on the top of my thigh. I'm too stunned to brush him off right away. I also want to avoid creating a scene. So far, we've both managed to keep our voices low, so as to avoid being overheard by the others, but I'm not sure how long I can keep this up.

'How about we go for a midnight swim on the beach tonight? Just you and I,' he murmurs seductively, caressing my thigh. 'It will be like old times.'

Before I can react or bat his hand away, he's up on his feet, being dragged away by one of the Balinese dancers to take centre stage on the dance floor. He attempts to mimic the dancer's dramatic eye expressions and intricate finger movements as she performs a traditional Balinese dance. Surprisingly, he has a natural rhythm and can move. I remain silently fuming in my seat while everyone else enjoys the performance, laughing and clapping along.

Is Nathan serious? Or is he winding me up? Is he really expecting me to sleep with him? He's not a stupid man, far from it, so what exactly is he up to? It's obvious that he doesn't want Sam to know about us, and if he lets on to Bartosz and the others, she's bound to find out as well. To tell the truth, I don't really care what other people think of me. If they're that bothered, they can refuse to have anything more to do with me. It would be no great loss in my opinion. I'm never going to see these people again after the honeymoon. It's Bartosz finding out that is my biggest concern. If he discovers that I slept with his brother's killer, he'll never look at me in the same way again. And I can't . . . *won't* let that happen.

CHAPTER 25: SAMANTHA

A sickening sense of shame engulfs me as I watch my husband dancing with the graceful Balinese dancer who dazzles us all with her gold headdress and gentle smile. When they first approached the diners for volunteers to join in, I cowered in my seat, not wanting to be picked. I despise being the centre of attention. I'm too socially awkward and self-conscious for that.

But it's not the dancing I object to. That is harmless enough. It's the fact that Nathan has humiliated me in front of everybody else by openly flirting with Angelika. I slump against my chair and gaze down at the floor. What will everyone think, considering we are newlyweds and currently on our honeymoon? And poor Angelika, she must be feeling terrible. I smile weakly at her across the table, wanting her to know that I don't blame her, and she sends me a grateful smile in return.

A sob lodges in my throat when I recall the predatory way Nathan was staring at Angelika, and I wonder if I should just get up and leave. But I know if I do that, Nathan will accuse me of embarrassing *him* just because he was having *fun*, which is something I'm not capable of apparently. You can have too much fun, in my opinion, and in my case, it's usually at my expense. Nathan will undoubtedly pass the whole thing off as harmless banter. He likes to boast that he's a red-blooded man's man, pink shirt or not. "You knew that before you married me," I can hear his defensive tone in my head, blaming me for creating a fuss over nothing. Given that Angelika appeared so uncomfortable sitting next to him — not at all her usual, confident self — I wonder if she felt it was *nothing*.

I look up, sensing a pair of curious eyes on me, and there's Bartosz, gazing down at me with a kind smile. I was wrong before when I felt that his gaze was too intense. He is just polite and considerate. It's not what I'm accustomed to at all. Mortified that he's seen me sniffing tearfully and wiping my eyes on my sleeve, I blurt out the first thing that comes to mind.

'I'm really sorry about your brother.'

He sighs deeply, head down, shoulders slumped, and murmurs, 'Angelika mentioned that she told you.'

'She did,' I concede, wishing I could erase some of his sorrow. Sadness clings to his face, like a long illness. 'I didn't know,' I stutter since it's important to me that he knows this. 'Nathan never told me.'

Bartosz shifts in his seat uneasily at the mention of my husband, and he clams up again. I instinctively extend my hand and give him a friendly pat on his bare arm. When our eyes lock, I whisper, 'I don't know what else to say.' He nods to express his lack of resentment and his belief that I am not to blame. Or anyhow, that's my interpretation of it.

Ever since Angelika told me what my husband had done, I have been curious as to whether his second wife, Cora (the one before me), knew about it. Did he tell her and not me? I could always ask her the next time she drops the kids off. Whenever we meet, we always exchange an understanding smile, before Nathan makes his boisterous appearance, that is, and covers her model cheekbones in loud, wet kisses. Upon learning about her husband's affair with the nanny, she had informed me pragmatically, "At least I know the children will be safe with you."

Another time, when she was a little tipsy, she admitted "I guess I should thank you for taking him off my hands". After that, we were in stitches. We call ourselves the *Wives Club*. The annoying thing is she has blossomed since the divorce. She's more beautiful now than when she first married Nathan — I should know I've seen the photographs — whereas I am more of a drudge than ever. When I'm with Nathan, people often look at me as if I'm stupid because I get so tongue-tied. I attribute this to our age difference and the fact that he is more worldly and knowledgeable than me.

'Would you like to see a picture of my brother?' Bartosz grunts stiffly in my ear, drawing me back into conversation. I watch him rummaging in his pocket to pull out a glossy black iPhone. He admits with tears welling in his eyes, 'I always keep one on me. To remember him.'

I nod because I can sense that it means a lot to him, and as I gaze into his troubled eyes, my heart bleeds for him.

I gasp in surprise when Bartosz places his phone with the picture of an attractive young man in front of me. Although he has dark eyes and dark hair, like Bartosz, he is nothing like his brother.

'I thought you were twins,' I say with a catch in my throat.

'We were. But we weren't born identical,' he explains, as if he's used to being asked this.

I run my finger over the image, feeling as though I am touching Stanislaw's skin for real. That's when I realise the dancing has stopped and Nathan is now approaching us. Talk about the worst possible timing. I drag my eyes away from the photograph and clamber awkwardly to my feet. Knowing that no good will come of Nathan seeing that picture and recognising the man whose death he is responsible for, as well as finding out he was Bartosz's brother, I stammer apologetically, 'Sorry, I don't mean to be rude but I think I'd better go—'

Bartosz fixes his steely gaze on Nathan who is happily receiving high-fives and enthusiastic applause for participating in the dancing. Because of this, his progress across the room is mercifully slow.

As Bartosz puts the phone back in his pocket and clenches his fists by his side, his voice crackles with rage, 'Yes, I think you'd better.'

My husband is left standing there looking perplexed as I move away, in the opposite direction to him, surprising even myself. 'Where the bloody hell is she going?' he is muttering to himself.

I can feel my heart thumping in my chest as I force myself to leave the restaurant with my head held high, ignoring Nathan's call to "come back" as well as the sea of curious faces that have turned to watch me go. I don't care what people think for once. Because I have never disliked my husband as much as I do right now. I would even go so far as to say that I feel like I could kill him. Life for the Prices might have been different if Stanislaw hadn't died when he did. But now I know that Nathan stole a young man's hopes and dreams without thinking it necessary to tell me about it, I'm not sure we'll survive another night.

CHAPTER 26: TIMOTHY

I check my phone once more, pawing through it in panic, before letting out an agonising groan. I can feel my pulse pounding in my head, *thrum, thrum, thrum* — as if it's about to explode — and when my head snaps up again, I find Putu glaring at me from across the room. *He's always there...* watching. Luckily, he's the only one to have noticed my distress. Taking in my frantic demeanour, his face takes on a pensive look and his Adam's apple bobs up and down. His tongue comes out then, like a lizard swatting at a fly, to wet his lips. Feigning a composure I'm far from feeling, I return my focus to the table, wishing Samantha were here. Hers is the only friendly face I've seen all night. And what a night it's turning out to be.

Shot glasses are piled up next to Jonah and Nathan, who are hunched over with their heads almost touching and are cackling like a pair of wild hyenas. Their eyes are red and blurry from alcohol. Connor has dozed off on an armchair that has been pulled up next to the table, his favourite soft blanket wrapped around him. I wonder if we are bad parents for allowing him to stay up so late. No doubt we'll pay the price tomorrow when he'll be tired and cranky. Angelika has since found her way back to Bartosz and they have cut themselves off from the rest of the group, speaking quietly, in hushed tones, to one another, leaving me feeling isolated. Jonah suddenly cries out, 'Come and join us,' as he finally notices that I'm alone. When I grind out through clenched teeth, 'Just going to nip to the bathroom first,' he doesn't exactly roll his eyes, but even in his drunken stupor, he realises something is up. That's a fucking understatement all right.

The money has gone. All of it. What the fuck. With only an hour remaining until I have to slip out under cover of darkness to meet Putu, I decided to double-check our bank balance to make sure no unexpected payments had gone out, and that there would be enough money to pay my blackmailer off if that's what I decided to do. Although I still wasn't sure exactly what to do about Putu, even at this late hour, I felt I still had some options. And now one of them has vanished. How in the world could the £200K overdraft — now showing as a minus amount — and £50K of our joint funds simply disappear?

Clambering to my feet, I square my shoulders and look around the room, focusing first on one face, then another. Jonah. Nathan. Angelika. Bartosz. Putu. Each one appears hazy as if I am also drunk. *The money has gone*, is all I can hear ringing in my ears. Feeling as if I'm about to pass out, I reach out to grasp the table for support. I gulp, hardly able to breathe. Then I take another look at my watch. I have fifty more minutes until I have to face Putu. When I tell him the money has gone, he won't believe a word I say. Somebody must have taken it. Our account must have been scammed because there are no outgoing transactions listed, pending or otherwise. Should I contact the bank? My thoughts return to Putu. If I go down on my knees and beg, will he take pity on me?

I stumble out of the room, conscious that all eyes are on me, and make my way to the hotel bathroom. Once inside, I promptly puke into the toilet, not able to close the door behind me in time. *What the hell am I going to do?* Retch some more, that's what. And so I do until there's nothing left to bring up. When I'm done, I stagger over to the sink and splash cold water over my face. I don't recognise myself in the mirror when I look at my reflection: blotchy skin, red-rimmed eyes and a shattered face. I imagine a younger version of myself gazing back at me. The one who was here, in Bali, all those years ago. What would I say to that callous young man who congratulated himself on getting away with a despicable act?

My whole body tenses and I have to tightly close my eyes when I picture that innocent little girl's limp body and bloody face. Ni Luh was such a happy child. Her face haunts me still. She had a smile for everyone, even me, although I wasn't into toddlers back then. I hardly paid her any attention because all I cared about was getting laid and smoking pot. It's a shame that things didn't stay that way. But, oh no, I had to show off in front of my friends. Prove to them that I was just as daring as they were.

When the door opens behind me and I hear a familiar, 'Ahem,' I turn around, expecting to see Putu, but it's Jonah. My Jonah. I want so much to glide into his arms and feel the comforting weight of his slight paunch against my body. I long to feel soothed. Instead, I bark louder than I intended, 'Jesus Christ. You scared me half to death.'

Oozing sarcasm, Jonah crossly puts his hands on his hips and snips, 'Well, excuse me for caring and coming to see if you are all right.'

My face crumples and I can feel the anger seep out of me, like blood from an open wound. 'Sorry.'

Jonah hesitates before timidly suggesting, 'Shall we call it a night?'

Seeing my husband's eyes clouded with worry, I want to say, "Yes please", but I can't so I mumble instead, 'I'm going to go for a walk.'

'At this time of night? Are you mad?' Jonah rants, shrugging one shoulder comically.

'It will help me unwind,' my words come out stilted and sharp.

Jonah rolls his eyes, before scoffing sarcastically, 'Good luck with that.' He then stomps out of the bathroom, banging the door behind him.

Alone again, I feel a knot of fear in my belly as I glance at my watch one more time. Twenty minutes have somehow elapsed. Tick Tock. Tick Tock. I have thirty more minutes until my life falls apart. Ignoring the overpowering smell of ammonia emanating from the urinal, I go back to staring at myself in the mirror. Right now, I'd give anything for a smoke. This is the first time I've craved a cigarette since giving them up five years ago. It was a condition of the adoption process. I wasn't alone in having to make sacrifices. Jonah had to shed two stone, which he found incredibly difficult. However, the weight has gradually crept back on. Biting my nails, I watch the hands on my watch go around, counting the minutes and then the seconds until it's time to leave.

When I finally step outside, into the unforgiving blackness of the night, I feel a flicker of unease, as if someone is watching me. The sea air is humid. In the distance, the ocean is as black and shiny as an oil spillage. I kick off my sandals and step barefoot in the scratchy sand and walk towards the water, my shirt sticking to my skin. I wait, hackles rising, by the jetty that we arrived on. Back when we were happy newlyweds with a privileged life of luxury ahead of us. When I didn't know who and what was waiting for us on this god-forsaken island. Putu . . . Bartosz . . .

My anxiety spirals out of control as I continue to wait. *Where is he?* My nerves can't stand this. I check my watch. It's ten minutes after midnight. A giant wave of relief — more forceful than the swell of the ocean — washes over me. He isn't coming.

CHAPTER 27: ANGELIKA

I wake up to screams. Based on the commotion going on outside our hotel suite, my initial thought is that something terrible must have happened. A Tsunami about to hit us! So I toss aside the white Egyptian cotton sheet I've been holding onto and spring to my feet. Bartosz is still asleep, his head lolls to one side and a trickle of saliva escapes from his partially open mouth. Honestly, he could sleep through an earthquake. Padding barefoot across the floor, I open the glass doors and step onto the balcony. Is it just me, or is there a crispness to the morning air that I haven't felt before? All I'm wearing is pants and a vest and I have goosebumps.

When I hear a man yelling, 'Go and get help,' my ears prick up.

'Oh, my God! I can't believe it. I just can't believe it,' whimpers a female voice with a distinctive Australian accent.

I lean over the balcony for a better look. That's when I see a couple gazing down at a seal-like mound on the beach, close to the water's edge. I recognise the man and woman as hotel guests. Newlyweds like us. My eyes bulge when I realise that what I'm seeing is in fact a crumpled body. My hand flutters to my mouth as I repeat the woman's words, 'Oh, my God.'

Bile rises in my stomach as I wonder who's lying there motionless and washed up on the sand. 'Bartosz, wake up,' I yell, urgently dashing back into the room to shove him awake.

'What is it? What's wrong?' He looks confused and bleary-eyed as he sits up, struggling to understand what's happening.

I sink onto the bed. My chest is so tight I can hardly breathe. Two thoughts simultaneously race through my mind. Firstly, if there really is a dead body out there on the beach, is it who I think it is? Secondly, if that is the case, then I have a good idea who is responsible.

'I think somebody has drowned,' I tell him bluntly, watching his face for any sign of guilt. But all I see is bewilderment as he stands up and follows my gaze to the balcony. I do not follow him out there. I've already seen enough. More voices have joined the Australian couple's. Help must have arrived, although too late from what I could tell.

'*Cholerne piekło*,' Bartosz exclaims in shock.

Although my husband generally abstains from swearing, I don't blame him for making an exception in this case — you don't see a dead body every day.

As soon as he returns inside, I question him sharply, 'Who do you think it is?'

He frowns, surprised by my tone, 'I have no idea.'

'You don't think . . .' I leave my sentence unfinished.

Eyes wide with disbelief, he asks, 'What?'

I change the subject. 'Where did you go last night?'

A twinge of guilt appears in his eyes. 'Last night? What are you talking about? I was with you.'

Knowing he is lying, I coldly correct him, 'I woke up and you were gone.'

'I was probably in the bathroom,' he says unconvincingly, and his face flushes with annoyance. Something else too, shame or anger, I can't tell.

'No, you weren't. I looked,' I retort accusingly.

He runs a hand agitatedly over his face before collapsing onto the bed. Without looking at me, he admits, 'I couldn't sleep so I went for a walk.'

'In the middle of the night?'

'Yes . . . in the middle of the night,' there's an edge to his voice now.

'And did you run into anyone on this walk?'

Looking stunned, he coughs nervously into his hand. He obviously doesn't like the direction this conversation has taken.

'Like who?' he asks incredulously.

I avert my gaze as I come to the point, 'Like . . . Nathan.'

His voice becomes unsure, 'Price, you mean?' Then, realising what I'm implying, he explodes, 'Jesus Christ, Angelika. You think it's him out there, don't you? And that I killed him?'

Backtracking, I mumble by way of an explanation, 'I don't know. I'm just thinking out loud, catastrophising. I think it's the shock talking.'

'You should never think or say such things,' he warns darkly. He stands up then and furiously tugs on a pair of shorts. I lower my head in disgrace. He seems so genuine. Clearly, I misjudged him. What kind of wife am I to accuse my husband, who is a good man, of murder? When Bartosz grabs his room key fob, still refusing to look at me, I panic, 'Where are you going?'

'To find out what's really going on, so my wife doesn't have to worry about me going to prison for murder,' he argues, thumping a fist on the nearest table.

'No, wait, I'll come with you.' I plead, wanting to make amends. 'And I'm sorry, Bartosz, I don't really think you would do anything like that.'

Even though I'm lying, he doesn't know that, so he softens towards me. You see, I *do* believe he is capable of killing someone. If he ever found out about Nathan and me, on top of what that man did to his brother . . . Price would be dead for sure. Christ, I had wanted to kill him myself, but thankfully I saw sense.

When Bartosz asks, 'Are you sure, Angie?' his fury somewhat subsides, but there's still hurt in his eyes and doubt in

111

his voice when he adds, 'It would kill me if you thought I was that kind of man.'

Shame moves me to tears, and when I whisper, 'You are the only kind of man for me,' I *am* speaking the truth.

He looks thoughtful as he rubs his jaw, musing sadly, 'I'm beginning to wish we'd never come to Bali.'

'It's turning out to be anything other than paradise,' I nod in agreement.

Grimacing, he observes, 'All we've done is argue since coming to this island.'

'Perhaps it's cursed.'

CHAPTER 28: SAMANTHA

A large group of hotel guests has gathered in the reception area and flustered employees are serving everyone calming tea in the hope that the situation does not get out of control. Rumours are circulating that a body has been discovered on the beach, so, understandably, we are all on edge. Even though Nathan didn't return to our room last night, I'm not unduly worried as I cannot imagine anything bad happening to my strong, self-assured husband who can handle any circumstance. Besides, if anything he'd be the aggressor, not the victim. He makes me feel safe yet terrifies me at the same time

Concerned, I watch, as a red-faced Connor, restrained in Jonah's arms, yells at the top of his lungs. Jonah won't let him do what he wants, which is to come to me. That man has taken a real dislike to me and now the feeling is mutual. Does he suspect something, I wonder? I no longer question that Connor is mine. *I sense it. I feel it. I know it.* Therefore, it's entirely feasible that someone else — and who better than one of his adoptive parents — has twigged that we are, in fact, mother and son. Our unique bond must be visible to everyone.

I gaze around the room, hoping to see the other members of our group and I feel immense relief when I spot Angelika rushing across the cool marble floor to greet me. She gives me the most intense hug. For someone so small, she is incredibly strong.

'I'm so glad you're okay. Did you hear the screams too?' she chatters on, not giving me a chance to answer. I notice then, perhaps uncharitably, that her breath smells of the previous night. She must have hurried down without having brushed her teeth. Bartosz leans in and gives me a brotherly kiss on the cheek. He, on the other hand, smells delicious. He throws me a wink that seems to be meant to reassure and I let out a giggle. But as everyone turns to stare at us, I fall silent. If the rumours are true, then someone has died. Possibly of drowning. This is neither the time nor the place for foolishness.

'Have you seen the others?' Angelika asks.

'Connor's over there with,' I can't bring myself to use the word "father", so I say 'Jonah' in a clipped voice.

'No sign of Timothy yet then?' Bartosz observes casually, accepting the offer of tea from one of the hotel staff. Angelika tosses her hair to one side and nervously tugs a strand of it behind her ear. Her eyes are all over the place, haunted even.

'There's Timothy,' I exclaim enthusiastically, waving at him as he stumbles into the room, looking gaunt and sick. But he doesn't so much as glance in our direction and goes straight over to join Jonah. He looks dreadful. Beat. Done in. World-weary. What is this island doing to us all?

'How about Nathan?' Angelika grabs my arm and pinches it too hard, her eyes staring into mine. Both pupils are dilated.

'What about him?' I squirm and pull my arm away.

'Where is he? He's the only one missing now.'

I wonder briefly why she gives a damn. It's evident that she detests him. Last night, while my husband was flirting with her and she was sending him daggers, she made that clear to everyone. I don't take it personally because I can't say that I blame her. I still want to be her friend.

'Don't worry about him. Nathan can take care of himself,' I shrug.

114

Her hand is back on my arm, more forcefully this time. 'But you don't understand . . . a body has been found. Someone is dead.'

'I'm well aware of that,' I remark primly, pointedly removing my arm once more. I exchange glances with Bartosz who appears to be just as worried about his wife's behaviour as I am. I get the impression that there is something going on between the two of them that I don't understand.

'Angelika worries too much, that's all,' he comes to my rescue by encircling his wife in his arms and keeping her out of reach.

'Yes, I'm sorry, Sam, please forgive me,' Angelika murmurs apologetically. And I do of course, instantly.

'Ah, here he is now,' I announce, not exactly with much enthusiasm. At that, everyone turns to watch Nathan rushing over to us, looking the worse for wear as if he'd gone ten rounds with Tyson Fury. Ignoring everyone else, he draws me into a tight hug that feels genuine for once.

'Darling, I was so worried when I heard what had happened,' he mumbles into my ear, 'Thank God you're okay.'

Cynically, I wonder if this display of affection is for my benefit or the Dabrowskis. I'd like to give my husband the benefit of the doubt but it's hard when his behaviour towards me in public is so different from how he treats me in private.

'Is there any more news about the body? Do we know who it is yet?' Bartosz blurts out bluntly to no one in particular. He certainly doesn't address my husband directly, but it's Nathan who answers for everyone. He can always be relied on to do so.

'No. But I mean to find out. Right now.' As he says this, he searches the room for someone to interrogate but he still keeps hold of my hand.

'Who can it be?' Angelika claps her hands together in prayer, but I notice that her eyes are less troubled now that everyone in our group is visibly safe. I'm touched by her concern.

When he turns back to face me, there is concern in Nathan's eyes too as he enquires kindly, 'Shall I take you back to our room first? Until we find out what's going on, I need to know that you are safe.'

'I'm fine, Nathan, honestly,' I protest. 'I'll just stay here with Angelika and Bartosz.' *Don't make a fuss*, is what I really want to say.

With a dubious glance in their direction, he ignores Angelika who is just a woman in his view and therefore not capable of being left in charge, and commands Bartosz, 'You will look after her, won't you? Until I come back.'

'Of course,' the words are dragged reluctantly out of Bartosz, who can barely bring himself to look at Nathan.

That's when someone from across the room shouts loudly so that we can all hear, 'It's the concierge's body that's been found.'

CHAPTER 29: TIMOTHY

'Did you hear that? The concierge is dead,' Jonah gasps, stunned. So much so that he lets Connor slip from his hold and slide onto the floor, where he starts to wail and purposefully hit himself around the head. Though it's a cry for attention, neither of us takes any notice, we are too shocked.

'Do they mean Putu?' I gulp nervously, hardly daring to believe it. What a stroke of luck. Does that make me heartless? Too right it does. But I've never pretended to be a saint. Far from it. And don't forget the man was blackmailing me and threatening to expose my long-kept secret. I remind myself that he was once a friend, and like me, he has a family. A wife and a son by all accounts. However, I am still unable to muster any sympathy for him. Jonah has oodles to go round. Enough for both of us.

Jonah looks pale and disturbed, 'They must do.' I see his hands shaking and I'm about to offer to go and fetch him a cup of tea for the shock when he turns to his neighbour and commiserates, 'The poor man.' In a split second Jonah transforms from a compassionate bystander to an idle gossiper as he exclaims, 'Does anyone know how he died?'

'By drowning apparently,' I overhear someone say. From somewhere else, another voice pipes up, 'But he was a good swimmer. He used to swim in the sea every morning.'

The black cloud hanging over me, that was Putu, has disappeared, along with our money, but the worry and fatigue from the past few days lingers. Ever since arriving on the island, I have not slept a wink. My head hurts, and I feel weak with hunger yet cannot bring myself to eat anything. My body and mind have both suffered as a result of the ongoing stress I've been under.

With Connor screaming and writhing on the ground and Jonah gossiping to just about anyone who will listen, I am unable to concentrate. Jonah will demand to know every graphic detail of Putu's death whereas I can barely listen to any of it without wanting to vomit. Even though I know it's not my fault — the Balinese police and Putu's family cannot blame me for his death any more than they could Ni Luh's — I feel like I'm somehow responsible. If it weren't for me, Putu wouldn't have been on the beach at all. But hold on, that must mean he was already dead when he failed to show up last night. But how could he have drowned if he swims well? With all these thoughts racing around in my head, it's no wonder my mind is a blur. I should be feeling deeply relieved. Instead, I feel dead inside.

I try not to get angry with Connor as I demand in a tight voice, 'Get up from the floor.'

'No,' he cries defiantly, folding his plump little arms across his body.

'Do as you're told,' I warn him, but he goes on ignoring me.

His terrible behaviour isn't going unnoticed. Or perhaps it's my shattered eyes and ghostly-white face that people are staring at. I look away from Samantha when I spot her waving to get my attention. She's standing next to Bartosz, and I can't be around him right now. Tentatively, as though hurt by my coldness, she lowers her hand. I like Samantha, but I have too much on my plate to worry about her. When, and if, Jonah finds out he's been socialising with the man who killed his loved one, how will he react? Should I even tell him? What's one more secret, after all? It will inevitably make him relive his grief all over again. Would his feelings for Noah also return?

The room is hot and overcrowded and sweat pools in the middle of my back. I'm still wearing yesterday's clothing so I must stink. Feeling claustrophobic, I look for a bolthole to escape to. That's when I feel a sharp pain in my ankle. I look down, wincing, to see what's caused it, and to my horror, I see Connor biting my skin, almost hard enough to draw blood. For a moment, I'm convinced my son hates me. Even worse, I feel like I hate my son.

And I respond instinctively, kicking out in an attempt to shake him off. But as my foot accidentally strikes Connor's head, he starts screaming uncontrollably and, looking absolutely terrified, he crawls away from me and back to Jonah, who glares at me like I'm a monster. As I watch him tenderly pick up our distraught child before stomping off dramatically, I am unable to move. *What have I done? Oh, God, what have I done?*

Putu is forgotten. Now everyone is focusing on me . . . The father who publicly kicked his son in the head. Individuals are whispering to one another. I imagine them saying, "If he can do that in public to the little boy, what must he be like beyond closed doors."

However, only one person approaches me. Samantha. For a brief moment, I think she has come to console me. She hopefully knows me well enough to know that I would never deliberately hurt my child — though I have to admit to wanting to in the moment, as my own mother would have done given the circumstances — but hope dies in me when I see her enraged expression.

'How could you do that to Connor?' she growls.

'I didn't mean to. It was an accident,' I insist, cowering under her fury. If Samantha isn't on my side nobody is.

'An accident?' she scoffs, with murder in her eyes. 'You kicked that little boy on purpose. I saw you.'

Did I? That's not how I recall it. Or am I deceiving myself? It wouldn't be the first time. Look what happened with Ni Luh. I've always maintained that her death was an accident and have never admitted my real involvement. Not even to the police. The other lads were just as much to blame, none of them came forward to testify either. But they were the ones who encouraged me to cruelly throw the little girl higher in the air, before catching her again. She liked it at first, but I kept tossing her higher and higher even after she started screaming. Only, I failed to catch her that last time and she landed on the harsh concrete steps, cracking open her skull. The others fled after that, and I was the only one left. It was me who was supposed to be minding the child for the family, just for an hour, and although I tried to convince everyone that Ni Luh must have scampered outside by herself when I wasn't looking and accidentally fell down the steps, Putu and his family saw through my lies. As Samantha does now.

She hisses, 'You don't deserve to be a parent,' and turns to leave.

CHAPTER 30: ANGELIKA

The resort is swarming with police officers brought over from the mainland. Although everyone's calling it "death by accidental drowning" they're here to investigate. And they mean business. Everyone is to be interviewed. Staff and guests alike. Naturally, Nathan has assumed the role of guest liaison officer, assisting the police with their enquiries, and ordering us all about. He's even been given a guest register with all our details on it and now stomps about as if he owns the place, with Sam flip-flopping along behind him. Apparently, he did not come back to the hotel last night, and instead took a speed boat to the mainland, so he was one of the first to be interviewed. But he has a solid alibi after spending the night drinking in a tequila bar with three young Swedish blondes. Ana, Freida and Agnes. That wouldn't have gone down well with Sam — the poor thing.

'Mr and Mrs Dabrowski,' Nathan announces, acting as if he doesn't know us. For now, he seems to have set aside our ongoing battle and the fact that I stood him up last night. *Get used to it.* I won't be blackmailed. I'd chickened out at the last minute, afraid of what I might do to Nathan.

As Bartosz and I walk hand in hand towards the reception area's back office, where the interviews are taking place, we exchange nervous glances. The main investigator, who is the only one not wearing a uniform, invites us to, 'Take a seat' as soon as we enter, so I assume he must be the most important. His twirly moustache gives the whole situation a ridiculous Hercule Poirot vibe, and while I want to giggle, I resist as he comes across as rather serious. A bureaucratic pen-pusher, one might say.

I reply graciously, 'Thank you,' and sit down in one of the chairs that have been pulled out for us. Bartosz follows suit.

Everyone falls silent while the policeman looks over his notes. I wonder whether this is done on purpose to make us even more anxious. If so, my sweat-slicked palms indicate that it's working. Eventually, he glances up, seeming startled to see us. As if he'd forgotten we were there. 'It's a pleasure to meet you,' he murmurs distractedly, darting me an apologetic look. 'My name is Kadek. I work for the Indonesian National Police. I'm here to ask you some questions about the incident that happened last night when a Balinese man died under suspicious circumstances.'

'Suspicious? I thought his death was an accident,' I say nervously, giving Bartosz a sidelong glance as if he were to blame for everything.

Folding his hands behind his head, Kadek reclines in his chair. I get the impression he does this often. 'Every death is suspicious until proven otherwise,' he exclaims smugly, before continuing more guardedly, 'How well did you know the deceased?'

'Putu? Not at all.' I look to Bartosz to confirm this, but he is choosing to remain silent as usual and letting me do all the talking, 'Did we?' I persist.

A look of confusion flashes across his face, before he responds, 'No. I didn't even know that was his name.'

When the inevitable question is posed, 'And where were you both last evening?' my heart pounds in my chest.

'We went to the cultural dinner, and then, just before midnight, we went to bed.' I maintain my composure since I haven't yet told a single lie, but I have a feeling that's about to change.

'And did either of you leave your room after you turned in for the night.'

Bartosz detests lying, but I don't operate under the same moral standards as him, so before he can stop me, I jump in with, 'No, we spent the entire night in our room.' I dare to look at Bartosz then, and he appears unusually flustered.

'Both of you?' The policeman wants to know.

My voice breaks a little as I answer for both of us, 'Yes. Both of us. We didn't leave our room until this morning when we went down to reception to report that we had heard screaming coming from the beach.'

Appearing satisfied, he nods. I twist around to see what he's written in his notebook, but he's too cunning for that, and he whips it out of sight with an amused expression. 'I appreciate your time. You may go now.'

'Thank you so much,' I exclaim, getting up immediately. Bartosz is too sluggish for my liking, and I want to prod him to his feet.

We're almost at the door when Kadek stops us with, 'Just one more thing.'

Bartosz and I slowly turn to gaze at him. Fearing the worst, I bite down on my lip, and I can taste the tang of blood in my mouth.

'Yes?' my voice wobbles ever so slightly. What can he have to say this time? We've told him everything. Except we haven't. Not really. Left to his own devices, Bartosz would most likely have admitted that he had gone for a walk by himself in the middle of the night. He claims not to have seen anyone, but we both know deep down that he was planning on bumping into Nathan. Who knows what would have happened then?

My husband claims not to be a violent man, but I witnessed, with my own eyes, him trying to shove Nathan down a mountain. Therefore, I think it's best if the police are kept in the dark about our respective connections to Nathan Price since they might also uncover my secret, and Kadek would be swamped with all kinds of paperwork then.

I find the policeman's smile more unsettling than his deadpan expression. 'Congratulations on your nuptials. You couldn't have chosen a more beautiful and peaceful island for your honeymoon destination.'

My gaze returns to Bartosz, and I get the impression that we are both thinking the same thing. *You have got to be kidding.* "Peaceful" is not the first adjective to spring to mind when describing our experience.

'Thank you,' Bartosz mumbles at last. He's naturally reserved, yet you can always count on him to be courteous.

I'll remember the policeman's next words for a long time to come.

'Stay safe,' He warns in a fatherly fashion, 'and keep in mind that even in paradise, there are criminals. Here, on this luxury resort, you are safe but, on the mainland, it is another matter. There are many unsavoury characters, scammers, sex workers, pickpockets and thieves. Don't fall for their tricks. On this island, people are not always who they seem.'

CHAPTER 31: SAMANTHA

'They've arrested your friend. Have you heard?' Nathan casually brings up this topic while I'm picking over my expensive seafood lunch. I usually have a good appetite but today I'm so worried about Connor that I can't finish a single bite. The poor child must be feeling traumatised after being kicked in the head by one of his adoptive parents, who are supposed to love and care for him, not physically abuse him. I want so much to remove him from their care, so I can comfort him, as only a mother can, but of course, I can't do that. Everyone would consider me crazy. But how much more insane is it that I'm having lunch in a romantic fine-dining restaurant overlooking the bluest of seas with a man who is meant to love me but may also have tried to kill me on Bali's second-highest active volcano?

I respond wide-eyed, 'What friend?' and quickly scan the restaurant as though the answer might be staring me in the face.

Biting into his suckling pig, Nathan murmurs, 'I knew there was a reason why I didn't like him.'

Spellbound by the trail of grease running down his chin, I push him again. 'Which friend?'

As though it should be obvious, he mutters, 'Nice-but-dim Tim, of course.'

'Timothy? For hurting his child, do you mean?' I gasp.

'What? No, of course not. That was nothing in the grand scheme of things. No more than the little brat deserved if you ask me.'

I want to scream at him, *I didn't ask you*. Naturally, though, I don't. However, I do insist in a tight voice, 'Then, why has he been arrested?'

Nathan shifts forward in his chair and murmurs insidiously, 'I have it on good authority, from a trusted source,' he pauses smugly to allow that information to sink in, 'that he is the only one who is unable to account for his movements last night . . . which makes him the prime murder suspect.'

Shocked, I sit up straight in my chair, setting down my cutlery and pushing my plate aside, giving up any pretence of being interested in my food. Assuming my husband is embellishing the truth, I take him to task by pointing out, 'I thought Putu's death was an accident.'

Nathan shakes his head knowingly and mumbles, 'The police have their doubts. Apparently, there were other injuries incompatible with drowning.'

'My God,' I gasp. Hitting Connor is one thing. But killing a man? 'They must be mistaken?' I shake my head, unable to believe what I'm hearing. 'Why on earth would Timothy want to harm a hotel employee?'

Nathan gives a one-shoulder shrug and feigns boredom as he scoffs, 'I don't know? Perhaps he was shagging him?'

I arch both eyebrows, 'On his honeymoon?'

'Why not? It's been known to happen,' he mumbles, as if it was not only possible but highly likely.

I toss my hair in irritation and clench my jaw. For some reason, this seems to please my husband, who taps his nose as if to insinuate that he knows more than he is letting on and is ready to fill me in, but only if I play the waiting game. I know I'm right when he puffs up his chest like an elephant seal and self-importantly confides, 'The police took a statement from the concierge's family to try and identify if he had any enemies and the wife broke down and admitted that Putu was blackmailing Tim.'

I try not to let my emotions cloud my clarity of thought. But this is outrageous. I snort disbelievingly, 'What on earth for? They hardly knew each other.'

'That's where you're wrong,' Nathan corrects me, pausing to swallow his mouthful of wine before belching noisily. I get a whiff of it across the table and it's not pleasant. He continues without any hint of a "pardon me" or any semblance of embarrassment, 'Because, it appears, that this was not Tim's first visit to the island.'

'It wasn't? But he said he'd never been before—'

Nathan eagerly jumps in with, 'I know what he *said*. But he was lying. And why would he do that if he wasn't guilty of something.'

Regardless of what my husband says, I'm convinced he is wrong about Timothy, but not wanting to get into an argument, I choose not to say anything. Rather, I inquire in some amazement, 'How do you know all this?'

'I have a nose for digging out the truth,' Nathan mumbles darkly, fixing suspicious eyes on me as if he were trying to read my mind. Shifting my attention elsewhere, anywhere but on his all-seeing, all-knowing gaze, I ask myself again: *Does he know something? Is he onto me? Is my secret about to be discovered?* On that depressing thought, my shoulders sag, and all the fight goes out of me.

Brow furrowing, Nathan breaks eye contact to gulp down the last of his wine. His fleshy pink lips are stained Merlot-red and there are delicate pink thread veins running down his cheeks. If he doesn't take better care of himself, he'll be dead within the next ten years. If excess doesn't kill him, stress will. Nathan is a businessman who likes to keep his enemies close and believes that information is power. He jokes about how he trades as much in secrets as he does business deals.

Down-on-their-luck former associates and rivals have labelled him an opportunist shark, a reputation he thrives on, although he maintains that nothing in business is personal.

He insists that he loves being a father and that his children are everything to him. He is open about wanting more. "The more kids the better," he's fond of boasting. I foolishly once dared to point out that he rarely spends time with his kids since he is always off gallivanting — golf, dinners at the club and business trips away. That warranted a lecture I'm not likely to quickly forget. "That's a man's job, Sam," he'd admonished, with an offended look. "I can't make money for my family if I'm at home being a hands-on parent," he'd added with conviction. "I'm a provider and a damn good one at that, even if I do say so myself. Put it this way," he had warned fiercely, "My kids will never know what it's like to be poor. I've worked damn hard to get where I am so the likes of you, Cora and Michelle can benefit from my wealth and good fortune. I'll be the first to admit that along the way, I've made some decisions I wish I hadn't. It might be a dog-eat-dog world out there, but that doesn't make me a bad man."

No, just a killer, I can't help but think, who took the life of an innocent young man. Nathan may not have plunged a knife into Bartosz's brother's chest, but he was otherwise responsible for his death. The irony is that he now feels justified in accusing others of the same offence.

'Aren't you going to ask me what it is I've found out?' Nathan lets out a sigh, no doubt irritated that I've checked out of our conversation again.

I think about how best to reply, before cautiously asking, 'Did the police tell you this, or have you come to this conclusion yourself?'

Taking this as a criticism of his investigative abilities, Nathan turns to glare at me. 'The most senior police officer has trusted me with this information, and it mustn't go any further.'

I nod gravely to show my agreement while hiding a smile that feels too motherly. I feel like my former status as a live-in nanny will never completely go away. Not when my husband acts like a spoiled child when he doesn't get his way. Are all men the same, I wonder? But when I think back to the connection I once had with Connor's father — before things went disastrously wrong, that is — I know this is not the case. There are men out there who regard women as equal partners. Not just ornaments, mothers and homemakers.

Nathan eventually tells me what he has been itching to tell me all along, with another gouty burp. 'You won't believe this, but it turns out your friend has killed before.' It strikes me then that he is enjoying himself far too much at the expense of someone else's misfortune.

It doesn't take me long to figure out why my husband seems to be getting such a kick out of this dreadful state of affairs. He is obviously jealous of the fact that I was able to make a new friend by myself without any help from him. That doesn't fit the image he has of me.

'When?' I mumble, still unwilling to accept what Nathan is telling me but beginning to feel uneasy. Timothy did strike out at his son, although, in hindsight, I don't really think it was intentional. I only said that to his face because I thought he deserved it and selfishly wanted to paint him as an even worse dad than he actually was. I had my own agenda for that.

With all the excitement of an executioner, Nathan exclaims sadistically, 'Eleven years ago on this island he committed, and got away with, his first murder, although it doesn't look as if he'll be that lucky this time around.'

'What? Who?' I whimper, fearing my husband might actually be telling the truth. His serious expression causes me to reconsider everything I thought I knew about Timothy. Could Nathan be right? Have I been spending time with a known killer? Worst of all, was my precious son ever safe in his care?

I have my answer when Nathan leans across the table and whispers dangerously in my ear, 'He brutally murdered a little girl.'

CHAPTER 32: TIMOTHY

I might as well have travelled back in time to eleven years ago, because I'm once again in a prison cell. Even though it's not as filthy and rat-infested as the previous one, at the end of the day, it's still a cell. I'm sweating profusely because there's no air conditioning, and even though I have already been interviewed — more like interrogated — I am still not allowed to leave. The reason I am here at all is beyond my understanding. I keep asking myself why Putu didn't show up to meet me on the beach last night. And, who stole the money from the joint business account? Should I mention this to the police or keep shtum? It's only day three of our honeymoon but it has already turned into a nightmare.

I let out a loud, guttural groan and drag a hand through my hair while looking past the bars and into the corridor beyond. There, I hear grown men, inmates like me, weeping like children. I fear the sound of booted footsteps approaching. Will the officers release me or bang me up for good?

Jonah is never far from my mind. What in the world must he be thinking? Does he believe I'm guilty as the others do? When I was marched out of the hotel in handcuffs, both guests and hotel staff gave me disapproving looks. There was no disguising the unmistakable morbid flurry of excitement in the air though, led no doubt by Price who, let's be honest, can't stand me any more than I can him. The mainland police are far more professional than the rural police force, who all those years ago thought nothing of roughing up a young foreigner visiting their island. The Java police are headed by an officer named Kadek who has, so far, kept his hands to himself. I recall boarding the flight back to the UK eleven years ago attracting worried glances from the flight crew because of my black eye, bruised face and cut lip. They must have thought I posed a flight risk since they watched me closely the whole nine-hour flight to Dubai.

The police have been quite clear that foul play is suspected in Putu's death and that it may not have been an accidental drowning as initially thought. Why did I have to get drawn into another alleged murder case? What could I have possibly done to deserve this? Strike that, I know what I did. I lied about the circumstances behind Ni Luh's death. Should I receive my karma and face charges, Jonah will fall apart. He'll already be utterly distraught.

The threat of being sent to prison for something I did not do makes me rigid with fear. I am innocent of everything I have been accused of. You could argue that I was innocent the first time around as well, though I was involved in the little girl's death in all the wrong ways. And now, according to the police, rumours are circulating that she was also sexually abused, which is an outrageous lie. This was never even hinted at before. And the family will attest to that if asked. However, since people would rather believe the worst, no one will bother to question them. I blame Price for spreading these slanderous rumours. Troublemakers like him have nothing better to do than exaggerate every small detail to stir things up.

I'm about to bury my head in my hands and start sobbing uncontrollably when on cue, the booted feet make their appearance. Scraping back my chair, I scramble nervously to my feet, fearing my knees might give way. A uniformed police officer with unforgiving eyes appears and gestures curtly for me to stand back, which I do, and the next thing I know, Jonah is being unceremoniously shoved into the room.

The policeman gives the command, 'No touching,' locks the door and turns his back on us.

'Jonah,' I whimper, bewildered by this unexpected development.

The policeman barks, 'Sit,' without turning to face us.

Jonah and I immediately do as we are told, and to be honest, it's a relief to be seated again. My whole body is shaking, and I feel queasy.

I want to reach for Jonah's hand, to reassure him that everything is going to be okay even though I don't really think that — but deciding to obey the police officer's instruction — I throw him a grateful look instead. But his expression doesn't soften. There is an awkwardness — no, a distance — between us that I have never felt before.

Lowering my gaze, I question incredulously, 'What are you doing here? I mean, how—'

With deadened eyes, he darts me a warning look, gesturing to the police officer, but when the guard walks away, keys rustling in his hand, and we hear the clanging of a door close by, Jonah hisses across the table, 'I haven't got long, so I'll come straight to the point . . . it was me.'

I frown, not understanding, 'What do you mean it was you?'

He can hardly bear to look at me as he shakes his head in disgust. I surmise from this that I have already lost him, and I feel my heart snap.

'I overheard you and Putu arguing and realised he was blackmailing you and that you were about to hand over all our money to him, so I forged your signature and moved it somewhere safe so you couldn't ruin us.' Jonah's unexpected admission comes across as harsh and stilted. It's no less than I deserve.

I gulp nervously before asking, 'Why didn't you tell me?'

'Why didn't *you*?' Jonah lashes out at me, fuming. He makes a valid point and has every right to be upset. His stance and eyes portray anger, and his clipped voice confirms it.

'Jesus Christ,' I murmur, my Irish accent returning strong and fast due to my current state of panic. Changing tack, I plead, 'I didn't mean to hurt the little girl. You do know that, right?'

'I wouldn't be sitting here now if I thought that,' he grimaces, folding his arms defensively across his plump chest. Jonah is vain and goes to great lengths to disguise his "man boobs" as he refers to them, by refusing to wear tight-fitting T-shirts or by going shirtless.

'And Putu — what about him?' I demand, dreading his next words.

'I intercepted him,' Jonah replies mysteriously with a dangerous gleam in his eye, as though he were rather proud of himself. He continues in the same vein, 'Before he could get to you.'

Startled, I gasp, 'Tell me you didn't?'

He rolls his eyes in a playful gesture, as though murder were just a game. He then switches to a vengeful mood, sneering, 'That was Noah's death money. There was no way I was going to let some blackmailing lowlife get his hands on it. Not while I was still breathing.'

I drop back into my chair, exclaiming in terror, 'Oh God, what have you done?'

'I've saved your arse is what I've done,' he scoffs. That's when I realise he doesn't understand the severity of his actions. As usual, he hasn't thought this through and has instead reacted impulsively and emotionally.

'You do realise I'm bound to go down for murder for this now,' I point out as gently as I can, aware that he naively believes he's saved us when nothing could be further from the truth. As for my husband being capable of committing cold-blooded murder when he was supposed to be looking after our child . . . that's not something I'm comfortable thinking about.

'That's absurd. You never went anywhere near him,' Jonah objects, wrinkling his nose in response.

I hiss loudly, 'But the police don't know that.'

Jonah's eyes fill with panic as it slowly sinks in that he has further implicated me in Putu's death even though all he was trying to do was protect me. For that reason, I can't be too hard on him, because he did this for us, demonstrating that Noah is nothing more than a distant memory and that he loves only me.

'I'm the only one without an alibi and the police think I killed Putu because he was blackmailing me,' I sigh despondently, feeling a life sentence in an Indonesian jail closing in on me. Jonah looks at me horrified, his small round eyes popping, when I go on to warn him in a tight voice, 'The only way they'll believe otherwise is if I tell them the truth . . . that it was you.'

CHAPTER 33: ANGELIKA

Sod it. Out of all the people on this island, I've been lumbered with Connor. The child from hell. When Jonah found me at the pool bar, minding my own business and enjoying an ice-cold gin and tonic, he begged me to take his son off his hands so he could go into town and find out what was going on with Timothy. I blushed at that because, since his sudden arrest, many of the hotel guests have already tried and convicted Timothy of the crime of murder after witnessing him kicking his child in the head in the hotel lobby. I did imply that Sam might be a better choice, as she's into kids in a way I'm not — not that I said so — but Jonah winced and murmured something about Sam being too preoccupied with assisting Nathan.

How could I say no after that? He was in a fix and required my assistance. He has asked for help before, so this is not the first time he's sought me out. Only yesterday Jonah asked to speak to me in private. He was after a huge favour and wanted to transfer a sum of money into my bank account for safekeeping. He assured me that everything was legal and that he wasn't attempting to avoid paying taxes or anything like that when he noticed the hesitation on my face. However, he went on to confide that he had received a tip-off someone was trying to defraud his bank account.

Since I saw no harm in this, I consented and provided him with my details, I reasoned, why not do a favour for a fellow hotel guest? Even so, I kept this from Bartosz since I knew he would not have approved. When I discovered that a quarter of a million English pounds had been transferred into my account, I was really taken aback. What the hell? No wonder Jonah decided to trust a stranger rather than a friend back home. He clearly had something to hide. Ill-gotten gains maybe?

Worried that I might be implicated in some way, I wanted to confront Jonah about this when he approached me at the bar, but he was so upset over Timothy's arrest that I didn't have the heart to do that to him. Instead, I agreed to mind Connor, insisting that we had a proper conversation about the money when Jonah returned. Because he nodded as if there was no issue, this calmed me down. Thus, I find myself at Jonah and Timothy's hotel suite, watching Connor as he destroys the Lego rainbow that I painstakingly constructed for him on the living room floor. Flashes of red, orange and yellow plastic fly everywhere. I flinch at the thought of stepping barefoot on those painful plastic edges.

'Lego is for small kids,' Connor angrily protests, sweeping away everything in his path with a clenched fist. He has felt tip all over his face and is wearing a toy Indian headdress. When I scowl at him, he gives me a cautious sidelong glance, as though he's still not sure about me. The little brat hasn't figured me out yet and I aim to use that to my advantage. He will never have met anyone quite like me before.

I'm scathing, 'Yeah, well, you behave as though you're still in nappies most of the time.'

'I don't!' he yells, pulling down his shorts to reveal his big-boy pants.

'Whatever,' I say, unimpressed, and then I purposefully make fun of him by observing, 'Big kids brush their hair and wash their faces.' With my lips pursed, I gaze at the door intently, wanting Jonah to walk through it. After just one hour of babysitting, I'm fried. It is impossible to amuse Connor for very long when his concentration span is non-existent. Despite my lack of experience with children, I'm convinced there's something wrong with the kid. Dogs are much easier to manage. And train.

Pouting, Connor runs a grubby hand through his matted hair and tugs on a knot. 'Ouch,' he complains, pulling a disgusted face.

'Want me to brush it for you?' I grudgingly offer, hoping he'll say no.

He snaps, 'No,' and adds, 'Stupid.'

'Fair enough,' I shrug and abruptly walk away before I lose my cool. I can tell by his stunned expression that he's not used to being ignored.

He gets up to follow me, demanding, 'Wait, come back,' but I hurry into the master bedroom — anything for a bit of peace and quiet — shut the door quickly and yell over my shoulder, 'Don't come in here or I'll take you to the woods and leave you there.'

Remarkably, he obeys, allowing me to explore the exquisite room by myself. Five minutes away from the kid is as good as the gin and tonic I gave up to be here. The room is not unlike ours; it just has a different layout. I chuckle silently as Connor begs not to be taken to the woods from the other side of the door. My mother used to threaten to do the same to me if I was bad, but she never meant it. We had a close relationship and were more like sisters. I still think about her every day. I feel so bad that I was unable to tend to her in her final hours. If only those spineless, greedy landlords hadn't thrown us out onto the streets I could have been there for her. However, she passed away in a hospice miles from where I was having to sofa surf, all by herself, without her only daughter by her side.

I've always been inquisitive by nature, so when I see a glossy black iPhone on the smooth white bedspread, I'm interested to know who it belongs to and what secrets it might hold. Everyone has them. Especially murderers! When I pick it up, the screen flashes immediately, indicating that it is fully charged, but it is locked. Of course, it is. Who doesn't keep their phone locked? Hmm . . . opening the door a fraction, I call out, 'Hey, weirdo, when is your birthday?'

I think I hear Connor smother a laugh. 'Why?' What a suspicious little creature he is.

'Never mind why. Just answer the question otherwise no more birthday presents,' I warn ominously. He instantly pipes up, 'The 1st of July.' Knowing that Connor is four, I return to the phone and tap in 01.07.20. I'm amazed when it unlocks. It worked. I'm in. Sinking onto the enormous bed, I browse through the phone and see a tonne of photos of an enormous glass-built three-storey mansion. This must be where Jonah, Timothy and Connor live. It has to be worth millions. I flinch when I see a familiar email address for info@brookesproper-tyservices.co.uk.

After that, nothing can stop me from digging some more. Next, I open up a slim, shiny laptop, and with the same pass-code, I'm browsing the internet in no time. That's where I come across the "Brookes of Brighton" website, a company that offers a wide variety of rental properties and who, accord-ing to their blurb, are constantly searching for investment properties to buy and sell. "Making profit is our business", the joint owners claim. The elegant office block on Lewes Street is familiar to me. I once sat on a cold brick wall outside it in the rain for three hours, waiting for the owners to appear so I could give them a piece of my mind for evicting us, but they never showed. When at last I see a picture of them standing under a sign that reads "Brookes Property Services", my mouth drops open. They have on sharp suits and money-grabbing smiles. I recognise them instantly.

I have always vowed to exact revenge on the cowardly landlords who sold my home from under my nose and refused to even have a face-to-face conversation with me about my mother's critical condition . . . *if they'd only given us a few more months in the house everything would have ended so differently*. And now that I know who they are, I can finally hold them accountable for their actions. If it weren't for them, my mother wouldn't have died homeless and alone. As I stare at Jonah and Timothy's hateful faces on screen, their fates are sealed. Starting with their money, which is now officially mine, I have big plans for them.

CHAPTER 34: SAMANTHA

I've been worrying nonstop ever since learning that the little girl Timothy is said to have killed all those years ago had also been sexually molested (something the police will neither confirm nor deny). So much for Nathan's grand claims of being kept in the loop. What if Connor has been experiencing something similar? Timothy might have adopted him with the sole intention of abusing him. I can tell my fears are running away with me when I find myself obsessing over whether Timothy is a paedophile, so I've decided to pay Jonah a visit. Since Nathan relayed the sickening news about Timothy with such relish, he cannot be trusted to tell the truth as he loves to exaggerate. I'm certain Jonah will be in possession of the real facts. Hopefully, this will ease my mind. I'm entitled to know. Connor is my son.

Even before I get to their suite, I hear Connor screaming uncontrollably inside. I place my hand over my heart and gasp, then I start to run. I swear I will murder Jonah if he is hurting my boy. Finding the door to their suite unlocked, I savagely thrust it open and swivel my murderous gaze around the room. Two startled faces turn to look at me. Connor and Angelika of all people. What is she doing here? My son wasn't in any danger at all, I realise foolishly. Instead of screaming for help as I imagined, he is giggling uncontrollably, evidenced by the grin lighting up his face.

'What's going on?' I growl, as though I'm entitled to be here, and Angelika is not. Even though technically, I have not been invited and she clearly has.

'Someone has finally come to their senses and is letting me brush their hair,' Angelika quips as she continues brushing Connor's thick red hair.

Connor cheerfully pipes up, 'It's knotted and Gelika is making it better,' as he imitates thunderous crashes and dive-bombs a Lego aeroplane.

'He's letting you brush his hair?' I bristle, stealing another furtive look at Connor, amazed and perturbed to find him enjoying her brush strokes so much. His brilliant blue eyes, so lively and clever, will be my downfall if I continue staring into them, so I fix my gaze on Angelika instead, who appears amused rather than offended, as I would be, by my barging in here unannounced.

'It appears that way,' Angelika asserts, taking control of the situation. I notice that her voice sounds different somehow. More urgent, with threads of apprehension wound through it. Or is it just me? Perhaps since Putu's body was discovered, everyone is on edge and feeling the pressure. Naturally, there is also Timothy's arrest which everyone is talking about.

I shakily continue, 'But he never lets anyone brush his hair,' . . . *not even me*, I refrain from adding.

Angelika chuckles, but I have a sneaking suspicion that she's faking it when she acknowledges, 'We came to a deal, didn't we, Tiger?'

Connor looks up at Angelika with adoring eyes and gig-gles before letting out a giant cat roar. My heart breaks at the glance they exchange. Tears sting my eyes, blurring my vision as I take in his smitten expression.

'Is everything all right, Sam?' Angelika asks, giving me an odd look.

I manage coldly between clenched teeth, 'Yes, of course.' But it's obviously not. Don't ask me why I am so upset. I just bloody well am. Any fool can see it, too. And Angelika is no fool, far from it. So I feel compelled to explain, 'I just wanted a word with Jonah. When I heard Connor outside, it sounded like he was crying, so . . .'

'So you broke down the door as if you were Miss Marple,' Angelika elicits another strained laugh. Then, slapping her thigh as if coming to a sudden decision, she suggests hesitantly, 'Jonah was meant to be back ages ago and I have some important things to do, so would you mind taking over minding Connor for me?'

'I'd love to,' I acknowledge with a grateful nod. She holds my appreciative stare for a few seconds before nodding slowly in agreement.

'I appreciate it,' she mumbles, gazing down at Connor's mane of red hair. She seems like she might be about to burst into tears, but as she glances up again, I realise I was mistaken. Her dark eyes are narrowed to mere slits, indicating that she is mad as hell. The ruthless determination on her face makes the hairs on my arms stand up. Seeing my shocked expression, she averts her gaze.

I gulp nervously, not liking the fact that she won't look me in the eye. 'Is there anything I can do to help?'

Her lips are pursed in anger as she demands, 'What do you mean?'

I remind her, 'You said you had some important things to do. Maybe we could all go together.'

'No,' she answers bluntly. Then, as if to reassure me that she is not upset, she seems to reconsider and adds, 'By important, I meant I've got a spa session booked.'

I aim to get her out of the door as soon as possible so I can be alone with my child. I do this by exclaiming, 'You don't want to miss out on something as important as that. You'd best get off now. So you're not late.'

'You're a star,' with a feeble smile, Angelika bends over and brushes Connor's pale white cheek with her mouth. He

142

doesn't wiggle away for once. He typically reacts to tactile affectionate gestures by striking out with his fists or even by kicking out with his ankles, but he happily accepts Angelika's kiss, behaving like a contended, purring kitten.

Sensing she is about to leave him, Connor looks up at Angelika and asks in a quivering voice, 'Where are you going?'

'That's for me to know and you to find out,' she teases playfully. 'Don't worry, your Aunty Sam is going to look after you while I'm gone.'

He turns ferocious eyes in my direction then, seeming to have completely forgotten that he once doted on me. Talk about fickle.

'I don't need looking after,' he scowls. More scathingly, he protests, 'And how can she be my aunty when she's not even related to me?'

His words are like a weight around my heart when he says this.

CHAPTER 35: TIMOTHY

After forty-eight hours, I am eventually released from police custody without charge due to a lack of evidence — even though I was the only one on the island *that they knew about* who had a motive — provided I turned in my passport and didn't leave the country. I would have agreed to anything to get out of that stinking hellhole. Being banged up again was like revisiting my past. After having my wallet and phone returned to me, I hailed a speedboat taxi and felt my heart sinking in my chest as it took me back to our honeymoon island. I've been trying to contact Jonah nonstop since being released but to no avail. Either he's out of signal range or is refusing to take my calls. Hopefully, it's not the latter, as I desperately want to make everything up to him somehow, in more ways than one.

First, I intend to come clean about Bartosz's true identity no matter the consequences. I owe Jonah that after all the secrets and lies I've kept hidden from him. I believe we still have a shot at being happy if we are completely honest with one another. According to Jonah, our money is safe, so at least we don't have to worry about bankruptcy or losing our home. Despite what I said, I never intended to hand him over to the police as the real murderer, especially after what he did for me. Us. I love him too much for that. If either of us ends up behind bars, I'll make certain it's me.

It would be an understatement to say that Jonah's confession shocked me. A tremor of anxiety goes through me, making me doubt all I thought I knew about my husband. This begs the question, when did he hear me and Putu arguing? Should I hold out hope that Putu's death was an accident, or did Jonah devise a ruthless plan to kill the concierge to prevent him from blackmailing me? The consequences of that fallout don't bear thinking about. How could I not know that Jonah was capable of murder?

As we get closer to the island's familiar ragged shoreline, it's almost dusk and, despite the sun having faded to a burnt orange, there are still far-reaching views of paradise. Palm trees. Pristine beaches. The white wooden jetty where I waited for Putu on the fateful night he was killed. It cuts me up to see newlyweds like me and Jonah strolling hand in hand along the beach. I get a sick feeling in the pit of my stomach as the boat's bow slices savagely through the white seafoam. Right now, everything in my life feels like an Agatha Christie novel being acted out for real.

I squeeze my eyes shut and count to three. When I open them again, my tired gaze is drawn to a small dark figure on the sand. They are wearing traditional Balinese dress and seem to be waiting for the boat to dock. I feel my jaw stiffen when I realise who it is . . . and my world goes black. It can't be Putu though, can it? *He's dead.* Has my former friend returned as a ghost to haunt me? The fading sun is directly in my face now, partially blinding me. When my vision returns, I frantically search the coastline, but there is no longer anyone there. I must have imagined it all along.

Rubbing at my temples with my fist, a wave of emotion floods through my chest and my eyes well up. I desperately want to go to a cheap bar and get wasted, so I'm tempted to urge the driver to run around quickly and take me back to the mainland. If I could, I would let myself get so drunk that by the end of the night, I would have multiple teeth missing and wake up with a crude tattoo on my arm. Anything beats having to return to that island, which is as destructively dark as any of the evil spirits the islanders are so anxious to keep at bay with their offerings to ward off demons.

As if reading my mind, the Balinese boat captain points eerily at the rocky shoreline and mumbles under his breath, 'Black magic island.'

Not only do his words grab my attention, but I also get the impression that he has been secretly observing me for some time, possibly trying to determine whether or not I am guilty of killing one of his kinsmen. Everyone within a ten-mile radius will have heard about the death of the concierge.

As the captain's gaze darts nervously away from the black contour of the island, I enquire gently, 'What do you mean by calling it that?'

He worriedly chews on his lip and looks closely at my face as if working out whether or not I can be trusted. With a lengthy, indecisive sigh, he says, 'I cannot say anymore. It is not permitted.'

Hackles up, I scowl, 'What do you mean you cannot say anymore?'

The boat radio crackles and, as if relieved not to have to speak to me, the captain talks to whoever is on the radio in Balinese. This leaves me wondering what he meant when he referred to our honeymoon destination as "Black Magic Island". Was there something inherently sinister about it? Hadn't I felt it from the start? No one can argue that since arriving on the island, everything has gone wrong — for me at least. Even the scent of incense, seaweed, grilled fish, coffee and frangipani flowers associated with the luxury resort is overwhelming. Sensing panic in the captain's voice, I turn to face him, and flinch when I see the dread in his eyes.

'We need to turn around. There's been an accident,' he cries, his voice full of urgency. But I grab his arm and force him to stop before he can turn the boat around. 'What's happened?'

'A man. An English tourist has died falling from Tegenungan waterfall. We have to go, *now*, so I can get everyone back to the resort safely. There is much blood. Much panic,' he mumbles with startled eyes, before continuing, 'This is not good for the Balinese tourist industry.'

Or for the English man's family, I refrain from saying since his skin has a white sheen to it that speaks of fear. Rather, I ask, 'English, you say. Was he staying here? On this island?'

He gives the smallest and humblest of nods, confirming. 'I picked them up and took them over this afternoon. Now I have to fetch them back.'

Letting go of the man's arm, I feel my insides lurch as the boat turns around in a tight arch, spraying water higher than the waves. Who is it that's died, I wonder? I know that our group talked of visiting the waterfall as it was on everybody's bucket list, but I figured it would have to wait because of Putu and my arrest. Our visit was scheduled for day five of our honeymoon, which triggers a spike in my blood sugar that makes my brain pop. What day is it now? We got here on Saturday. On Monday, Putu died, and I was arrested. It's been two days since then. That means today is Wednesday . . . Day Five.

CHAPTER 36: ANGELIKA

One hour earlier

At Tegenungan waterfall, Jonah and I split from the rest of the group and I'm the first to admit this wasn't accidental on my part. We almost hadn't come at all, but after Timothy's arrest Jonah needed cheering up, so Nathan insisted we continue with our planned itinerary as if nothing had happened. However, I suspect this was more because he wanted to go than any genuine desire to help Jonah. Selfish as ever, that's Nathan. Since neither of us was into nature in the way Sam was, Jonah and I left her with Connor to construct a stone tower to go with the hundreds of other piles built by tourists over the years. Where Nathan disappeared to is anybody's guess.

Directed by me, we ventured off course and up the steep, slimy, slippery slope that led to the very top of the waterfall, though Jonah, with his short, stocky legs needed some convincing to get to this point. He struggled, but I bided my time and waited patiently. "Good things come to those who wait" was a saying of my mother's. Prior to that, Jonah insisted on stopping at every location that might make a good Instagram selfie, such as the giant swing overlooking the waterfall. With curiosity, I watched him taking photo after photo and deleting the ones he didn't like. Talk about vain.

Being a chef, Bartosz was naturally interested in every restaurant we encountered and after taking one look at the enormous waterfall and the serene turquoise pool below it where people were swimming, he shrugged in an unimpressed way and made his way back up the two hundred plus steps that led to the street food cafes. With so many menus to mull over, I didn't expect to see him any time soon, which suited my purposes.

The sound of white-water thundering over the black stone cliffs deafened us as we climbed. We didn't say anything until we reached the top as you had to shout to be heard. By then, Jonah was complaining about the green mould stuck to his Ralph Lauren T-shirt. He also told me something I'd rather not have known. He was desperate for a shit having refused to use the dirty public toilets located at the entrance.

'You can go here,' I informed him tetchily. But when I saw the disgusted look on his face, I quickly reassured him that no one would see him as we were the only ones up here.

Ignoring the breathtaking vistas of our surroundings and the fact we were so close to the tranquil clouds, I resolved to hurt him as much as he had hurt me when, earlier in the day, and prompted by me, he'd made callous remarks about how he'd made his fortune, proving he was a money-grabbing bastard who only cared about profit. I had wanted to punch him when I heard that. But hadn't I always known this? The man is a parasite.

So, with a sudden catch in my voice, I ask him, 'Back down there, when you said most of your tenants were scum, did you mean it?'

When Jonah responds, 'There are exceptions, but most tenants trash the places they live in leaving landlords like me to pick up the bill,' he is still trying to catch his breath back from the climb.

I argue, 'But people have to live somewhere,' giving him the chance to see things from a different angle.

He stomps all over my argument by muttering, 'True. And as long as they pay their rent on time, that's all that matters.'

'But you said yourself your company has increased rents by at least twenty per cent this year. How can your tenants afford that?'

Putting on an expression of indifference, he shrugs, 'Not my problem. The going rate is whatever people are willing to pay for it and if they can't afford it, social housing is the council's responsibility, not mine.'

I pick at the scab once more — I can't help myself when my mother's grey, cancer-ridden face is in front of me — by protesting, 'But what about families who fall behind with their rent through no fault of their own?'

Jonah arches a cynical eyebrow as if he could never experience falling on hard times. 'Tough luck, I'm afraid. I'm not a charity.'

I think he has finished trying to justify himself when he snidely snaps, 'I don't believe for one minute that you give away meals to the homeless in your posh chain of restaurants or translate for free for poor people.'

I bristle and growl, 'Actually, I do. Bartosz and I both volunteer for charitable organisations. We enjoy giving back to the community.'

With a couldn't-care-less attitude, he scoffs, 'Well, good for you.' His eyes then brighten when he catches sight of a small worn grass path that swiftly vanishes from view. 'Now if you don't mind. I need to take a shit.'

I glower ferociously after him as he delicately picks his way over large boulders, trying not to stumble, before vanishing over the edge where the path drops down. I can't help but tremble when I replay in my head the image of my mother being taken away by social services after the bailiffs evicted us. She was already very ill by this stage, but I never imagined this would be the last time I ever saw her. Everything we owned was piled up in the street outside for everyone to see which caused her even more distress. Even though I had worked as a sex worker for years and been called every name under the sun, I'd never experienced such crushing humiliation as this. The rage I felt earlier is still present. I'm not done yet.

Risking everything, I shout over the whoosh of the waterfall so Jonah can hear me, 'Does the name Anzela mean anything to you?'

A pause, and then he yells back, 'No. Should it?'

'She was one of your tenants,' anger fuels my voice as I realise that he most likely forgot about me the moment I ceased being a tenant. He hasn't wasted years thinking about me as I have him, longing for revenge.

He climbs back up the cliff's edge, doing up his trouser zip as he comes into view. Seemingly perplexed, he racks his brain, 'Who?'

I grit my teeth and repeat, 'Anzela Novak,' feeling as though I'm gasping for air and drowning. I have waited so long for this moment.

'The surname rings a bell,' he says, shaking his head and wracking his brain, until a flash of uneasiness passes over his face. 'Wait a minute. Wasn't that the name on the bank account I made the transfer to?' In the next breath, he pulls a distrustful face, 'Is she a friend of yours?'

'No, not a friend,' I mumble. As I continue, I can't stop my mouth from twisting into an unpleasant scowl, 'Guess again.'

He frowns as he runs his hands through his tight blond Shirley Temple curls, 'Now that you mention it, I do remember an Anzela who lived in one of my houses. She left owing me money.'

'Apparently, she's now a quarter of a million richer than she was a few days ago and isn't giving that money back.' I respond icily, slowly advancing on him so that we are standing in front of each other. I watch as a range of emotions pass over his face until realisation hits. His voice is cloaked with incredulity as he cries, 'Wait. You. You're Anzela Novak.'

We are nose to nose, and even though my heart is thundering in my chest I take great delight in grinding out through clenched teeth, 'I was.'

His face turns a shocking scarlet red, and beads of sweat form on his forehead as he realises what I'm insinuating. Also, that I'm blocking his exit. It seems to me that he knows not just my name but also who I am, and that obviously frightens him. When he stammers, 'You were the tenant with the sick mother who we had evicted,' I know I'm right when he continues, eyes wide with shock, 'And you were a prostitute back then.'

I step forward menacingly, forcing him to retreat a step. Then another. He is wise enough to understand that right now I have all the power. He knows he can't outrun me. I am slim and super fit whereas he is flabby and weak. His terrified gaze flits over and around me as if searching for an escape route. But there's only one place for him to go . . . down. Angrily, I stab him in the chest, causing him to flinch and let out a whimper as I scream in his podgy face, 'Right again, another of your scum tenants.'

And then, before he can respond, I shove him even harder. He doesn't immediately disappear. Rather, he hovers midair, arms flailing wildly and hands splayed. His eyes pop with fear, as if they might explode out of his head, and his mouth opens and closes as he silently begs for help, *not a chance*, and then, just like that . . . he is gone.

CHAPTER 37: SAMANTHA

Now

Everyone is pointing, shouting, shaking and crying, not knowing what else to do. Everyone but Connor, that is, who is gawking at his adoptive dad's broken, bloodied and twisted body spread out on the rocks, with something akin to morbid curiosity. Jonah's right leg is bent at an incomprehensible angle and pointing in the wrong direction, while one arm is behind his head as though he were resting against it. His rainbow striped shorts and vivid pink Ralph Lauren T-shirt, now splattered with blood, make him easily identifiable. While a few courageous locals have already made calls to the police and approached the body, the majority of us are in shock from seeing Jonah fall from the top of the waterfall and remain at a distance.

Though I am just as distressed as everyone else, my first thought is to protect my son, who could be permanently scarred by this horrific scene, so I cover his eyes with my hands and gently turn him around. He's probably too shocked to say anything, which explains his silence. I cast my eyes up to the top of the waterfall, where the jagged outcrop juts out like a clenched jaw. Jonah must have fallen while he was up there by himself. Or did he take his own life? Only yesterday, Angelika confided in me that the couple were facing bankruptcy and would have to sell their beloved home when they returned to the UK. "That, on top of Timothy's arrest and not knowing if he will be released, must be incredibly traumatic for Jonah," Angelika had said, making me promise not to tell a soul, and I did what she asked. But somehow, the other hotel guests found out, and now everyone is talking about it. Jonah's mental state must have been affected by that. Would he have actually plunged twenty-five metres to his death, though, knowing his son would witness it?

Feeling queasy, I take hold of Connor's hand. Mine is shaking like mad, but his is still and calm. 'Come on, Connor. Let's go back up the steps,' I encourage in a voice meant to sound normal but comes out strained.

With a hopeful grin, he cheekily asks, 'To the ice cream shops?'

That's when I realise he's not at all indifferent. He's simply too young to comprehend what has happened, so I nod and muster a weak smile, confirming, 'To the ice cream shops.'

I'm relieved that the body is no longer visible as we turn to go. Our view is obstructed by the throng encircling it, and someone has tactfully covered Jonah's corpse with a picnic blanket. But some strands of blond hair escape from underneath it. This instantly moves me to tears, but I wipe them away, not wanting Connor to see. For his sake, I have to be brave.

When a familiar but agitated voice suddenly screams, 'Not Jonah!' everyone stops what they are doing, including us. Fascinated, we all turn to watch Timothy frantically scaling the wet rocks to get to the body, a Balinese guide scrambling after him. The crowd makes way for Timothy as he drops to his hands and knees with a heart-stopping thud next to Jonah.

Even though the light is starting to fade, Connor is still able to see his other dad sobbing uncontrollably as he pulls

Jonah's mutilated body into his chest and cradles it in his arms, all the while crying, 'This island is cursed.' I have to avert my eyes from the grief on his tormented face.

My heart breaks for him but I am hesitant to get involved because my last words to him were not kind. Rather, I scan the area for Angelika and Bartosz, who I'm sure will know what to do for the best — maybe they can persuade Timothy to return to the resort with us — but they're nowhere to be found. I've never felt so clueless in my life and my heart is going at a steady gallop. I think it's about to burst when an arm snakes around my shoulders and a voice murmurs, 'There you are.' How could I have forgotten about my own husband? And now that Nathan's here, I'm ridiculously pleased to see him.

'Thank God you're here,' I murmur as he pulls me into a comforting hug. 'Did you see what happened to Jonah?'

He nods gravely, before saying, 'It must have been upsetting for you to see that. I should have been here,' and gives me a gentle pat on the back.

'Where *were* you?' I tilt my head back to look at him. He cannot miss the deep burning question in my eyes, and he clicks his tongue in frustration, before replying forcefully, 'Let's talk later.'

Having masterfully sidestepped my question, he continues, 'Let's get Connor out of here. He's already seen more than most children his age should.' As Nathan says this, his worried eyes fall on my son, and for once, I am so grateful I want to shower him with kisses.

Even though I have an overpowering urge to scoop Connor up in my arms and sprint up the steps with him, far away from here, I force myself to ask, 'But what about Timothy? Shouldn't we wait for him?'

Nathan's forehead furrows as he turns to face the scenario playing out in front of us. A sea rescue helicopter is hovering noisily above us, mercifully drowning out Timothy's pitiful cries as a paramedic is lowered, signalling that help is on its way. Too late for Jonah, though. When I next look at Nathan, his jaw is set. 'We need to leave before the police arrive otherwise they'll keep us here for hours,' he takes charge. 'Tim will have to stay and speak to them, but they can reach us at the hotel if necessary. He's not in a fit state to be around his kid so we'll take Connor back with us.' With that, Nathan places a firm hand between my shoulder blades and presses me forward. To Connor, he booms playfully, 'Up you come, young man, for a piggyback,' and hoists him onto his back.

We've barely made it to the steps that lead up to the exit when we see Angelika and Bartosz barrelling towards us, their faces a picture of panic and confusion. When Nathan sees them . . . or rather her . . . his entire body tenses. I suspect something has happened between them. Only a couple of nights ago he was all over her and now he's barely civil. I don't want to consider what this might mean so I try to shake the dark thought out of my head. This is not the right moment for that. Even so, nothing will prevent me from watching them more closely in future.

I can feel my eyebrows pinching together and my head buzzing with anticipation as Nathan quickly fills them in on what has transpired. Eyes bulging with horror, Angelika clasps her hands to her mouth and laments loudly, 'First Putu and now Jonah. What in the world is going on?'

Lips pressed together in disapproval, Bartosz shushes his wife. But she is merely expressing what we are all thinking. Was Timothy right when he claimed the island was cursed, and if so, whose life will it take next? It could be any one of us.

156

CHAPTER 38: TIMOTHY

I can feel the heat of Kadek's investigative stare boring into me as he murmurs from the other side of the table, 'Either we have a murderer on our island, or two people have committed suicide in as many days.'

As I meet his gaze, I get the impression he wants to neatly explain away Jonah and Putu's deaths as suicide so he can move on.

'But why would Jonah kill himself?' I give an exasperated groan, feeling as if my heart is about to explode. And then, on cue, anger sharpens my words as I exclaim, 'He had everything to live for! We'd just got married for Christ's sake. We have a child together.' My voice breaks as I add pitifully, 'Connor's only four.'

I hang my head, thinking of Connor, who I'm told witnessed the whole thing and is now back at the hotel under Samantha's care, so at least I know he is safe and in good hands. Kadek offers me a box of tissues, which I accept with gratitude. My hands shake as I dab at my eyes.

Kadek glances apologetically in my direction before advising, 'In my experience, money problems are often to blame for people taking their own lives.'

I give a triumphant snort, 'That's where you're wrong because we weren't short of money. Together, we run . . . ran . . . a successful business. How else do you think we could have afforded a honeymoon in Bali?'

Wracked with uncertainty, I wonder if my guilty expression tells Kadek everything he wants to know. Should I tell him what Jonah did? Now that he's dead and *gone for ever* the truth no longer matters. He can hardly serve a prison sentence for murder now. What if Jonah was lying, though? For him, making things up was nothing new. I was not blind to Jonah's shortcomings and usually took whatever he said in my stride. However, he was as shrewd as anything when it came to business — usually, that is — but, when I think back to our last encounter when he paid me a visit in the police cell and claimed to have killed Putu, I believed him. I still do.

Since Jonah's body landed at the bottom of the waterfall, my mind has been tying itself in knots, so I nearly jump out of my chair when I hear the slam of a door outside the police interview room. Jaw working from side to side, I'm brought back to earth with a devastating thud when Kadek says, 'And yet, your joint bank account is showing that you are two-hundred-and-fifty-thousand pounds in debt.'

My first thought on hearing this is how the fuck does he know that? However, I suspect Indonesian detectives have different powers from the police back home. Or maybe Kadek thinks he is above the law. I know I sound aggrieved when I remark tetchily, 'Technically yes, but Jonah only moved our money temporarily and clearly hadn't gotten around to moving it back again before he . . .'

Kadek tosses me a cynical look and cuts in with, 'Are you familiar with the name Anzela Novak?'

'No,' I shake my head. 'Why?'

'Are you certain?' he offers me a second chance. It isn't necessary.

'Yes,' I tell him firmly.

'And yet, Jonah gave this individual a total of a quarter of a million pounds. Everything you had in fact.'

158

I actually gasp in shock. I've never heard of Anzela Novak before. How did Jonah know her? Who is she? I have almost as many questions for Jonah as the policeman has for me. Thinking aloud, I ponder, 'I assumed Jonah had opened up another bank account to transfer the money into, but on second thoughts, I realise he wouldn't have had time to do that.'

'Why was it so urgent that he transferred the funds?'

Feeling a stab of guilt, because this is all on me, the words stick in my throat as I try to find an appropriate response. In the end, I drop my gaze and run with, 'We got word that we were about to be scammed.'

'By whom?' Kadek asks politely, as if he were enquiring after my health.

My head stays down. I can't look at him while I ramble, 'I don't know. Jonah never said.'

'And yet, you never once considered that he might have been the one scamming you?'

'No, of course not. What are you suggesting?' I blabber nervously, breaking out in a sudden ice-cold sweat. 'Jonah loved me. He would never do anything like that.' I feel like a fool talking about my feelings in front of this couldn't-be-any-straighter male cop, and it makes my whole face burn.

'And yet,' he pauses to stroke his chin thoughtfully, leaving me to wonder how many more "And yets" I have to endure.

'We have not been able to trace an Anzela Novak either here or in the UK,' he continues, oblivious to my frustration.

I'm grasping at straws when I rush in with, 'It sounds like an Eastern European name to me.' But Kadek has already anticipated my response—

'The truth is she doesn't exist. The account was opened years ago and closed yesterday, hours before Jonah's death.'

'And you have no idea where the money has gone?' I ask in a broken voice, feeling like a part of me has died.

With a shake of his head, Kadek uses his most persuasive skills to insert an unsettling thought in my head, 'We can't even be certain the account holder was a woman. It could very well have been a man.'

I feel something inside me snap then. If I find out who has our money, there's no telling what I might do. Is Kadek right? Did Jonah betray me by giving away our money to another man? Someone he knew, and I didn't. When he claimed to have "transferred it somewhere safe," was it a lie? What if, all along, he was having an affair with this person? Did they intend to run away together once they had the money? Was that the plan? Nothing makes sense anymore and if I thought things were bad before, they're now ten times worse. Without that money, I'm finished. I'll be made bankrupt. Never mind the cost of a funeral, how will Connor and I manage financially? We'll have to sell up. Everything will have to go. The house. The cars. The extravagant lifestyle. I'll need to enrol Connor in daycare and get a proper job.

Jonah, what have you done?

CHAPTER 39: ANGELIKA

A smile creeps onto my face every time I secretly open up the banking app on my phone to check the £250K is still there. And why wouldn't it be? It's not like anyone can take it away from me. Not now Jonah is dead and I've transferred those funds to another hastily opened offshore banking account. Naturally, I didn't kill Jonah for the money. That was about my thirst for revenge. However, I consider the small fortune a bonus, because I know how much Timothy will suffer when he discovers he has been left with nothing. Although I don't suspect him of operating quite as ruthlessly as Jonah, he still needs to be held accountable as a business partner in the same unethical company that was responsible for evicting a dying woman. He's lucky to escape with his life but I couldn't leave Connor an orphan. I'm not that cruel.

As for Jonah, I refuse to feel even the slightest pity for him. It's not that I'm heartless, but he called us scum and my mother was an angel, a devout woman who was kind and gentle. She was adored by all, including those in the red-light area, for whom she made bread and cakes. Had it not been for Jonah, she would have passed away peacefully at home with me by her side. As it was, she didn't like to make a fuss, so the nursing staff in the hospice mostly ignored her throughout her silent, agonising final days. When I went to see her in the chapel of rest, she didn't resemble my mother at all. Her skin was so loose and thin you could see her bones beneath it.

The resort is teeming with law enforcement again, and rumours are circulating that some hotel employees have packed up and fled, citing the island's supposed curse, much like Timothy had done. Some are even suggesting "black magic" was responsible for Putu and Jonah's deaths and warn that more lives will be taken. I'm not superstitious at all, but if it helps to avoid anyone pointing the finger at me, I'll happily pass on any gossip, no matter how false. Once more, the majority of guests have gathered in reception to try and figure out what's going on. These days, I am quite the helper, assisting Nathan with "information flow" as he likes to call it. It caught both Bartosz and Nathan off guard when I offered to help, but with Sam looking after Connor it made perfect sense. The two men are both slyly observing me, wondering what it is I am up to. If only they knew!

As I give the Australian couple who found Putu's body a tray of tea and biscuits, I pull a sympathetic face and utter conspiratorially, 'They're saying Jonah's death was a suicide,' I add credibility to the lie by pointing to Kadek, who is chatting to the hotel manager by the desk, as if he were the source of my information.

'Really?' With a gasp, the woman clasps and unclasps her hands in her lap. 'How awful. And to think that little boy saw it all.'

'Oh, I know,' I agree wholeheartedly, 'But it seems that Jonah was about to be made bankrupt due to money problems.'

'Yes, I heard that too, but apparently Timothy was unaware of it, and it came as a complete shock to him,' the man concurs, putting a protective arm around his wife's shoulders. They seem more shaken this time as if they can handle one dead body but not two. The honeymoon they'd been promised is not going as planned. If I was them, I would ask for a refund.

'No?' I act shocked, as I move across the room away from them, but of course, I know all of this already, because I was the one who spread the reports of financial difficulties in the first place. When rolling out lies, the best course of action is to assure each confidante that the information you are sharing is absolutely top secret, even though you know that at least two-thirds of them will tell someone else right away. Unfortunately, that's how the world operates. I should know. As a former sex worker, I've encountered some of the most unscrupulous people. Like the one and only Nathan Price, who's coming at me right now armed with a downturned mouth and a clipboard.

'What are you up to, *Anzela*?' he growls.

I smile warmly, not for his benefit but for everyone else's and toss my silky brown hair over one shoulder, before muttering back, 'I could ask you the same question.'

He puffs out his chest and grimaces, 'I was perfectly clear about what I was up to the other night, but you stood me up, remember.'

'A lot's happened since then,' I remind him.

'Yes, quite,' he acknowledges with a serious look.

Bartosz is staring at me accusingly from across the room, making me squirm guiltily. "Traitor", he'll be thinking, seeing me talk to Nathan. He can't come to me because the Australian couple is now holding *him* captive.

I pull a sympathetic face, knowing how much my socially awkward husband detests being monopolised by strangers.

Darting a quick glance at Nathan, I say, 'I think we should agree to call a truce for now.'

'For the time being,' he grudgingly agrees, adding, 'but I'm not done with you yet.'

My breath catches when I notice Kadek marching purposefully towards me. When he snaps his fingers in the air and a uniformed cop chases after him, my fear ramps up another notch.

Kadek's gaze is fixed intently on me. Has he found out about the offshore bank account I opened years ago in a fake name, when I was working as a sex worker, with the express intent of money laundering? I couldn't take the chance of depositing Jonah's money into our joint bank account because Bartosz would have found out, so I'd put all of it in there temporarily, where it wasn't traceable, until it could be moved.

When I contemplate being arrested — for theft, fraud or murder . . . take your pick — I experience a feeling of terror so powerful it takes me back to the nights when I used to get picked up in a police car for soliciting. I was usually let go but I occasionally had to perform a "favour" for the arresting police officer. Judging by the determined expression on Kadek's face, I may have celebrated getting away with my crime too soon. Every hair on my body stands on end as I wait for his heavy hand to come down on my shoulder and for the cold metal of the handcuffs to surround my wrists.

CHAPTER 40: SAMANTHA

'I'm back, darling,' Nathan calls as he enters the garden where Connor and I are having fun splashing around in the private pool. Because neither of us can swim properly, I won't let him go in the deep end and I've also insisted he keep his armbands on. The rumours about black magic and evil spirits are making me anxious and I'm afraid that something terrible will happen to my precious son. Nathan assures me that this is nonsense, and I shouldn't take any notice. He likes to boast that, "You are perfectly safe with me around," which makes me worry about the times he's not, which happens frequently. To be fair, though, since assuming responsibility for Connor — and there was never any doubt of my doing that — I've seen a new side to Nathan. Whenever there are children around, he becomes a kid again. It's such a shame he doesn't get to spend much time with his own children, who'll be grown up before he knows it.

Forgetting that we have an on-call butler, Nathan pops the cork of a bottle of expensive red wine and strolls across the grass barefoot to kiss me on the cheek mumbling, 'Love you,' in my ear.

'I love you too,' I dutifully respond, reflecting on how wonderful it is when Nathan pays attention to me when no one else is around to witness it because that makes it all the more sincere. Having kissed and made up last night it's as if we are finally on our honeymoon, although we are already six days into our holiday. So what if he occasionally vanishes to attend to business calls at the strangest of times? Sometimes during the night.

'How did the meeting go in reception?' I enquire like a good wife should.

'As expected,' Nathan grumbles, looking suddenly defeated, which is not like my powerhouse of a husband at all.

Sensing his need for attention, I lead Connor out of the water and smother him in a towel. He has been very quiet since seeing Jonah plummeting to his death at the waterfall. That's to be expected. The poor love mostly communicates with gestures now. Pointing to the jug of iced juice on the patio table, he does so now. I pour him a glass and resist the urge to pull him into a hug because I know it would make him uncomfortable. Realising that Nathan is waiting for me to pour his wine, I fill his glass to the top as if he'd just completed a twelve-hour shift in a coal mine. He blows me a kiss and settles into the chair across from Connor.

'The police aren't saying much. Not even to me and I'm meant to be the guest representative,' he mutters, staring dejectedly into his wineglass.

'Don't you think you might be taking your role in the investigations a little too seriously?' I dare to suggest.

At that, his head snaps up. 'No,' he barks. 'Two men have died in case you haven't noticed.'

'Sorry, Nathan,' I mumble, suitably chastised.

'No, *I'm* sorry, love,' he reaches apologetically for my hand and strokes my palm with his thumb until it tickles. 'It's just that we find out more from Angelika than we do the police. She seems to know everything.'

Do I imagine it or is there a trace of admiration in his voice? I scrunch up my face and warily ask, 'What could she possibly know that you don't?'

166

'Everything,' he sighs, his shoulders slumping in defeat. 'It's a good job she's on the case, that's all I can say.'

'What do you mean by that?' I ask in alarm, sensing there is something he isn't telling me.

'Just that she's been helping me in your absence.'

I make a conscious effort to smile and not feel disheartened when he tilts his head back to observe me. 'What?' He demands, narrowing his eyes.

'Nothing,' I reply over brightly, pretending to dry my wet hair.

'Don't give me nothing,' he chuckles, watching me closely, 'I know you better than that, Mrs Price. You're jealous.'

'Of Angelika?' I pull a face and shake my head in denial. As much as I like Angelika, I wish she'd stay away from my husband. I feel like if he prioritised spending time with me over her or any other woman come to that then we might have a slim chance at making our marriage work. I'm forgetting for the moment that he is responsible for a young man's death and capable of keeping dark secrets. Something I can't forgive.

Sensing that it might be wise to change the subject, Nathan slips off his shirt, revealing a slightly flabby chest scattered with dark-blond hair. With temperatures approaching thirty-five degrees, it's the hottest day of our holiday so far. Sliding on dark shades, he remarks, 'It's a scorcher.'

The next minute, he's belching loudly to make Connor giggle. It works. Before long, they're engaging in a fight to see who can finish their drink first. Nathan surprises me by allowing Connor to win. Normally, he's really competitive. Affectionately, Nathan ruffles Connor's hair and jests, 'Vitamin C will put hairs on your chest like mine,' while pointing to his chest.

Connor pulls a disgusted face, 'Ew . . .' which makes us both laugh.

I feel a rush of contentment flood over me as I watch Nathan tickle Connor's stomach until he's roaring with laughter. He then manages to escape Nathan's grasp to gallop around the garden, taunting him with, 'You can't catch me. You're not fast enough.' Never one to back down from a challenge, Nathan gets up and chases after him, deliberately not running fast enough to catch him. Connor keeps laughing harder and harder.

Observing them together, I begin to feel hopeful that Nathan will forgive me and agree to raise Connor as his own if I tell him that he is my son. Ignoring the fact that Connor already has a father who is also his legal guardian, the concept sounds less ridiculous than it did before. However, I'm perplexed when Nathan stops, panting for air, and remarks breathlessly over his shoulder, 'It's a brave thing what Tim and Jonah did.'

'How do you mean?' I frown.

He points out the obvious, lowering his voice so Connor cannot hear: 'Well, he's not theirs, is he? Technically, that is.'

I cross my arms across my chest and squirm uncomfortably. 'Isn't that the whole point of adoption?'

'Yes, I am aware of that,' he observes cynically, as though I am being intentionally stupid, before continuing, 'It might be an alpha male thing but there's no way I could bring myself to love a kid that wasn't my own.'

CHAPTER 41: TIMOTHY

It was a mistake coming. I see that now. I ought to have waited till the morning after I had taken a shower, changed into fresh clothing, and grabbed some sleep. I must look awful because I'm still dressed in the same T-shirt and shorts that I was wearing when I was arrested in connection with Putu's death. Although no one suspects me of being involved in Jonah's sudden death, the police held me for hours questioning me about him. Eventually, I was so exhausted that I nodded off at the table and jerked awake wondering where the hell I was, only to find Kadek sitting in front of me, staring at me quizzically. After that, they released me and I crept back to the island under the cover of darkness, like a thief in the night, not wanting to see anybody other than Connor. I had to be sure he was okay. Selfishly, I felt seeing him would make me feel better. How mistaken I was.

It was Nathan who answered my persistent knocking and when he came to the door, eyes bleary with sleep, he seemed so serious that I was stumped for a second. When I explained that I had come for Connor, he gave me a wary look and asked robotically, 'Do you think that's wise?'

'I don't care. I just need to see him,' I angrily objected. With that, he opened the door, and I trailed behind him into the living room, which had a magnificent view of the pitch-black ocean. But in my mind, I was imagining the moment when Jonah fell from the top of the waterfall and landed with a sick bone-crunching clatter on the rocks below; blood seeping out from beneath him and staining the otherwise grey rock scarlet. If I'm honest, I'm still finding it hard to accept what has happened. *Why? Oh God, why?* Who the fuck kills themselves on their honeymoon?

Nathan grunts, 'Get that down you,' and sets down a tumbler of brandy on a table next to an elegant bridal-white corner sofa that faces an imposing prestige TV mounted on the wall. The entire space is teeming with cutting-edge amenities. Like Jonah, Nathan is evidently fond of his technology.

'Is Connor awake?' I enquire, gulping down my drink all at once.

Nathan motions for me to take a seat across from him, then wrinkles his nose, as if at a bad smell. Could that bad smell be me? Only then does he ask, with a hint of amusement, 'Do you have any idea what the time is?'

I groan and bury my face in my hands, 'No.'

'It's almost three o'clock in the morning.'

My head shoots up in shock, 'It can't be.'

Behind me, a hard voice says, 'I can assure you it is.'

I turn around to see Samantha standing in the doorway, watching me. Her face is pale and her red hair cascades down her shoulders, giving her a ghostly appearance. In contrast to Nathan, who I could tell had just woken up when I knocked on his door, she appears to have been awake all night tossing and turning. A frown creeps onto her smooth, unlined forehead as she asks, 'You don't mean to take him now, do you? At this hour.'

My frown matches hers as I stutter, desperate for understanding, 'He's my son. He needs to be with his dad. Especially after what happened.' I swallow and struggle with my next words . . . 'What he saw.'

Samantha appeals to me with tearful eyes, 'You've been through so much, Timothy, and we are both here for you,' she pauses to shoot a back-me-up look at Nathan, but he just blinks back at her, not understanding what is required of him. Then, in an attempt to reason with me, she protests, 'But it's so late and Connor is asleep.'

Refilling our glasses, Nathan orders impatiently, 'Go and get the boy.'

'But one more night won't hurt. Timothy can collect him in the morning,' Samantha bargains, contradicting her husband, and my jaw drops. While a part of me wants to applaud her for finally defying him, another part of me wants her to do as she's told without further delay.

When she doesn't move, Nathan growls, 'This is none of our business, Sam.' He stands up and agitatedly runs a hand through his hair, warning. 'Tim has every right to take his son, no matter what time it is.'

I think for a moment she is going to continue to argue with him, but instead, she sniffs, sounding offended, before stomping off.

'I'm really sorry, mate, about Jonah,' Nathan sighs, retaking his seat and staring out of the bi-folding doors. 'I really liked him.'

'I could tell,' I mumble, finding this conversation uncomfortable. Nevertheless, I think Nathan is telling the truth. He and Jonah did get along.

Nathan shoots me an awkward look and asks, 'Have the police said anything? Given you any indication as to what made him do it?'

'No,' I get up. My legs threaten to buckle beneath me as I shake my head and grit my teeth in frustration. I am unable to do this right now. The image of Jonah's crushed body on the rocks is too painful for me to revisit. I carefully set down my glass before it slips from my grasp, feeling a strange chill crawl over my skin as I think back to Jonah's words from three days ago, 'I moved the money somewhere safe so you couldn't ruin us.' He had sounded accusing and nasty as if he wished to punish me.

With a scowl on her face, Samantha comes back into the room. Connor is curled up in her arms, clinging to her like a little monkey, legs wrapped around her. I shrink back in alarm when I see him because for an instant I don't know my son. He doesn't look like Connor at all. Even in his semi-conscious state, he seems more content than I've ever seen him, and his wild hair has been tamed. But when his eyes sleepily open and settle on me, all that changes. I know it's my son when he lets out a piercing scream.

Taken aback, I ask Samantha, 'What is it? What's the matter with him?'

'I don't know,' she replies, looking deeply distraught. I suspect then that she cares too much for my son, though I recall that she told me she was a nanny before she married Nathan so it must come naturally to her.

Connor's cries dissolve into sobs and his little shoulders hitch up and down with every breath. He points at me with terror in his eyes. Glancing down at my soiled shirt, I realise that it's Jonah's blood he can see.

'You killed Dad!' he accuses, more tears welling up in his eyes.

Stunned, I try to calm him down, saying, 'No, Connor, that's not what happened. Jonah had an accident.'

'You were meant to catch him, like you do me when I jump off the swing, and you didn't.'

Suddenly, I can see Ni Luh's battered face instead of Connor's since what my son is accusing me of is right in one way. *I did fail to catch her.*

When I try to comfort Connor by moving towards him, he violently whips his head away from me, as if he can't stand to look at me or even be in the same room as me. It makes me feel like throwing up.

'No!' he screams, pressing his scrunched-up face into Samantha's shoulder. 'Don't come near me. I hate you,' he hisses, eyes burning.

Nathan says quietly, 'I think you'd better leave it for now,' putting a reassuring hand on my back and patting me in a manly manner. He then turns me around and leads me to the door. I

172

swear I see a disturbing glimmer of victory in Samantha's gaze as I cast one last long look at my son.

As I'm led away, Connor's crying becomes muffled. Just a few hours ago, I thought life couldn't get any worse. And now it has. Because my son hates me and blames me for Jonah's death. He must think I'm some kind of monster as did Ni Luh's family, and with good reason. If Putu were here, he would quite rightfully point out, "That's karma for you".

CHAPTER 42: ANGELIKA

I'll admit that I peed my pants a little when I thought Kadek was going to arrest me. It wasn't until he casually sidestepped me and smiled politely before continuing on his way that I realised how paranoid I was. Although I don't feel bad about ending Jonah's worthless life because the scumbag deserved it, I also don't want to be punished for it, so I'm willing to lie, cheat, fabricate and dupe — all excellent English terms — however much is necessary to prevent my being discovered. Especially by my husband, who is among the most moral and honest people I have ever met.

Bartosz would disown me if he knew what I had done. I'd wager my life on it. Luckily, he seems unable to tell when I'm lying. All I can hope is that the police detective is just as gullible. It's therefore a nerve-wracking moment for me when we're asked to return to the small office in the hotel lobby for another audience with Kadek. I reassure myself that we are not being singled out because every guest who was at the waterfall when Jonah died is being questioned but it does little to calm my nerves.

'Ah, Mr and Mrs Dabrowski, come in,' Kadek motions for us to sit with a deceptively friendly wave.

As we take our seats, I'm shocked to see him tucking into an elaborate spread of side dishes arranged on the desk in front of him. The sight of it makes my stomach recoil, even though it looks delicious. Bartosz and I exchange bewildered looks as Kadek noisily continues to gulp down his food. This is not the conduct we expect from a police officer investigating a man's death. No, strike that, multiple deaths.

Kadek sighs, sensing our disdain and reluctantly pushes his food aside. Using a napkin to wipe his mouth, he grimaces, 'Don't mind me. You have to grab food when you can in this job.'

Thinking it might earn me some points, I treat him to a charming smile and say encouragingly, 'Please don't stop on our account. Having such an important job means it's vital that you keep your strength up.'

Bartosz stares incredulously at me and I cringe internally. He knows I'm not usually one for flattery and will be wondering what I'm up to. This makes me even more agitated.

But Kadek doesn't resume eating. Rather, his expression hardens, and his stare becomes more intense. Suddenly, he drawls, 'So, here we are again. Another man has died. What do you have to say to that?'

With a look of astonishment, Bartosz raises one eyebrow and looks to me for a response. I gulp nervously, and stammer, 'Sorry, I don't understand the question. We don't have anything to say.'

'You two were present at the scene when each of these deaths occurred,' he points out, seeming pleased to have finally rattled me.

I'm ready with a feisty retort, 'Us and dozens of other hotel guests.'

'True,' Kadek nods, seeming to lose interest with this line of enquiry, but I'm able to see past this ploy. I'm not fooled by the air of unprofessionalism he likes to give off.

As it becomes apparent that he is deliberately trying to unnerve us in an attempt to identify the true criminal among a plethora of possible suspects, I respond heatedly, 'You can't think we had anything to do with poor Jonah's *accident*. He was our friend.' Though, not strictly true, it'll do.

Kadek eyes me suspiciously as though he is having trouble believing what he is hearing and means to trick me into confessing to murder, but he isn't nearly as subtle as he thinks he is, and I aim to take advantage of that by stating truthfully, 'Neither of us saw Jonah fall. You'd have to ask the others about that.' And since this is the first time that I've been honest with him, I hope to persuade him of this with ease.

'I understood you were both there at the waterfall when the death occurred,' he scowls, as though angry at someone for misleading him about our whereabouts. A junior officer I'd like to bet. Most likely the one that rushes over whenever Kadek clicks his fingers.

Just as I'm about to speak, Bartosz beats me to it, which is rare for him, as he's usually very happy to let me do all the talking.

'Yes, we were both there, but we didn't see anything.'

Kadek shuffles through some documents on his desk, and when he doesn't locate what he's looking for he heaves a pragmatic sigh. He gives the impression that he is cursed by the incompetence of others.

'You were at the waterfall with the others, and yet you didn't see anything?' he quizzes impatiently, clearly unconvinced.

This time, I stay silent, not giving anything away as I wait to see if Bartosz will come to my rescue once more. I don't have to wait long.

'We went with the rest of the group to see the waterfall, but it wasn't our thing, to be honest, too touristy for us,' Bartosz shrugs apologetically to avoid offending Kadek, who takes great pride in his country's culture and heritage, 'so we spent our time looking around the shops instead.'

Kadek is mildly scathing, 'Isn't it unusual for a man to enjoy shopping so much?'

'By shops, I meant restaurants,' Bartosz explains effortlessly. Then recognising Kadek's incredulous expression, he adds, 'I'm a chef, you see. With my own chain of restaurants back home.'

'It's an obsession with him,' I attempt a laugh, but it sounds absurd, bordering on manic to my ears.

I breathe a sigh of relief when Kadek switches his attention to my husband. His face brightens with curiosity as he notes, 'My son is also a chef. It is a great profession, is it not?'

Bartosz nods, 'None better.'

'My son is eager to gain more knowledge about cooking international cuisine. While you are here, maybe you could give him some advice.'

'Of course, any time,' Bartosz obliges.

The tension in the room disappears as they continue to talk enthusiastically about their mutual interest in food and cooking, and I can at last focus on why Bartosz would lie to the police about my whereabouts given that he knew I was at the waterfall with the others. Is it because no one, not even the Balinese, trusts the police in Bali, and he fears that one of us could be falsely accused? Or does he know something — *how could he unless he saw me, oh God, is that what happened* — and he is now providing me with an alibi as I did him?

I could argue that if this is the case, he has taken this action to protect me, and for that, I should be grateful; but now that he's shown he's capable of deceit this means he is not the honest, trustworthy person he portrays himself to be, which suggests that we don't really know each other.

CHAPTER 43: SAMANTHA

Nathan suggested that rather than isolating myself away in the suite, I go to the hotel restaurant for breakfast, saying it would do me good to be around other people. I reluctantly gave in to his request to leave Connor behind, as I wanted Nathan off my back. Since making that devastating statement about not being able to love a child who wasn't his — *if only he knew the truth* — he's picked up on my coldness. I had been deluding myself into believing my husband would forgive me for the lies I told him and that Connor, he and I would go on to live happily ever after. Now I know there's no chance of that happening, I can't hide the fact that my heart has hardened against Nathan. He on the other hand appears to be putting in a lot of effort and is more infatuated than he's ever been. I'm at a loss as to why, given that the majority of the time I just annoy him.

As soon as I enter the open-air room, which smells of ground coffee and cinnamon, I notice how empty it is. Usually, you have to wait for a table but today most of the guests are absent. As are the hotel staff. According to Nathan, a lot of employees have left the island with no plans to return, and other honeymooning couples have also fled, scared off by the number of unexplained deaths. I look around, hoping to see a face I recognise but none of our crowd is present. I try not to think about how our group of six has shrunk to five. I wasn't a fan of Jonah, because he tried to keep me away from my son, but I wouldn't have wished that on him. I hope Timothy isn't losing his mind with worry. Poor man. We could have been the best of friends if he wasn't Connor's dad although I think he doted on Jonah more than he did his kid. And I still think that Connor is better off with me for now. For ever, in fact.

Feeling queasy and unsettled after last night, when I stubbornly slept in Connor's bed and not my husband's, I realise I can't handle food today, which is rare for me because I usually eat like a horse. Instead, I wander down to the rice fields for a walk. I'm hoping that practising some mindfulness in nature will lift my black mood. But I feel a twinge of guilt when I see how hard the locals are working. It's a backbreaking job, even though they look content enough and grin pleasantly at me. You have to admire their resilience, it rarely drops below thirty degrees in Bali.

I put my hands together in traditional greeting and repeat 'Swastiastu,' to everyone I pass. However, as soon as they pick up on my English accent they respond with a cheerful 'Hello.'

There's no denying the beauty of the island as I admire its spectacular views. The lush green valley has a small silvery river running through it and many intricate stone statues and temples line the terraces. Still, it has crushed all of my dreams. If we hadn't travelled to Bali for our honeymoon, I wonder how things might have worked out differently. I never would have come across my son then. I also would not have discovered Nathan's involvement in a man's death, a fact that continues to haunt me.

On my way back to the hotel, I accidentally step on an offering left at the base of one of the Ganesha statues that are found almost everywhere in Bali. The elephant god with a human body is believed to symbolise protection and the removal of obstacles from one's path. Since I have destroyed the colourful flower and palm leaf offering, does this mean that I am now cursed with bad luck as well? Just as Putu and Jonah were? My mouth is dry as I try to put the offering back together and hide it somewhere where no one can see it. But I can't shake the knot of fear in my stomach or the sensation that something horrible is going to happen.

I can't think straight, I'm trembling all over, but my subconscious is urging me to return to the room. Sensing Connor is in danger I start to run, faster and faster, gently nudging other guests out of my path as I head back. Gasping for air, I fling open the door of our royal honeymoon suite, to see . . . Nathan seated by himself at the dinner table, preparing to tuck into a hearty English breakfast. My heart stops as if someone had torn it out as I register there's just one place setting. One plate. One glass. One cup. Served no doubt, by room service. After a moment of staring at my husband's blank gaze, which tells me everything, I demand. 'Where's Connor? What have you done with him?'

He seems uneasy even as he takes a sip of his fruit juice before answering in a patronising tone, 'Now, now, don't get upset. But I reasoned that, after last night's performance, it might be best for you *and* Connor if you weren't here when Tim picked him.'

Tears well up in my eyes as I lament brokenly, 'Timothy has been here and taken him? But I thought we agreed he was better off with me, us.'

With a pitying gaze, he sighs, 'Darling, nobody agreed to that. However, what Tim and I did agree on is that you are becoming overly attached to that boy and vice versa.'

'What's wrong with that?' I plead pitifully, wanting to curl up on the ground and sob until my tears run out. Knowing that Nathan went behind my back is like having a knife drawn across my throat.

'Nothing at all if you were the boy's mother,' Nathan decides not to say anymore and takes a piece of crispy bacon from his plate to gnaw on. How can he eat when my heart aches?

'I know how much you love children,' he sighs compassionately, 'and I've always said that you'll be an amazing mother someday, so I think we should get you checked out by a doctor when we get back home.'

'What for?' I gasp.

'To find out why you can't get pregnant. And don't worry, I won't hold it against you if it turns out you need fertility treatment. It's fairly common these days. Cora went through it early on as well.'

I realise as I glare at him that I have the power to destroy his whole world, but I can't bring myself to break a promise, so I grit my teeth instead, and snap, 'I'm going to find Connor and bring him back.'

He stands up angrily. 'No, you're not. I absolutely forbid it.'

I pause to enquire, 'Why not?' since I'm used to blindly obeying him.

When he says, 'Because Connor is not yours,' his eyes soften a little.

'Yes, he is!' I rage before I can stop myself.

CHAPTER 44: TIMOTHY

On my way back from picking up Connor, who is more tolerant of me this morning and happy to accompany me back to our room — by this stage he is missing his toys — I run into Bartosz, who is returning to the hotel after a jog on the beach. When he sees me approaching, he stops and glances around as if trying to decide what to do. With no obvious escape route, he reluctantly walks towards us. Earlier, Nathan had surprised me with his thoughtfulness by arranging a time for me to see Connor when Samantha wasn't present because he knew it would be easier without her. Easier for Connor that is, not so much Samantha. She's going to be pretty upset when she finds out her husband has gone behind her back. But in this instance, Nathan *did* know best, and I owe him one. Just shows you shouldn't judge a book by its cover. As for Bartosz, I have no reason to be so forgiving.

Irrationally, I can't help but think that if it weren't for Bartosz, Jonah would be alive today because he would still be with Noah and would have never met me. The husband who ruined everything. Now that Kadek has planted those insinuating suggestions in my head, I'm unable to even grieve Jonah properly. Was he really going to leave me for someone else, and did he plan to take Connor with him? I guess I'll never find out.

'Timothy,' Bartosz acknowledges abruptly, standing motionless in front of me. Dressed all in black, he reminds me of a paid assassin, trained to kill quickly and silently. Following the direction of my alarmed gaze, he turns to look at the distant seashore, where a small, dark figure is observing us. A part of me wants to ask Bartosz if he can see the lone shadow that has been following me ever since Putu died, but I'm afraid he'll answer "No" and I'll have to accept that it's all in my head. A place I don't want to be.

Since I can't afford to let my guard down with Bartosz, I ask with affected brightness, 'How is everyone?'

His intense stare swiftly swings back to me, shocked, as he counters, 'Never mind us. How are *you* doing?'

Irritation courses through me — *how dare he pretend to care?* — and I answer snippily, 'As well as can be expected.'

With a guilty sigh, Bartosz presses a hand to his temple and stammers awkwardly, 'I'm so sorry about Jonah.'

Although he's clearly struggling with his emotions, I am not going to make this easy for him, so I plaster on a sarcastic smile and ask, 'Are you?'

Bartosz sucks in his breath, taken aback by my response. 'Of course,' he mutters, adding for good measure, 'very much so.'

'And yet,' I venture, sounding like Kadek, 'You are the only one who stands to benefit from Jonah's death.'

'What do you mean by that? How could I possibly benefit?' Bartosz gasps, wild-eyed.

'Because I know who you are and what you did,' I hiss vehemently.

Bartosz takes a step back from me and murmurs in a low voice so Connor cannot hear, 'I have no idea what you're talking about.'

I raise my voice a notch, 'No? You don't remember meeting Jonah before coming to this godforsaken island?'

Bartosz blinks rapidly as if racking his brain. Frowning, he shakes his head in bewilderment, muttering, 'No. Not at all.'

'That's bloody convenient, don't you think?'

Bartosz gestures subtly to Connor, who is peering up at us with concerned eyes. He clings tightly to my hand, as though worried about losing me too. I think Jonah's death is only now beginning to sink in with him, and I'm devastated once more. By the time my son grows up, he won't even remember Jonah. Even though it was my fault in the first place for getting us into financial difficulty, Bartosz is also to blame. I certainly don't need the man who broke Jonah's heart to tell me how to care for my son.

After a beat of silence, Bartosz enquires in an urgent tone, 'What makes you think I had already met Jonah? Surely, he would have said something.'

'You would think so, wouldn't you?' I say in a voice that is dangerously quiet. In the middle of my speech, I halt and consider whether or not to continue. Maybe I should just walk away before anyone else on this island gets hurt? What would Jonah have wanted me to do about Bartosz? In my head, I hear him baying for blood and wanting revenge. That's good enough for me, so I attack him with—

'For all I know, you were the one who pushed Jonah off the cliff.'

'Woah, just a minute,' Bartosz raises both hands in surrender, but his eyes are fiercely indignant as he demands, 'Why on earth would I do that?'

'According to the police, you weren't at the bottom of the waterfall with the others, which means you could have been up at the top with Jonah.'

Bartosz puts both hands in his short's pockets and groans, 'I wasn't anywhere near the waterfall. I was checking out the restaurants.'

'We only have your word for that,' I sneer, wanting to slit his throat.

Another hefty sigh from Bartosz, 'Mate, why would I want to kill Jonah?'

I bark, 'Don't *mate* me,' pausing to scoop up Connor as he starts to whimper at our raised voices. As I jiggle him up and down on my hip, his tiny face seeks out the comfort of my neck and he soon falls quiet again.

I hiss at Bartosz, 'Because you killed his boyfriend, and you don't want anyone to find out about it.'

Bartosz laughs incredulously, his dark eyes gleaming with what appears to be disgust. His next words are spiteful and uncalled for as he leans in to scoff, 'Are you sure it wasn't you who fell off the cliff and bumped your head and not your boyfriend because you're fucking delusional.'

Even with everything I know about Bartosz, his response shocks me. Typically, he's quiet and kind but now that I've seen a much darker side to him, I wonder if I should challenge the suicide claims which largely depend on the fact our money vanished into thin air. A moment ago, I was simply trying to rattle Bartosz with my accusations as I wasn't really convinced by them, but now I'm beginning to believe that he actually killed Jonah.

I grind out through clenched teeth, 'You can laugh all you want to,' and my eyes narrow to mere slits as I add. 'But your incompetence killed a man.' With saliva flying everywhere, I snarl, 'I don't know how you can call yourself a chef, let alone live with yourself when you can't tell the difference between a prawn sauce and a red pepper hummus.'

He flinches at that and his expression changes. As he starts to work it out for himself, his eyes widen in astonishment. He glances down at his trainers before stammering brokenly, 'What was the man's name?'

I rage sarcastically, 'Hah. That says it all. If you have to ask me that, how many more people have you poisoned?' Never before have I wanted to kill someone as much as I want to kill Bartosz now. Maybe if I did, my guilt over my role in Jonah's death wouldn't be as overwhelming. It would be so much easier if there were someone else to blame.

Bartosz, who appears to be shrinking in front of me, repeats, 'The name?' with weary eyes. I can see Angelika coming up behind him. She's frowning too, like me, so she must be able to hear our raised voices.

When I finally exclaim, 'Noah Brookes,' a weighty sensation descends upon my chest. I continue, very softly, 'He was the love of Jonah's life.'

CHAPTER 45: ANGELIKA

I assumed Bartosz had gone for his morning run without me when I woke up and saw that his side of the bed was empty, so I quickly showered, got dressed, and headed down to the beach to find him. I knew something was wrong as soon as I saw him and Timothy arguing. *What now?* That was my first thought. I was already on edge after being interrogated by the police. The fear of being discovered as a killer is almost worse than committing the act itself. Furthermore, Bartosz is acting strangely. He's more distant than ever and it seems like his finding out Nathan was responsible for his brother's death is having a bigger impact on him than I could have predicted. Should I be worried about him? By murdering Jonah, have I unintentionally set Bartosz off into a deep dark depression over the death of his brother? I'm told grief has an accumulative effect, so I can't completely rule this out.

After a very terse, 'Excuse us,' Timothy hurried away, with Connor constantly glancing back over his shoulder as if he wanted to stay and talk to me, but it was clear Timothy was not in the mood for conversation. And who could blame him? Not me, that's for sure, not when I keep experiencing twinges of regret that I could never have anticipated. Not over Jonah exactly — I'm still too angry for that — but I'm starting to imagine this might change in the future. It isn't as though I planned to kill him. It happened impulsively. But Connor is a different story. The little bruiser has unexpectedly grown on me, and I feel a great deal of remorse over him.

After overhearing part of Timothy and Bartosz's conversation, I snap to attention and turn sharp eyes on my husband, demanding, 'Are you going to tell me what that was all about?'

When he bites his lip and mumbles, 'Nothing,' a sick feeling of betrayal rolls around my stomach.

'Don't give me nothing,' I reply indignantly as I glare at him. I want him to argue back, but he won't even look at me. As soon as his eyes hit the sand, I press my lips together and scold, 'I heard what Timothy said.'

He starts in surprise, and this time he does look at me, but I don't recognise the blackness in his eyes. My heart leaps into my chest upon realising that I might as well be talking to a stranger.

'The guy's crazy. You can't believe a word he says,' Bartosz gives an exasperated growl.

Rage bubbles up inside me as I realise that he is lying. He's clearly not going to admit to anything, not without a fight anyway. 'Is it true what he said about you poisoning Jonah's previous boyfriend?'

He stretches out a calf muscle, knotted from his run, and gives a derisive laugh, 'He obviously mistook me for some other chef. It happens.'

'No, it doesn't,' I seethe, angrier than ever now because I can see right through his pathetic attempt to deceive me. Once again, he has underestimated my intelligence. I'm far too wily to fall for that.

The delicious smell of the salty sea, coconut oil and frangipani flowers fills the air between us. Secrets too. The bewitching ocean view, the flawless blue sky and the golden sun should be uniting us, but instead, we can hardly look at one another. Is our marriage over before it's even begun?

Bartosz's expression is one of mock horror, as he stammers, 'You don't really believe for one minute that I killed Jonah, as Timothy does.'

Because I know without a shadow of a doubt that Bartosz did not kill Jonah, I jump in with, 'No, I don't. But you never did explain why you quit working on the cruise ships and now I know why . . . because a man died.'

'Keep your voice down,' he cautions, his voice growing hard. 'People will hear you.' With that, he signals with his eyes for me to check out the beach.

I take a cautious look around. That's when I see the Australian couple who discovered Putu's body on the shore. They were clearly heading towards the sea because they're dressed in swimwear and are carrying snorkelling equipment. But they're now standing motionless and staring at us, obviously shocked to see us arguing. Irritation courses through me. It seems to me that they are everywhere. Like hard-to-get-rid-of bedbugs that take over hotels. Although not luxurious five-star ones like ours.

Without really meaning it, I exclaim petulantly, 'I don't care if they do. I can't believe something like that happened and you kept it from me.'

Bartosz turns to face me with a quizzical look, and I wonder whether this is when he will reveal to me that he witnessed me pushing Jonah from the cliff or that he is aware of my past sexual encounters with Nathan. I realise that by accusing him of hiding secrets, I am being hypocritical, but I have never pretended to be perfect like he has. It's a huge betrayal.

'I'm telling you it wasn't me. I didn't do anything wrong,' he snarls through gritted teeth. His jaw is set and there is a hard glint in his eyes that sends shivers down my spine. 'Why won't you believe me?'

Fury erupts in my chest as I scream, 'Because I can tell when you're lying. Besides, why would Timothy make up something like that, about getting the dishes mixed up and a man dying because of it?'

'You'd believe him over me?' he barks, so incensed that he kicks out at the sand. Realising that the Australian couple is still watching us, he yells, 'What are you looking at?' even though he had just seconds before wanted to prevent them from hearing our fight. With astonished eyes, they grasp hands before scurrying fearfully away, with the woman casting quick glances over her shoulder, much in the way Connor had done.

I sigh in disgust and shake my head, muttering, 'Oh, well done. Now the whole island will know we were arguing.'

'I'm sorry, okay,' Bartosz sniffs, rubbing a hand over his stubble. 'It's this place. It's getting to me.'

I don't buy his fake tears, even when he pretends to swipe them away. 'You want me to feel sorry for you?' I cry. 'When all this time you've been blaming Nathan for what he did to your brother and you're just as bad!'

His shoulders go rigid and his whole face tenses as he warns darkly, 'Don't say that. I'm nothing like him.'

In response, I roll my eyes and shrug one shoulder, implying that he is *exactly* like Nathan. I realise my mistake when, without warning, Bartosz lashes out and strikes me hard across the cheek.

CHAPTER 46: SAMANTHA

An exotic choir of songbirds can be heard outside, accompanied by teasing glimpses of tropical plumage darting amongst the pink and white flowers. The tops of the palm trees sway seductively in the distance and then there's the soothing sound of trickling water as bubbles rise to the surface of the pool. The sun is high in the sky, bouncing golden rays through the glass doors onto our faces, warming our skin, and I can hear a monkey's eerie treetop call in the nearby jungle. These sights and sounds of paradise are not the kind you hear every day at home, although the dreary, wet UK is where I long to be at this moment. Inside the room, there is only silence. Tense. Awkward. Stilted. Silence. Nathan has set his cutlery back down on the table and removed the napkin from around his neck. With his arms folded, he raises a provocative eyebrow and asks in a surprisingly calm manner, 'What do you mean, he's yours? What are you talking about?'

I brace my shoulders, fully alert, but I'm unable to meet his intense stare, so I look down at my sandal-clad feet and see that the orange gel nail polish on my big toe is chipped. I murmur softly under my breath, 'I had a son before I met you and had him adopted,' and push a long strand of hair back behind my ear.

Nathan stiffly rises to his feet. He takes a deep breath and exhales slowly as his eyes fill with deep disappointment. It's a look that I've come to dread. 'You're not serious?' he asks in a deadly tone.

My silence speaks volumes as I move towards the corner sofa and sit down shakily, feeling as though my knees could give way beneath me. I place my trembling hands in my lap and keep them there.

Nathan's cold, accusing gaze is palpable. It burns every inch of my skin. 'Well?' he persists icily as he comes to tower over me. I think he does it deliberately, to intimidate me. 'And you didn't think to tell me?' He sulkily demands, as I squirm under his enraged look.'

I don't say anything, *I can't*, but I shrug my shoulders as if to imply, "obviously not."

He lets out a puff of exasperation, turns his back on me and goes to stand by the glass doors. Accusingly, he laments, 'How could you?'

I dare to risk a quick peek at him. His hands are on his hips, his buttocks clenched firmly together. Looking at his erect shoulders and stiff jawline, his posture screams resentment. 'How could you lie to me about something as important as that?'

I'm on the verge of tears when I exclaim, tellingly, 'That's ironic coming from you! You haven't been completely honest with me either.'

He looks at me strangely, as though he's trying to figure out what I could have found out about him. If I didn't know any different, I would say he was afraid of being a disappointment to me. But that is just too ridiculous for words. Still, I can tell he isn't going to admit anything, so I point out, 'You didn't tell me that you were responsible for another man's death.'

That does, as I predicted it would, get him in the gonads. In the silence that follows, I wring my hands nervously and find myself holding my breath, as I try to guess his next move.

He scowls at me as if he were still angry with me, but I can also see that he is being evasive as he sits down next to me. His weight pulls me towards him, which is not where I want to go, so I lean back in my seat. 'Who told you that?' he asks.

I shake my head, mumbling, 'It doesn't matter.'

'It does matter!' he roars, too near to my ear, making me flinch.

'What matters is that we've both been keeping secrets from each other,' I murmur primly, as I lower my gaze once more.

It clearly isn't the response Nathan was hoping for as it's not nearly apologetic enough, so he growls irritably, 'What happened to that man, as you well know, was an accident.' He pauses to gulp nervously, before continuing, 'A road rage incident that went horribly wrong.'

As he stares at me, I notice a glimmer of shame in his eyes and am moved by it. My husband might have a conscience after all. As I move to console him with a stroke on the arm, he knocks me back down to earth with a painful whack, as he accuses spitefully, 'It's hardly the same thing as hiding from your husband the fact that you already had a baby.'

I'm about to respond when he turns to face me with startled eyes and coldly states, 'But what has this got to do with Connor?'

'He's mine. The boy I gave away,' I sniff tearfully, but when our eyes collide, I see he's not convinced. Beneath his piercing blue gaze is doubt.

Bewildered, Nathan stands up to pace the room. Agitatedly, he runs both hands through his floppy blond hair, unintentionally exposing the bald patch he despises so much. Wide-eyed, he stutters, 'Are you sure?'

I nod, once, and then a second time as a tear lands on my cheek. I quickly bat it away and wipe the wetness on my linen shorts.

He can't help but cynically add, 'And is Tim aware that Connor is your long-lost son, or rather, that you believe he is.'

'Oh, God no,' I reply, shaking my head vehemently.

'If he *is* yours, which is extremely unlikely, what did you think you were going to do about it?' he asks, flabbergasted.

I snippily answer, 'I intended . . . *intend* to take him back to England with me and officially adopt him.'

'That's insane!' he laughs bitterly, jabbing an irate finger at me. 'He has a legal father! *You're* insane if you think that's going to happen. And even if he is your kid, I meant what I said before. He's not going to move in with us. There's no way I'm going to raise, support and pay for a kid who isn't mine.'

Deeply wounded, a darkness and a desire to fight back washes over me. I've always known I have the power to destroy him, and I do so now by saying smugly, 'You have no idea, do you?'

'About what?'

'Your kids aren't yours.'

He raises a brow, suggesting once again that he has no idea what I'm talking about because I'm mad, crazy, doolally — all of those things. And yes, at this precise moment, I am. I prove it by cackling hysterically, 'The children you have been raising, supporting and paying for, as you call it — Jordan, Will and little Elouise — they're not yours.'

'That's absurd,' he argues. However, I can sense a hint of uncertainty in his gaze. The fact that he is less sure of himself has me laughing even harder. Since I can't seem to stop, Nathan is getting even more irate with me. 'Seriously, Sam, when we get home, I'm taking you to see a therapist,' he warns with a frown. 'There's something wrong with you.'

That's when my horrible, scary laughter stops. Incensed, I retaliate by screeching, 'No. There's something wrong with *you*. You're not able to have children due to your low sperm count.'

'You're talking in riddles again, Sam.'

'When you were married to Cora and nothing was happening pregnancy-wise, you took yourselves off to the fertility clinic, remember, assuming it was her fault? But it turned out you were the problem, not her. Only Cora kept that bit of news from you.'

His face goes pale, and perspiration breaks out on his brow. He tries to appear indifferent, but he can't keep the mounting anxiety out of his voice when he barks, 'That's outrageous. If I were infertile, I'd have a right to be told. Besides, if the kids aren't mine, then whose are they?'

'It really is hilarious, isn't it?' I scoff, but neither of us is laughing anymore. 'That Cora was having a long-term affair with Nick behind your back while you were out chasing other women, including me, the nanny.'

'Nick who?' he asks in shock.

My chest erupts with fury as I scream, 'Your brother Nick.'

CHAPTER 47: TIMOTHY

Samantha is nowhere to be found, even though I've spent the entire afternoon looking for her. She's not at the resort's restaurants or shops, spa, beach or pool area. Angelika and Bartosz are also nowhere to be seen — not that I want to run into that bastard again unless it's on my terms. Nathan was right when he said there was something strange about the man. I ought to have listened to him. Come to that, I haven't seen Nathan since the wee hours of this morning. Where is everyone?

I've hauled Connor around the entire island in search of our group, and by now he's hot, exhausted and grumpy. I've never seen the beach so empty. Not only are there no towels on the sun loungers, but there are no cocktails being served today. I head to the Price's hotel suite, realising everyone must be staying in their rooms, where at least it's cool *and* safe. Even though Samantha is probably still mad at me for removing Connor from her care, I'm sure she won't say no to having him for a few hours.

When I arrive on their doorstep I hear angry voices inside. Nathan and Samantha are having a heated disagreement about somebody called Nick. My first impulse is to leave and return later, but I've rung the bell already, and since I can't hear them arguing anymore, they must have heard it.

I grimace and tell Connor, 'It's okay. It's just grownups being grownups,' and I wiggle his hand reassuringly. He looks at me with suspicion, probably because I am one of those "grownups" and then the thumb on his other hand disappears into his mouth. He starts making that annoying sucking sound that grates on me. What can I say? I'm a bad dad.

I awkwardly hover at the door, wondering if anyone will answer soon, or if I should simply leave. Christ, this is embarrassing. I had no idea their relationship was this bad. Why get married if they don't get along? No wonder Samantha is miserable, and Nathan is drunk most of the time.

As the door eventually clicks open, Samantha's pale ivory face peers out. Once again, I am dazzled by her stunning blue eyes which are a match for my son's. Thankfully, I can't see any bruises or black eyes since I'm not in the right head space to save her from an abusive situation. She has been crying, though, as evidenced by the tears in her eyes. She looks me up and down, more flustered than I've ever seen her, but as soon as she sees Connor, her demeanour relaxes.

'Hello, big man,' she coos, getting down on his level and ruffling his hair. At that moment, I spot Nathan in the background, tugging on a shirt as if he wants to tear it to pieces. Anger has turned his face a brilliant red.

'Is everything okay?' I ask over brightly, knowing it isn't.

She lets me off the hook by failing to answer. Rather, she asks of me, 'Why are you here?' with what seems like abruptness.

'I was hoping you could help me out,' I am deliberately vague, not wanting Nathan to overhear my request in case he tells me to "Piss off".

'How have you been?' she remembers to ask, seeming to have woken up from a deep sleep and realising that I have recently been bereaved.

'Oh, you know, up and down,' I sigh.

'Mostly down I imagine,' she smiles sympathetically at me.

I'm so grateful for her concern that I could burst into tears, but I control myself and go on to explain, 'I need to go to the mainland for the night. There's so much to sort out. For starters, Jonah's body,' I mumble the last bit to keep Connor from hearing. 'And there's a tonne of documents to sort through.' Embarrassed, I choke and haltingly add, 'Financial stuff mostly.'

She dismisses all of my explanations with a polite wave as if she doesn't need to know the details and comes straight to the point, 'How can I help?'

'Could you have Connor for me? I know it's an imposition, but you're the only one who—'

And with that, her face brightens and, for the first time, she smiles properly. 'Of course, I'd love to,' she interrupts. She even partially opens the door, as if about to welcome us inside. I was right when I suspected she'd take my hand off for the chance to babysit my boy. I speak too soon, because the door is then abruptly flung open, and Samantha is shoved aside.

'I'm leaving,' Nathan announces gruffly to Samantha, ignoring me. However, he does a double take upon seeing Connor, as if the mere sight of him increases his anger. Samantha glares at her husband as if daring him to say something. They're an odd couple, it has to be said. I've never seen this side to her before and, even though I've always felt she needed to toughen up — especially with Nathan — I'm not sure I like it.

Irritated, I find myself biting my lip. Leaving Connor with them doesn't seem like such a good idea anymore. What choice do I have though? When Nathan suddenly storms off without another word, I'm relieved. Without him around, there can be no more arguing. Samantha is standing in the open doorway, so Nathan doesn't even get to enjoy the satisfaction of slamming the door behind him.

'Has someone been out in the sun too long?' I joke.

'Take no notice,' Samantha advises, before turning to Connor and saying, 'We can order fish fingers for tea if you like, from room service.'

'And orange juice', he murmurs happily — his thumb still inhabiting his mouth — causing her to chuckle.

Unlike Samantha, I am not amused. It's not easy trying to instil manners and politeness in a four-year-old. 'Take your thumb out of your mouth when you're speaking to Samantha,' I tell Connor.

Surprisingly, he does as he's told and then exclaims, 'I haven't cried about my dad.' With a disapproving sideways look at me, he whispers, 'Unlike my other dad who cries all the time. Like a baby.'

Samantha is trying not to giggle at my expense. 'That's because you're a big, brave boy.' She gives Connor a big, encouraging smile and gestures for him to enter, which he does. He doesn't look back to see if I'm following.

'Unlike me, he means,' I shrug helplessly, trying to make light of my situation.

Samantha looks at me questioningly, as though she senses something is wrong. When her reply comes, it's businesslike. 'How long do you need me to watch him?'

I pull a face, fearful of her response. 'All night.'

I kind of expect her to ask me questions or say she can't keep Connor that long, but she doesn't do either of these things. She merely nods in acknowledgement before silently closing the door in my face.

CHAPTER 48: ANGELIKA

I have no idea how many margaritas I've had today because I'm not counting. All I know is that I intend to have another and another, until the oblivion I'm looking for eventually finds me and puts me on my back, comatose. With whatever dignity I had left, I stormed off after the altercation with Bartosz, ignoring his pleas to "Come back" and his worried cries of "I'm sorry. I didn't mean it. You know I'm not that kind of man". I didn't even bother screaming back at him, 'So what kind of man are you?'

I barely smile in appreciation as the waiter brings me another drink. Still, as soon as my trembling hand curls around the chilled glass, I feel a wave of emotion building inside me that travels up through my stomach and into my throat until I find myself back in the murky past, where I was once knocked out by a punter who wanted "it" for free. I vowed afterwards that no man would ever hurt me again, so I armed myself with pepper spray and kept an illegal Taser in my handbag. Never in my wildest thoughts did I think my loving, patient and kind husband would raise his hand to me. I still find it hard to accept that Bartosz did that. Until I get another sickening flashback of his hand lashing out. As I recall the ugly, sharp sting of it, I quake all over.

Bartosz hasn't come looking for me, as far as I can tell, and I've been gone all day. I lingered on the beach for hours, mulling over what had happened while gazing out at the still ocean. As I squinted up at the sun, which was a brilliant yellow in the sky, and burned fiercely through my eyelids, I bid a heartfelt farewell to my short-lived marriage. It's over. Bartosz and I are no more. When we finally depart this cursed island, we will also be leaving each other. I can overlook a lot of things, but not this. Never this. And yet, my heart is breaking. I could have handled the situation better, of course. I should have used a less combative approach and encouraged Bartosz to talk instead of calling him out on being as awful as Nathan Price. That's what did it, and now I'm cursing myself for it. Still, I'm not one of those women who, like Sam, hold themselves responsible for the behaviour of their men. This is all Bartosz's fault.

'I fucking hate Bali,' a voice complains as a man slides onto the bar stool next to me. My eyes go straight to his sunburned face. It's Nathan and he looks as traumatised as I feel, so I signal for the waiter again.

'What are you having?' I ask, smiling to disguise my anxiety.

'The usual,' he grimaces, obviously in a dark mood.

'What happened to you?' I ask matter-of-factly, even though that's the last thing I'm feeling right now.

Seeming offended, he snaps, 'What do you mean?'

I curtly respond, 'You look like shit,' and take a sip of my cocktail, slurping on the straw and blowing bubbles like a kid.

When he grins at me, I am reminded of the younger man I once knew. He was always handsome and, when the situation called for it, charming and even funny. He's a distraction from my suffering, I realise, when my heart finally stops hammering. I remind myself that I have every reason to hate this man, but there's something about his boldness that is endearing, and so I find myself laughing when he turns to me and says—

'The other night when I asked you to meet me on the beach, I wouldn't have gone through with it. I just wanted to see if you'd show up,' and coughs apologetically into his hand, almost blushing.

I scoff as I lean back on my stool to observe him, 'You so would.'

At that, he laughs good-naturedly, agreeing, 'I so would.'

Our drinks come quickly because we are the only customers at the beach bar. Talk about tumbleweed! The barman knows Nathan well and has served him his usual tipple without being asked.

'What shall we toast to? Old times?' he suggests with a swagger, sliding a shot glass towards me and winking.

I shake my head and pull an annoyed face. Putting the glass to my lips, I exclaim angrily, 'To fucking Bali.'

'To fucking Bali,' he curls his lip and smirks, while downing his drink in one.

When he blinks at me blearily, before glancing up and down the beach as if looking for someone, I begin to think that he has been on a similar journey to myself this holiday, and I find myself warming to him.

The next thing I know, I'm spluttering, 'Jesus, what is this?' into my drink. 'It feels as though I've lost my virginity all over again.'

Laughing heartily, he slides in closer, nudging me and saying smuttily, 'You were a virgin? I find that difficult to believe.'

'Piss off,' I hiss playfully, leaning into him and elbowing him back.

'It's arak,' he gestures to my drink. 'A Balinese spirit that contains sixty per cent alcohol. You've just got to make sure it's not the black-market kind as that stuff can kill.'

'Shit. That's stronger than our best Polish vodka.'

'You Poles are not the best at everything.'

I roll my eyes as if to say "Whatever."

He falls silent then and looks at me thoughtfully. With a sympathetic tone, he asks, 'Want to talk about it?'

'Who are you, my friendly but perverted uncle?' I am deliberately sarcastic but when I see his face fall, I heave a sigh. He clearly means to be kind. 'Not really,' I choke out, blinking back tears. 'You?'

'Nah,' he shrugs, face crumbling as he glances quickly away.

Pinching my nose, I scrunch up my face and keep one eye closed as I knock back the rest of my shot. As it goes down, I let out a shudder, 'Fuck.'

He follows suit, 'Fuck,' afterwards banging his glass down on the counter and telling the barman, 'Same again, please.'

Once we've been served, Nathan twists in his seat to look at me and he says softly, 'I'm pleased I ran into you. Right now, I'm glad of the company.'

'Ditto,' I mumble, realising that he is not the same Nathan Price I previously knew. Like me, he appears broken.

Scowling, I raise my glass, 'To fucking honeymoons.' He knocks his glass against mine, grimly nodding in agreement, 'To fucking honeymoons.'

CHAPTER 49: SAMANTHA

Connor's angelic little face puckers into a frown as he wonders, 'Who is the man in the photo?' I squirm on the bed beside him and nervously pluck at imaginary hairs on my nightdress, questioning whether now is the right time to tell him who I really am — his mother — and that the man in the photo is his father. But, deciding that it is too soon after Jonah's suicide and that the shock will only traumatise him further, I reply, 'Somebody I loved very much,' instead.

'What's his name?'

'Never mind,' I tell him, unable to peel my eyes away from the image on my phone. 'All you need to know is that you look just like him.'

Appearing immediately interested, Connor sits up in bed and demands, 'I want to see better.' I tilt my head to one side and smile. It's impossible for me to say no to him. 'Okay,' I say, handing him the phone.

I search his expression for clues as he squints at the photo. It's the only one I have of his real dad. I wonder if he'll notice the resemblance. Finally, he asks, 'Is he your boyfriend?' with a hint of jealousy.

'No. I'm married to Nathan, remember?' I chuckle, but in my mind, I'm secretly thinking, *Am I?* 'But he used to be,' I add, in a dreamy tone.

Connor scrutinises my face closely, as though he wants to know what's going through my mind. Suddenly bored, he tosses the phone to the bottom of the bed, and I'm taken aback when he pouts, 'He's nothing like me.'

Mouth wide open, I'm about to exclaim, "How can you say that when he's your double?" but since he's still a little child, I reconsider. However, I struggle to find the right words as I remark casually, *too casually*, 'You do think you look like me though? Everybody says so. Even your dad.'

When he says, 'Which dad? The dead one or the other one?' my heart bleeds for him. This little boy has been through so much already that I take what he says about his real father with a pinch of salt. While it's true that Connor looks more like me than his biological father, the similarity cannot be ignored. Connor is too young to see it, that's all.

Whispering, 'It's time to go to sleep,' I tuck him in and kiss his forehead, not wanting to bring up the subject of Jonah's passing.

'I'm not tired,' he complains, pulling a face. But he grudgingly lies back down and closes his eyes. A few seconds later they flicker open again, and he looks frightened as he pleads, 'You'll stay here with me?'

'Of course, I'm not going anywhere,' I reassure him. And I mean it. I have no intention of ever being apart from my beloved son again.

'Night,' he yawns, turning over on one side and sighing. I can tell he's asleep when I hear his breathing get deeper. I keep my promise and remain where I am. There was never any danger of me leaving. Watching my son sleep is a privilege, not a chore. Keeping him safe is what I was born to do. If only I hadn't given him up. But there is only one person to blame for this.

It's shaping up to be a truly incredible day, and not in a good way as I am being forced to confront my past. I am like a rabbit in the headlights, much like I was when I first discovered I was pregnant. Unknowingly, and in a way I never could have imagined, Connor has revived my love for his father. Every time I look at him, he's there, in his eyes. I recognise too late that my love for him has never faded. He was my first and only true love and this makes me wonder how I could have said "yes" to Nathan.

I had married the Joker, but the joke was on me. When Nathan, who was married to Cora at the time, began pursuing me relentlessly, I mistakenly believed that I had discovered love again. I even convinced myself that I had finally met a man who would not abandon me as Connor's father had done. But it turns out it wasn't me that Nathan wanted but an upgrade, something he did every few years, according to his ex-wives.

Even the poor deceived Cora seemed relieved to be rid of him and doesn't hate me anywhere near as much as she should for stealing him off her. I'm ashamed of what I did to her, but try telling me that at the time, when all I could think about was the security of being with Nathan, instead of worrying about his wife and three children who I was nannying for. Nathan said he wanted to take care of me, which was something I had never experienced before — I later found out the reverse was true. I'm not trying to make excuses, but this made me easy prey. Easy full stop.

Now that I know better, and I realise that Nathan is no prize, I'm much kinder to Cora than he would have me be. Because of me, she received a far better divorce settlement than Nathan would have agreed to. Given what I knew about her, she didn't put up much of a fight for him. She must have regretted making those drunken confessions about her children's paternity. However, at least I knew going into my marriage there wouldn't be any kids. And I felt okay with that after losing one child.

I have now betrayed her as well and she will undoubtedly suffer the consequences and Nathan's wrath. As for my husband, I am sure he is inconsolable and probably quite drunk by now. I wish I could take back what I said, but after hearing what he had to say about Connor, I was unable to control my desire to hurt him as he had hurt me, even if only momentarily. Nathan, like a hunter holding up the lifeless jaw of a shot animal, has always taken pride in his masculinity and bragged about being a "man's man". I have deprived him of that as well as his children.

As Nathan's third trophy wife, I consider myself the weakest to date. I'm aware that I'm not his usual type. I don't have curves, or any fashion sense nor do I wear makeup. Also, unlike Cora, I'm not materialistic, fancying myself as more of a free spirit. I'm not the mouse everyone takes me for though, I just like to stay in the background. So, I object to nothing and say very little when Nathan is around. He's a man that needs a lot of attention and it's sometimes exhausting being his wife. When I said yes to marrying him it felt like a fair exchange at the time, for hadn't I wrecked his marriage to Cora and ruined the lives of his three young children?

And now, well, now things have changed. A week ago, if you had asked me if I wanted my marriage to succeed, my answer would have been an instant and enthusiastic "Hell yes." However, knowing how Nathan feels about my son, it's now a "Hell no."

CHAPTER 50: TIMOTHY

As I step off the speed boat, I am unsteady on my feet and almost stumble into the dark swirling ocean. The driver comes to my rescue, escorting me onto the jetty and fussing over me as if I were an old woman. He knows I've had too much to drink. He can smell the booze on my breath. Vodka. Gin. Red wine. A whisky sour. You name it, I've had it.

'Are you all right, Sir?' he wants to know.

'Fine,' I mutter unconvincingly. Isn't that what grieving people are meant to say? Even when they're clearly not fine.

He appears to be about to say something else, but then he seems to change his mind. 'Good night,' he mutters, eyes averted.

'Night,' I slur, as I watch him leap into his boat with the energy of a competitive athlete, making me envious. As I turn to walk sluggishly away, head down and hands in pockets, the sudden movement causes my head to spin, and I stagger onto the beach before collapsing face down in the sand. Ouch. And double ouch. Though it happens incredibly slowly in my mind, the reality is I hit the ground fast. Thank God nobody saw.

The last time this happened was when I was chasing after Connor on the beach back when Jonah was still alive. All I have left of him now are tainted memories. The rage I felt after learning he lied to me about the money and had taken his own life instantly bubbles to the surface.

'Fuck,' I shout at the top of my lungs, wanting to lash out with my hands, feet, and teeth. Everything I've got! Nothing happens because nobody can hear me. I am alone on the beach. I spit out the salty particles, wipe my mouth with the back of my hand and roll onto my back, coughing up blood and sand.

Across the water, I can make out the bright lights of Ubud in the distance. A hazy glance at my Smartwatch indicates that it's just past two in the morning. There aren't many bars open this late — or early, depending on how you look at it — and I managed to find them all before returning to the island. *Or they found me.* The corners of my mouth twitch and I find myself grinning at the discovery that the LGBT community is thriving in Bali even though same-sex marriage is illegal in Indonesia. There aren't any official gay bars in Ubud, Bali's Cultural Centre, but a night at the gay-friendly CP Lounge smoking sheesha, getting wasted, and enjoying live music was exactly what I needed. Anything to take my mind off Jonah's betrayal and the awful way Bartosz spoke to me. The bastard's words haunt me. "Are you sure it wasn't you who fell off the cliff and bumped your head and not your boyfriend because you're fucking delusional," he'd scoffed.

I'm not proud of myself for lying to Samantha and telling her I was going to the mainland to make the necessary arrangements for Jonah's body to be returned to the UK and to take care of the finances. There are no finances to take care of since there isn't any money. How in the world am I meant to pay for anything? How will we live? *Where* will we live? I find it ironic that Connor and I will probably end up living in rented accommodation once we've sold our beautiful home. At least my credit card hasn't been declined by the bank yet. But that will change when they find out that all of the money is gone and I'm unable to pay off the £200K overdraft.

A strange sound, like bare feet running along the beach, has me on high alert. 'Hello?' I call out nervously, sitting up. Nothing. Except for an eerie silence. The gentle lapping of the sea against the sand becomes invisible in the background, like white noise. That's when I hear it again — a swishing, splashing sound — and this time, I know I'm not mistaken. Someone is out there, running in and out of the water and playing tricks on me. Since Putu died, I have felt their ever-watchful presence. I knew I wasn't imagining it. Even amid the brightly illuminated, busy streets of Ubud, I could not stop looking over my shoulder, convinced that someone was following me.

Hot and sticky with fear, I clamber to my feet, feeling very sober now considering how much I've drunk. 'Who's there?' I growl. Silence, again . . .

It's obvious that whoever is out there doesn't want to identify themselves, so I decide not to stick around and head towards the safety of the resort, hands clenched into fists at my sides, just in case. Since I'm terrified of being attacked from behind, the hairs on my body stand on end and sweat pools in the middle of my back, soaking my shirt. Only when I reach the dimly lit pool area of the hotel, do I breathe a sigh of relief.

After a night of burning incense and spicy street odours in Ubud, the blast of tropical scent flooding my nostrils is a wonderful change of pace. The sweet creamy fragrance of the coconut trees that surround the pool isn't strong enough to mask the unpleasant smell of bleach in the water though. The trees themselves are smooth and slender, like the majority of Balinese women I've met and have wide, glossy, pleated leaves. Diamond-white slivers of light ripple across the bubbling water by uplighters. Nature's white noise — the sound of crickets chirping — provides a soothing background that I find comforting after the scare I've just had.

Though I'm tempted to curl up on one of the rattan sun loungers and enjoy this tranquil scene until dawn, I accidentally rub my ankle on something prickly. Startled, I jump back, ready to flee, but when I see that it is a large but innocent-looking coconut, I can't help but smile wryly. This island has turned me into someone who is scared of a bleeding coconut. I pick the woody thing up and inspect it, realising it must have fallen through the safety netting on the trees. It could have dealt someone a nasty blow to the head if they had been sitting under it.

My thoughts spiral from there. What if Connor had been playing out here at the time? I'm about to angrily walk off in the direction of reception, in the mood to vent to hotel management despite the late hour, when I notice the dark silhouette of a man sitting in one of the sun loungers, as I had wanted to do. However, he isn't soaking up the atmosphere. Rather, he is holding his head in his hands and softly crying.

Could this be the person who has been following me? What will I do if that's the case? Should I confront him or walk away now, while I still can? However, I reject that idea as soon as I realise they couldn't have possibly reached the pool area before me. Armed with nothing but the coconut, I sneak up behind them to take a closer look. I have to know who it is.

CHAPTER 51: ANGELIKA

I wake up to a crime scene or at least that's what it looks like. Through half-closed eyes that refuse to open all the way, I can just about make out the sun shining in through the blinds, blinding me. The bed smells of sex, alcohol and bad breath, and there is a jumble of his and her clothes all over the ivory marble floor. 'What the fuck,' I groan, tugging at the sheet that defies orders. Mainly because it's tightly wrapped around someone else. The bulk of a man who is selfishly stealing the sheet for himself. But that can't be right, can it? Because I had absolutely no intention of kissing and making up with Bartosz last night or any other night, come to that. I must still be drunk and therefore hallucinating. That's what I tell myself, anyway.

I have the feeling that someone is screaming inside my head. That's no surprise considering that fireworks are going off inside it, melting my brain. I have to go to the toilet. And I really, really want a glass of water. I can't move though. My legs are like jelly. When the screaming doesn't stop, threads of anxiety begin to tug at my insides. After a few more minutes, I suddenly realise that this is not my hotel room and that the screaming is coming from outside rather than from my hungover brain.

'Jesus fucking Christ, not again,' I shriek, jolting upright in bed.

The body beside me, which does not belong to my husband, mumbles into his pillow, rolls over on his back, and smacks his lips thirstily.

Eyes bulging in alarm, I exclaim, 'God, Nathan, tell me we didn't.'

One unrepentant eye opens. Then the other. And suddenly he's looking guilty, which would indicate that *we did*.

'Oh, shit. We're both in trouble now,' he moans, sitting up in bed and massaging his sleep-deprived eyes.

'Put some clothes on,' I screech as the sheet comes away from his patchy red and white sunburnt body and I realise he's bollock naked.

'You put some clothes on,' he chides, unable to resist a cheeky wink.

That's when I realise I am also naked, so I cover my breasts with both hands, swing my feet out of the bed, and bend down to gather up my clothes that have been discarded on the floor. The screams from outside continue. There are voices too. Lots of panicked voices.

'What the hell is going on?' Nathan demands, pulling a disgruntled face as he wanders over to the patio doors and peers through the blinds.

He's still as nude as the day he was born, so I turn away and manage to put on yesterday's clothes — a black sundress, a thong and flip-flops — while his back is turned.

'You don't think they've found another body?' I ask, nibbling worriedly on my fingernail and blinking in confusion.

'Bloody hell, I hope not,' he says with a scowl.

I avert my gaze from his manhood, look around the room and gasp, 'Isn't this Timothy's room?' I almost said *and Jonah's* but caught myself in time.

At last, Nathan puts on his shorts, watching me with interest as he ponders, 'I think you're right.'

'Oh, my God. What are we doing here? And what if Timothy comes back and finds us?' I'm in true panic mode now, scrambling to make the bed and cover our tracks. My heart is racing so fast that I think it's about to burst. *Will whoever is screaming outside please stop?* My nerves can't stand it.

Comically, Nathan replies, 'I seem to recall you telling me last night that Tim was staying on the mainland and wouldn't be needing it.'

My stomach is doing cartwheels, and I want to vomit. 'Are you saying that this was my idea, and I brought you here?' I bark.

'We were both hammered,' he explains, as though that justifies what we've done. I doubt if that will be good enough for Sam, but don't say so.

'Too drunk for you to . . .' I gesture hopefully to the bulge in his shorts.

He flinches at that, insisting, 'Drink never has that effect on me.'

My face falls. 'So we did have sex then?' I wail.

'Both times,' he beams, obviously hoping to get a rise out of me.

His comment throws me, and I groan out loud.

Pulling on his shirt and doing up his buttons, he mumbles conspiratorially in a mocking tone, 'I won't tell if you won't.'

'This isn't funny, Nathan,' I grumble petulantly as I frantically run my hands through my hair to get rid of the knots. Before I sneak out of here, I need to make sure I look half-decent in case I run into someone. The hotel staff perhaps. Or even worse, Bartosz.

'No. You're right there,' he agrees, seeming preoccupied, as though he's trying to figure out a way to get out of this mess. That would take a miracle.

My hand flutters to my mouth as I lament, 'What are we going to do?'

'I don't know,' he mutters, clearly irritated. 'I don't have all the answers just yet, but there will definitely be a lot of lying involved.'

I scowl and protest, 'You can't lie your way out of every situation.'

'Watch me,' he flashes me a loan shark smile. Same old Nathan. And with that, he sheepishly moves towards the door.

'Wait for me,' I cry in a panic.

'It's best if we don't leave together in case we're spotted,' he suggests sleazily, acting as though this kind of behaviour is nothing new to him.

'Fine,' I sigh, feeling incredibly let down by myself. Nathan fucking Price had to be my vengeful, drunken one-night stand, didn't he? You couldn't make it up. I flex my chin in disdain and urge, 'Let me go first.'

'Be my guest. Ladies first,' he adds, politely indicating that I should lead the way. But I'm no lady. Certainly not after last night. More like trash. Before I get the chance to walk out with my head held high, there's a sharp rap at the door. Then another. And another. Similar to a burst of gunshots.

Nathan and I stare wide-eyed at each other, unable to move, as a key is quietly inserted into the lock from the other side of the door. The handle slowly turns, and the door begins to open, inch by dreadful inch . . .

CHAPTER 52: SAMANTHA

After storming off yesterday, Nathan didn't return to our room last night. That means we have been apart for two of the seven days of our honeymoon. This must be a record for a newlywed couple. However, it's not entirely unexpected. When it comes to marriage, Nathan invariably gives up when things get difficult. In business, he's ambitious and determined to see deals through until the bitter end, but when it comes to relationships, he'd sooner bail than admit he's a failure. When my phone pings for the third time in a row I fish it out of my bag and groan irritably when I see that it is Nathan, wanting to know where I am. I toss it back into my bag with childish abandon. I don't feel like talking to him right now.

Connor and I have made the best of our time together. We were up bright and early and are now seated in the rooftop restaurant overlooking the rice fields. Although the resort has three restaurants, due to the lack of staff, only one is currently open. As a result, the waiters that *are* left, surround us like vultures as we are the only ones eating. Even the morning yoga class was cancelled due to a lack of attendees.

As Connor tucks into pancakes and maple syrup, with my help since I've cut everything up into small pieces for him,

I sip my black coffee and nibble at my delicious jam-filled sweet pastries. Honestly, I don't know what Timothy and Jonah used to make all the fuss about when Connor is as good as gold. He is a well-behaved angel while he is with me. The morning air is filled with the smell of dew and earthiness, but there's also a faint tang of eggs, bacon and porridge. I notice that the waiters have now formed a huddle and are whispering to each other, along with the chef who has emerged from the kitchen. Their horrified faces unnerve me. *What now?* Every time I see them glancing furtively at us, my heart skips a beat.

When they turn to stare at the entrance as if someone important had just marched in, and then quickly disperse, pretending to busily wipe tables but secretly keeping one eye out, I shift in my chair to see who it is. I should have known. It's my husband. He's red in the face and appears unusually dishevelled with his unwashed hair and creased shirt. His lips twitch at the corners when he sees me and his erect shoulders drop in relief.

Sweating profusely, he hurries over to join us at our table and slumps exhausted onto a chair. The faintest smell of floral perfume catches in my nose and, suspicious as ever, I feel myself scowling.

Connor chirrups brightly, 'Hello, Nathan,' and gives him a sticky grin.

Though he doesn't look at my child, Nathan has the decency to acknowledge him, 'Hi, Connor.' It's a start. He's not ignoring him at least.

To me, he asks irritably, 'Why aren't you answering my messages?'

I shrug, 'Isn't it obvious?'

Nathan appears wounded as if he can sense my growing indifference to him. His face is etched with anxiety, and he looks like he is about to cry.

'Have you heard the news?' he comes straight to the point.

I shake my head, shooting him a warning look that reminds him there are little ones present. 'No, what is it?

'It's Bartosz,' he announces abruptly, raking his fingers through his hair.

Fear lights up my eyes as I stammer, 'What about him?'

Nathan shakes his head, a flicker of panic in his gaze. It's a universally accepted gesture that implies, "He didn't make it".

'Oh, my God,' I exclaim in horror, covering my mouth with both hands. I sensed something was wrong the moment Nathan sat down but I never imagined this. We exchange grim expressions, and I allow my gaze to stray to the waiters who appear to be watching my reaction. I guess then that they already knew about Bartosz and that's what the whispering was about.

'How?' I stammer, shocked to my core.

When Nathan murmurs, 'Either a coconut fell and hit him on his head or someone bashed his brains out,' he doesn't meet my eye.

I let out an agonising groan, 'Oh, no,' feeling the familiar sting of loss. 'Poor Angelika. She must be going out of her mind.' I hesitate before continuing, 'Do you think I should go and see her?'

'No,' Nathan growls, shifting uncomfortably in his seat. In a softer tone, he says, 'I don't think it's a good idea. The police are questioning her.'

'Why?' I gasp, incredulous. 'They can't think that she had anything to do with his death, surely?'

'They were seen arguing on the beach yesterday morning and, apparently, blows were exchanged,' shrugs Nathan.

'Never. I find that hard to believe. They seemed so in love.'

Glancing down at his joined hands, Nathan gulps and states the obvious, 'Yes, well, looks can be deceiving.'

I feel like a bitch when I probe, 'What was the row about?' because I wouldn't be a bit surprised if it had something to do with my husband. Whenever I think of Angelika and Nathan together, I feel a prickle of jealousy at the back of my neck and have to force the unwelcome emotion away.

He admits with a guilty-looking shrug, 'I don't know. Nobody does.'

'Is there any chance it had something to do with the incident involving you and his brother?' I ask cynically.

'I doubt it. That was years ago.'

'Try telling that to Bartosz,' I exclaim bitterly. Nathan narrows his eyes at me then, as if to caution me to keep my voice down. I don't heed the warning, and cry even louder, 'Oh no, we can't, can we? Because like everyone else around here, he's dead.'

Everyone stares at me then, including Connor, and I start crying. They must think me callous to come out with such a thing, and maybe I am.

From across the table, appearing like he wants to comfort me, Nathan whispers, 'Take some deep breaths, Sam. You've had a shock. We all have.'

I nod tearfully, but when he reaches for my hand to give it a reassuring squeeze, I yank it away. It no longer pains me to see hurt in his eyes.

He licks his parched, cracked lips and declares urgently, 'I think we should leave this island.'

'You mean run away?' I ask in astonishment. A sick feeling of dread rolls around in my stomach as I try to work out what he's up to. Nathan isn't a quitter. He's never run away from anything in his life, except for his last two wives. The penny suddenly drops. 'Where were you last night?'

'Me?' He puffs out his chest, offended. However, I get the feeling from his blank expression that he's keeping something from me as usual.

'Who else?' I sarcastically murmur, unimpressed.

With a pang of regret, he confesses, 'I got wasted on arak and slept it off on the beach.'

'All night?' I raise an eyebrow.

'All night,' he nods curtly.

It does sound plausible, so perhaps he is telling the truth. We'll have to wait and see. The jury is out on that one, as they say.

'You don't have an alibi, then for last night?'

With his arms folded across his chest, he boasts, 'I don't need one.'

As Kadek loudly bursts into the room, accompanied by a pair of uniformed police officers who march two steps behind in perfect synchronisation, I impulsively grab my husband's hand and gaze devotedly into his eyes. I can see that Nathan is surprised by my unexpected rush of affection but we really don't want the detective to see us fighting in public, as Angelika and Bartosz did. We cannot afford to make the same mistake. Even if it is fake, we must put on a show of love and support, otherwise we could fall under suspicion ourselves.

CHAPTER 53: TIMOTHY

It's midmorning as I saunter from the jetty towards the hotel, turning to wave appreciatively at the boat driver, calling, 'Thanks, mate,' but rather than wave back, he stares curiously at me, before shaking his head in irritation. Unlike last night, when I was alone in the dark, afraid someone was going to stab me, today people surround me. However, they are going in the opposite direction . . . towards the dozen or so taxi speedboats that are bobbing around in the water, each with a smiling driver on board. There seems to be a mass departure of guests and hotel employees from the island, including the Australian couple who are barrelling towards me, loaded down with suitcases.

'What's up? Where's everybody going?' I ask.

They make it clear they don't want to be delayed but are too polite to just walk on by, so they pause reluctantly to speak to me. The man seems to shrink before me as he says, 'We're leaving. There's been another death.'

I pull a suitably horrified face, but before I can get a word in the woman adds tearfully, 'The poor man had his head bashed in.'

I drag my eyes away from her unconsolable stare and, for a split second I glimpse a dark silhouette at the end of the jetty. Murmuring an abrupt, 'Our boat is waiting,' the couple moves around me and scurries towards their boat, not caring that items of clothing are spilling out of their hastily packed suitcases. Now that they are no longer blocking my view, I search for the stranger's menacing shadow again, but all I see is Kadek. He flashes me a toothy grin in greeting, and I groan inwardly when I realise that he is waiting for me. Even though I knew to expect this, my heart is thumping wildly inside my chest — as if a herd of beasts were stampeding over it — but I manage to keep my composure as I stroll casually towards him. Not too fast. Not too slow.

'Mr Taylor-Davies,' exclaims Kadek, pumping my hand in an overly friendly fashion as if he were pleased to see me. But I can tell this isn't the cordial conversation he is making it out to be when I see the two uniformed police officers standing behind him with hard, bullet-like eyes.

'Shall we go for a walk and a chat?' Kadek suggests, leading the way.

Despite his small stature, I can't match his quick pace, and I catch myself fearfully glancing over my shoulder at the policemen pursuing us, whose hands rest warily on their gun belts. There's no mistaking their dark, unsmiling eyes mean business.

'Why are your men armed? I haven't seen them carrying guns before.' I observe worriedly, biting down on my cut lip and wincing.

Kadek looks at me questioningly, giving me the benefit of his golden gaze. 'We've never had a murder on the island before.'

Wide-eyed, I gulp hard before responding. 'Murder? So the Australian couple were right when they said somebody had their head bashed in.'

'Aren't you going to ask who?' Kadek scowls, trying to trip me up.

I'm ready for him though. Last night I was drunk and out for revenge. I had royally screwed up and I kick myself once again for my sloppiness. It won't happen again. 'That was going to be my next question,' I tell Kadek confidently, perhaps a bit too arrogantly, as he's now glaring at me with something like disapproval.

'This way,' he cuts me down to size by insisting on taking me towards the pool area, which I notice is cordoned off and under police guard.

Kadek abruptly stops, and the two policemen behind us nearly collide into him in a style reminiscent of a comical Keystone cops sketch. He then looks down at the ground, which has an unsettling yellow outline of a body drawn on it, and thoughtfully rubs his chin. Very Columbo-like.

'Does the name Bartosz Dabrowski mean anything to you?' Kadek poses the question while pointing to the horrific murder scene as though the body were still there. *Thank Goodness it's no*t. I can't even bring myself to look at the blood stains and bits of splintered bone on the concrete.

'Angelika's husband?' I give a sharp gasp, unable to look Kadek in the eye. 'Yes, of course. We are all friends. Are you implying that he was the one who was murdered?'

'Unfortunately, yes,' Kadek nods with the solemnity of an undertaker.

'Wait. You said that this was the first murder on the island. Does that mean you've decided Putu's death was an accident after all? And that Jonah's death was . . .' I can't say the word out loud and look to Kadek to help me out.

Kadek nods, appearing uneasy, 'A suicide, yes, I'm afraid so.'

I murmur incoherently, 'I still find that hard to believe,' as tears well up in my eyes.

Kadek informs me, 'We're interviewing all the hotel staff and guests again to ascertain alibis,' while fixing his scorching-brown glare on me.

'There don't appear to be that many left,' I observe with a cynical shrug.

Kadek points out smugly, 'Naturally, those that are of no interest to us have been allowed to leave,' which makes me want to slap him. *Is he implying that I am a person of interest, or that I am not allowed to leave?*

'Naturally,' I reply cuttingly, becoming increasingly uncomfortable with Kadek's intense gaze. It seems like he's waiting for me to fall to my knees any second, confess to murdering Bartosz, and beg for forgiveness all at the same time. We both know that's not going to happen.

'And I am at your service anytime you wish to speak to me,' I offer grandly — *I might as well have bowed* — adding, 'But would it be okay if we picked this up after I've taken a shower, changed into clean clothes and spoken to my son? As you can see, I've been out all night and have only just returned.'

And there you have it — my alibi — right there.

CHAPTER 54: ANGELIKA

'Would you say you're a difficult woman to get along with, Mrs Dabrowski?' Kadek wants to know. He is facing away from me, staring out of the balcony doors at the blue sea, and although I think he squares his shoulders at the sound of my name, I may have imagined it.

'No,' I protest, with hot tears streaming down my face, 'Ask anyone.'

'Oh, I have.' He turns to look at me, his eyes rolling cynically. 'And I must say, I've received a mixed response from the other hotel guests.'

I cross my arms defensively across my body and purse my lips stubbornly, 'Do tell.'

'How about we do this sitting down?' he suggests, gesturing to the plush white sofa that Bartosz used to enjoy sprawling on. My poor Bartosz. I can't believe he's gone. And in such a way. The victim of a brutal, unprovoked murder. Because of what he did to Noah, the only person that comes to mind who may have wanted to hurt Bartosz is Jonah, but he's already deceased. The police now suspect me. His wife.

Reluctantly, I do as I'm told, collapsing onto the sofa, and shoving one of my dead husband's missing socks aside.

Kadek comes to join me. He's afforded me the comfort of conducting this interview in our, *my* hotel suite, given how distraught I've been since learning about my husband's death. After Bartosz hit me on the beach, I might not have seen a way forward for us, but that didn't mean I wanted him dead, or that I no longer loved him. The reverse was true, and my heart is breaking.

Kadek is watching me as I bow my head and take several deep breaths.

'May I proceed?' he prompts, not unkindly.

I wipe away my tears and nod. My face stretches in surprise when he comes out with—

'You were seen flirting with another woman's husband at the cultural dinner a few nights ago.'

I recoil at his words and burst out indignantly, 'The opposite is true. Nathan was the one flirting with me. He was at it all night.'

Kadek replies hesitantly, which is out of character for him, 'I see.'

'But I don't think you do,' I comment darkly. 'Why on earth would I want to kill my husband?'

'Hmm,' he ponders, rolling the word around on his tongue as if he were only now giving this some thought. That's when I realise that he is playing with me. I'm immediately on my guard. *What does he think he knows?*

'What's that supposed to mean?' I bark.

Ignoring me, he continues, 'Yesterday morning on the beach, you were also observed arguing with your husband.'

'I bet it was that bloody nosey Australian couple who told you that,' I snap, drumming my fingers on the glossy surface of the coffee table.

Eyes lowered for once, instead of blazing with certainty, Kadek mumbles, 'I also heard that he hit you.'

Upon hearing this, my hand immediately flutters to my cheek. *That slap was the last time my husband ever touched me*, I realise brokenly.

226

When I don't respond, Kadek probes, 'What was the argument about?'

I spring to my feet, wailing, 'It was nothing. Just a typical argument between newlyweds getting to know each other,' I lie.

Kadek glances at his notepad, but when he smirks at me as if he had just scored a goal, I realise he's not fooled. He proves it by pointing out, 'It says here that you lived together for three years before getting married.'

'Things change when you're married due to the pressure,' I argue. 'People who've been together years often break up after marriage.'

'And did you change?' he wonders.

'No,' I sigh and shake my head. 'Bartosz did.'

Kadek frowns, 'In what way?'

I glance moodily out of the glass doors, catching a glimpse of the coconut tree tops in the distance. I will never be able to look at another coconut again without picturing the horrifying scene of Bartosz having his brain smashed in. The poor bastard. What a way for him to go!

'He said the island was getting to him,' I murmur tearfully, recalling his last words. "I'm sorry, okay. It's this place. It's getting to me."

For a moment Kadek doesn't speak, and then he is on his feet, nodding silently. 'Some know this resort as Black Magic Island.'

'You don't say?' I scoff bitterly, giving him a menacing look that makes him back away from me. 'And somebody thought it would be a good idea to turn it into a honeymoon resort. How many bodies has it racked up so far? Three, if you include my husband. And I'm curious as to how many more there will be as the police continue to waste everyone's time questioning his widow.'

The force of my yelling has me stumbling forward, and Kadek is forced to save me. A sob lodges in my throat as he holds my arms and tells me, 'Stay calm, Mrs Dabrowski. You are causing yourself unnecessary distress.'

'Unnecessary distress!' I shriek hysterically as I push his hands away. 'Is that what you call it?' Wave upon wave of grief pours out of me in anguished howls.

Unable to look me in the eye, Kadek shamefacedly bows his head and implores, 'Please sit down and have a glass of water. If you like, we can take a short break.'

I look at him through my tears. Although he's obviously uncomfortable dealing with an emotional woman he's not a bad person. I believe he means to be compassionate, but as a translator, I should know better than anyone else that words uttered in a second language frequently lose their meaning.

'No,' I shake my head firmly. 'I want to get this over with.'

'Perhaps if we can establish an alibi for you for last night, we can let you get some rest?' Kadek prompts, sharing a worried look with the uniformed policeman standing by the door as if he's now fearful of saying the wrong thing. Given my situation, they won't want to be accused of being heartless.

'If that's all you want from me, why didn't you say so? I can't believe your colleague failed to mention it.'

'What colleague?' Kadek asks, baffled, as he exchanges another cautious glance with the policeman at the door who refuses to look at me.

'The one who let himself into the room this morning checking to see if anyone was inside and alerted us to the discovery of another body.' *Duh. Isn't it obvious?*

Incredulous, he queries, 'Us? Were you with someone?'

'Someone other than my husband, yes,' I hang my head in shame.

The words are dragged out of the darkest, saddest part of me as I'm forced to admit. 'I'm sorry to disappoint you, detective, but I do have an alibi. I was with Nathan Price. We spent the entire night together.'

'But you can't have,' Kadek fumbles his words as he flicks through the pages of his notebook to check something, 'Because we've already interviewed him, and he said he was alone on the beach all night.'

'The fucking liar. I'll kill him,' I seethe.

CHAPTER 55: SAMANTHA

So much for all the promises of five-star luxury in paradise. Since all of the restaurants are now closed, we can only order from a limited menu through room service. The butler, who was supposed to be on duty around the clock, left for the mainland yesterday along with the majority of staff. After another death and further talk of vengeful demons, they deserted us, leaving us to fend for ourselves. The hotel's main areas, including the pool, are off-limits to guests — not that anyone would want to go there after what happened. When it became known that all of the boats had disappeared this morning, Nathan's hopes of escaping the island also vanished. I have no intention of leaving. Not as long as Connor remains on the island.

Because of the ongoing murder investigation, there is a continual police presence. Even though I have done nothing wrong, I still feel like I'm being watched all the time. I know the police are simply doing their job and I hope they get their man or woman. I feel bad for Angelika, who I don't believe for one moment harmed Bartosz, but from what I've heard, she's staying in her room and refusing to see anyone. It's been two days since Bartosz died and with only forty-nine civilians remaining on this island, they still don't have a suspect in custody. You could argue that my husband is the closest thing they've got since he is the only other person without an alibi for the night Bartosz was killed, but the bar staff claims he was too inebriated to have overpowered someone as young and healthy as Bartosz. To the best of my knowledge, the police are unaware of the men's past or that Nathan was responsible for the death of Bartosz's brother.

After losing Jonah, Timothy has undergone a transformation. Not only has his physical appearance deteriorated, but so has his attitude. He suddenly has a darkness about him that I never would have thought possible. As might be expected following a recent bereavement, he seems quiet and melancholic, but I worry that there is more to it than that. He talks only of murder and death, and he comes across as obsessed and paranoid, claiming a "dark and menacing stranger" is pursuing him. It's hardly surprising that a lively little boy like Connor dislikes spending time with his adoptive father when he's like that. Timothy is done fighting and doesn't object to Connor spending most of his time with me. I suspect he prefers being by himself so he can brood as much as he wants.

This means that before we have to travel home, I get to spend five more days with Connor — or even longer if the police force us to stay. I've taken Connor paddling in the sea to make the most of our time together, and to divert his mind from Jonah. We can't keep ourselves cooped up in our room all the time since it's unhealthy for a young boy like him. And we are perfectly safe given that the island is crawling with cops. As for my husband, he comes and goes as he pleases. He periodically asks about Connor, and we are courteous to each other, but other than that, it seems like we have already parted ways. I won't lie, I find this upsetting, but every time I think back to what he said about my son, my heart gets harder.

When Connor suddenly exclaims, 'It's Nathan,' and pulls his hand away from mine to sprint in his direction, I feel myself freeze.

This section of the beach is truly stunning. Its jagged jungle-lined cliffs drop down to magnificent turquoise waters that form a curved bay, where Nathan is fishing from the shore. He waves and stoops to speak to Connor.

Since our argument, we have maintained a chilly demeanour towards each other, but today Nathan seems warmer and more approachable. He is actually smiling as I get closer to him, making me suspicious.

'Where did you get that?' I motion grumpily to the enormous fishing rod that he has to hold in both hands due to its height.

'One of the locals must have left it behind. I thought if I could catch a fish, I could barbecue it for supper.'

'Very Robinson Crusoe,' I scowl.

'Want a go?' he offers.

I wince and shake my head, then giggle as Connor joyfully leaps up and down while begging, 'Me. Me.'

'Come on, then,' Nathan gives in and gently moves Connor into the proper position so that the rod is between his little legs. Of course, he's too small to hold it by himself. Nathan has to do that for him.

I watch them with self-pitying tears welling up in my eyes. All I've ever wanted is a family of my own. I don't care much for status or money, which are things my husband cherishes above all else. We were never a good fit, I realise bitterly, and I was naive to think I could make our marriage work. We never stood a chance. Any more than Jonah and Timothy. Or Angelika and Bartosz. Perhaps the locals *are* right, and this island *is* cursed.

'I was hoping we could give it another go,' Nathan mumbles self-consciously while shooting me a questioning look.

'Give what another go?' I shrug, confused.

'Us,' he says, his cheek lifting into a mischievous grin.

As my back goes up, I hiss, 'Are you serious, after what you said?'

He hangs his head. 'I've had time to reflect on things since then.'

'Since when do you reflect on anything?' I bristle.

'All I'm saying is, give me another chance, Sam . . . please. I don't want to lose you. I know I don't say it anywhere near enough, but I do love you.'

Warily narrowing my eyes, not daring to think I heard him correctly, I demand, 'And Connor?'

Nathan affectionately tousles Connor's hair, admitting. 'The kid's kind of grown on me.'

'Are you saying what I think you're saying?' I splutter.

'Without you, there's only me. And I can't stand me,' he chuckles dirtily, reminding me of the clown I married. I can't help but smile back at him.

Up until a few minutes ago, I thought there were two people in this world who were preventing me from getting my son back. Nathan was one of them. But if he means what he says about being a father to Connor and is genuinely on my side, then . . . that only leaves Timothy.

CHAPTER 56: TIMOTHY

There is a bonfire smell in the air and the horizon glows orange as I walk barefoot in the sand towards the fire on the beach. What first caught my attention was the crackling of flames and the creaking and groaning of wood. As I strike a match and light a cigarette, I can't help but wonder who built the fire. Fascinated, I inhale greedily on the toxic fumes of tobacco and then toss the still-burning match into the leaping flames. It's been five years since I quit smoking, and I feel like me again. It's good to be back.

As I stare moodily at the burning pile of wood, I wonder if it has any significance to what is going on. Maybe an SOS to a neighbouring island? I've been thinking a lot about Putu tonight and debating whether Kadek was right about his death being an accident. But if so, why would Jonah confess to killing him? Except Kadek doesn't know that. It could all be part of a police cover-up. Anything to disguise the fact that honeymooners are being killed because, without tourism, this island wouldn't survive.

Not my problem, of course. My problem is getting up the nerve to tell Samantha that Connor and I are leaving early tomorrow. According to my solicitor, the police can request me to stay, but I can refuse, so they cannot prohibit me from leaving. I'm not under arrest and haven't been charged with anything. Once again, I will be leaving Bali under a cloud of doubt.

Although having to say goodbye to Connor will break Samantha's heart, it's for the best. She's becoming increasingly attached. This afternoon, when I spent an hour with Connor — under strict supervision, of course — it was an even more tense encounter than normal. Nathan compensated with corny jokes and an invitation to a barbecue. He bragged about catching an enormous tuna fish and told me he intended to cook it tonight. I turned the invite down, saying I was waiting on an important call. I was able to have five minutes alone with Connor before I left, and when I told him about my plans, his small face lit up with excitement. He's always loved horses.

For context, I had already taken the anticipated call by this point but didn't want to mention it to Samantha. It has been two years since I have spoken to my father. I never forgave him after he cheated on my mother when she was dying, and I've refused to have anything to do with him or his new wife since. But now that he's offering me a lifeline, beggars can't be choosers and I'm in no position to refuse. Call it guilt money if you like, but Dad is wealthy and can afford it. Back home in Ireland, he is a well-known racehorse trainer. Of course, he was saddened to learn of Jonah's passing and has pledged to handle everything on my behalf.

True to his word, he has already booked our flights and transferred a sizeable amount of money into my bank account. Even now, he is arranging for Jonah's body to be flown home once the coroner releases it. He says he can't wait to meet Connor and has insisted that we take a flight to Ireland before returning home, in order to reunite as a family. "Will Ruth be there?" I had asked petulantly, still the troubled teenager that I was, to which he had sighed and said, 'Of course, she's my wife.' Acceptance is difficult at any age, but I am ready to swallow my pride. Not only are we getting off this hateful island tomorrow, but good old Dad has assured me that I won't have to sell my house, which is the only home Connor has ever known. He says I might as well have my inheritance now rather than later. That's when I started crying and told him I loved him for the first time in my life. I could actually be happy if it weren't for leaving Jonah behind.

A rare breeze strokes the back of my neck, prickling my skin. That's when I start to feel as though someone is watching me, and the sound of footsteps behind me increases my dread. Expecting a figure to emerge from the shadows, fear flutters at the back of my mind and my mouth suddenly feels dry with nerves. I whirl around and mumble, 'Who's there?'

But, as before, there is no one there. I still haven't recovered from the previous time this happened, when I ran back to the hotel shitting my pants in fear and came across Bartosz by the pool. Feeling enraged, I acted impulsively, striking violent blows down on his head until the coconut split in two. The poor bastard never stood a chance. I now regret my drunken act of revenge. But at the time I believed I was doing it for Jonah.

Angrily, I shout, 'I know you're there. Why don't you come out, or are you a coward?'

A man's voice cries out, 'It isn't me that's the coward. It's you.'

'In that case, why don't you show yourself,' I scream, aware on some unconscious level that his accent gives him away as being an islander.

I can't even begin to describe how scared I am when he emerges slowly from the shadows and walks towards me, grinning unconvincingly. This makes him seem even more sinister.

'So, I take it you're the one who's been following me?' I stammer, as my eyes sweep his face, searching for clues. *Who is he?*

'I am Made,' he states simply, bowing in greeting.

My face puckers into a frown as I ask, 'Is that supposed to mean something to me?' But even as I say this, something in my memory stirs. I smooth a hand over my hair and risk a quick look in his direction. He's small and slight, even for an islander, and he's young, most likely only in his early twenties. He has a headdress on and is bare-chested, as if he's about to go into battle. When our eyes lock, I am the first to look away.

'Only if you want it to,' he replies in a deliberately vague tone.

I realise with sudden clarity that I do know him. 'You're one of the speed boat drivers. You've driven me to and from this island numerous times.'

He torments me by saying, 'You may have left the island on the night the Polish man was killed, but you came back twice. Once in the early hours of the morning and again, much later when the police were waiting for you. I know this because I was the one who brought you back both times. I helped you onto the jetty, remember when you were too drunk to stand.'

Saliva flies from my mouth as I demand, 'Who are you?'

'I told you; I am Made. And I saw what you did,' he hisses venomously.

Panicking, I take my wallet out of my pocket and begin to count notes in my hand. Gulping nervously, I insist on knowing, 'What do you want? How much money? Name your price.' I can feel my freedom slipping away from me, so I'm willing to give him anything he wants. No matter what he knows, I refuse to go to prison. I have a son to raise.

He moves quickly, like a ghost, to knock the notes out of my grasp. 'I don't want your money. It's revenge for my brother and niece that I seek.'

'Your brother and niece?' I'm momentarily stunned so I rack my brains. *Think, man. Think.* I eventually figure it out. Made is a name I vaguely recognise. 'Do you mean Putu?' I ask incredulously.

'And Ni Luh,' he growls, his eyes shining menacingly.

'I remember you now. You were just a boy when I knew you.'

He juts out his chin to proudly inform me, 'And now I am a man, and the Gods have sent me to punish you.'

'If that's the case, why didn't you kill me on the boat two nights ago when I was drunk and couldn't defend myself?'

'Because there is no honour in such a killing,' he replies coolly.

I raise my eyebrows and fold my arms before saying sarcastically, 'What makes you think you can take me? I'm twice your size and in case you haven't noticed, I'm sober this evening.'

'This,' he chuckles softly as he draws a severe looking dagger from his waistband and runs his finger along its ragged blade.

CHAPTER 57: ANGELIKA

My tone is harsh and confusing — it has every right to be — when I confront Sam at her hotel door. 'Don't act as though he's not here,' I warn. Although her eyes swirl with instant panic she cautiously invites me inside.

'Where is Nathan?' I give a caustic bark.

She points silently to the folding glass doors, and I give a resolute nod before making my way over to them. Rightly or wrongly, I believe Nathan is to blame for everything. If I hadn't slept with him, Bartosz would still be alive. *Oh, my God, I hate Nathan almost as much as I do myself.* He not only stitched me up good and proper with the police, but he got me so wasted I ended up cheating on my husband.

'What's wrong, Angelika?' Sam trips along after me, no doubt wanting to alert her arsehole of a husband to the fact that they have an unwanted visitor. He must have known I wouldn't keep my mouth shut for ever. Admittedly, it's taken me twenty-four hours to pluck up the courage to barge my way in here but that's because I didn't want to hurt Sam. I understand now that this was unavoidable, and she may thank me for it in the future.

I ignore her and walk outside to see the pool has been lit up in fibreoptic colours. Summer anthems play in the background and scented candles and fairy lights adorn their gorgeous jungle garden. However, I want to throw up because of the overpowering coconut scent. Fury erupts in my chest when I see Nathan playing happy families with Connor, without an apparent care in the world. He has his back to me and is barbecuing a large fish.

'You,' I jab an angry finger at his spineless backbone.

Turning around, his face flushes as he blusters unconvincingly, 'Angelika, we weren't expecting you. How are you?'

My voice wavers uncontrollably as I give an impatient toss of the head, 'You lied to the police about your alibi, and I bet you lied to Sam too.'

Nathan projects an air of self-righteous innocence, mumbling, 'I'm afraid I don't know what you mean.'

'I might have known you'd say that,' I seethe, turning to confront Sam. 'He always was a good liar even before he made his money, back when he went by the name of Damian and was little more than a two-bit crook.'

Sam wrings her hands nervously and looks from me to her husband, unsure who to believe. 'What is she talking about, Nathan?' she implores.

'I don't know, love. It's the grief talking. She's clearly not herself after what happened to Bartosz.'

On hearing my dead husband's name, I burst into tears, but my voice continues to crackle with rage as I cry, 'For fuck sake, Nathan, man up and tell your wife the truth for once.'

When he purses his lips together and refuses to answer, I heave a frustrated sigh, 'Your husband and I knew each other long before we came to this island. In fact, we fucked many times, isn't that right, Nathan?'

'Sam, don't listen to her,' Nathan warns, 'She's a troublemaker and always has been.'

'So you did know each other before?' Sam whispers brokenly.

'Aren't you going to tell her what you were really doing, and who you were doing it to, on the night Bartosz died?' I scold bitterly.

'You're a lying little slut,' Nathan explodes, shocking everyone in the room and frightening Connor who cowers wide-eyed beside him. In the silence that follows, Connor scurries over to Sam and she puts her arms around him in a protective manner, while angrily narrowing her eyes at Nathan. There is a glimmer of resolve in her gaze as she asks, 'So, he wasn't alone on the beach that night? He was with you?'

'I'm so sorry, Sam, but he had it coming,' I whimper, my shoulders heaving with grief as I bend my head in shame and nod regretfully.

With eyes as wild as a deer, she looks at me silently for a moment and then says with considerable dignity, 'Please go.'

Five minutes later, I'm trudging along the sandy shore with tears streaming down my face. I want nothing more than to collapse upon one of the sand dunes, rest my head in my hands, and sob uncontrollably. So when I hear two male voices arguing, my head snaps up in irritation. Then, my curiosity takes over and I move stealthily to take a closer look. The men are pursuing each other around a small bonfire whose flames are dying out. A pungent fragrance of male sweat permeates the air, as they kick up sand around them. Every time I hear a testosterone-fuelled grunt or a sharp intake of breath, I make myself smaller to avoid being noticed.

In the darkness, I see that one of the men is tall, and the other is small. Sometimes I can hear the smack of a hand hitting flesh, another time, the crunch of knuckle on bone as they battle it out. I try not to think about the moment when Bartosz struck me across the cheek or the sting it left behind.

I flinch when a Balinese voice cries out triumphantly, 'That's for Ni Luh,' and as a sliver of silver sparkles in the moonlight I realise the smaller man is holding a knife and is jabbing it at his opponent. In fear, my hand instinctively flutters to my mouth. I ask myself, *am I in any danger?* And then I kick myself for being such an idiot and coming out here by myself when everybody knows there is a murderer at large.

A body sinks onto the smooth sand with a dull thud. It descends gradually, as though it isn't in a rush. I want so badly to run away, but I'm too scared to move in case the person wielding the knife chases after me. It could be me next.

'And Putu, my brother,' the smaller man hisses, bending over the larger one and spitting on him. I may not be able to see his face, but he sounds as angry and vengeful as any of the Gods the islanders whisper about.

The larger man, whose accent I recognise as being Irish, writhes in agony on the ground and clutches at his chest as he moans, 'I never touched him. You've got to believe me.'

'Even if that's true, you have blood on your hands. You killed my niece, and I saw you beat the Polish man to death with my own eyes.'

My ears prick up at that. Suddenly, all of my body's nerve endings are firing with adrenaline. What have I stumbled upon? Am I hearing right? Is the smaller man referring to Bartosz? If so, does that mean his murderer is thrashing on the ground in front of me, pleading for mercy? A sick feeling of dread rolls around in my stomach as I try to figure out what's going on.

When everything goes quiet, I realise the smaller man has disappeared. My eyes are puffy and wet from crying, and I have to strain to see properly, but I reluctantly emerge from my hiding place in the inky blackness and move closer to the body on the ground. The man's face is illuminated by the fading firelight. When I see who it is, I stifle a scream.

'Angelika, is that you?' Blood spurts from Timothy's mouth as he chokes on what he is saying. He tries to sit up zombie-like only to slump back on the ground, giving up. It's while he clutches at his chest, gasping for air, that I notice the dagger sticking out from under his rib cage.

'Thank God you're here. You have to help me,' he mumbles weakly, glancing down at the knife in complete dread. I stare at its carved, sandalwood handle, hypnotised. The blade itself hasn't been inserted all the way in which suggests that the attacker wanted his victim to suffer a long, agonising death. Timothy looks at me incredulously when I do nothing. Panicking, he stammers urgently, unable to bear my silence any longer, 'I think my lung is punctured. If you don't do something, I'll die.'

He shudders in relief when I kneel next to him and remove his sticky hand from the knife, which he has been clutching to stem the bleeding. As our flesh touches, electricity crackles across the air. He watches helplessly as I place both of my hands over the knife's handle and unintentionally press lightly on the wound. He flails about in agony as a result, screaming, 'You mustn't pull the knife out. If you do, I could bleed to death.'

I nod to assure him I understand. He seems to settle then. But when I whisper, 'This is for Bartosz,' in his ear, his entire body stiffens up like a corpse. As realisation dawns in his terrified eyes, I plunge the knife in as deep as it will go before he can scream again. As I do, I feel the knife piercing through layers of bone and flesh all the way up to my palm.

CHAPTER 58: SAMANTHA

Hearing about Timothy's stabbing shook us all terribly, but I was particularly affected because I stood to gain the most from his passing. I became really anxious about this, fearing that if the authorities found out I had been planning to bring Connor back to the UK with me all along, I might be charged with murder as well as kidnapping. Fortunately, Angelika spoke up at the eleventh hour to say that she had witnessed a strange man on the beach near the scene of Timothy's death. She also said that the man appeared to be injured and had blood on him.

After that, the police worked quickly, and within a few hours, they had their suspect in custody. Finally, after a protracted hunt, Kadek has found his killer, whom he holds accountable for every death except Putu's and Jonah's, which he still believes were caused by accidental drowning in the former case and suicide in the latter. Who would have guessed that Putu's younger brother, a native, was the one carrying out the murders? Apparently, he was motivated by a desire for vengeance against the visitors to the island, whom he blamed for his brother's and niece's deaths.

Two days later, we're among the last ones left on the island. But not for long, because I am packing for our flight home tomorrow. I won't be sorry to leave Bali. It isn't the paradise I imagined it would be. Even in Indonesia, it's a small world, where everyone knows someone, and we are all connected without realising it. I believe in karma, just like the islanders do, and it's obvious that the Gods are angry with us and want us gone.

I feel a lump in my throat and have to wipe away a stray tear as I look down at all the swimming suits, sunscreen, paperbacks and flip-flops I've packed neatly in my case, realising that all my dreams about marriage have been dashed. Childishly, I haven't packed Nathan's case as I usually do. After finding out he slept with another woman on our honeymoon, I'm done waiting on him. When I hear the quiet shushing of the door opening onto the carpet behind me, I muster a smile, thinking Connor has come to find me. He rarely leaves my side and avoids Nathan at all costs since the other night when he raged at Angelika and called her a "slut".

I gasp in alarm when I hear Nathan mumble miserably, 'Can we talk?'

'Not again, Nathan. There's nothing left to say,' I answer gloomily.

'Don't leave me, Sam. I haven't got anyone else. Not even the kids are mine.'

I scowl and turn to confront him. 'You should have thought of that before having sex with Angelika.'

'You knew what I was like before you married me,' he replies evasively, gazing at the floor.

'I have Connor to think of now,' I tell him haughtily, 'and he needs positive role models in his life.'

Nathan brightens and exclaims, 'I can be a good role model,' with all the enthusiasm of a schoolboy, seeing this as a challenge.

I give a sarcastic harumph to let him know how much I doubt this.

He grimaces a little and insists stoically, 'I can still fix this.'

At this point, I realise he's like a spoiled child in a sweet shop, desiring everything he's not supposed to have. Me. Angelika. Soon it will be someone else. Ever the showman, he considers everything to be a contest, in which he is the victor. Like the ocean, he draws you in with his magnetism, yet just like the cold unforgiving water, he can also be deadly.

As I ignore him and return to packing, he cries out in desperation, 'It was a huge mistake and I can't tell you how sorry I am.'

I purse my lips and ask through gritted teeth, 'Enough to promise you'll never do it again?'

When he doesn't reply I turn to see that his once-smiling countenance has vanished, and he's scrutinising me as though I were a stranger.

'What?' I ask, rattled.

He clears his throat and shrugs his shoulders, 'Nothing,' before shoving his hands dejectedly in his short pockets.

I throw him a weak, unconvincing smile and remark, 'It doesn't sound like nothing.'

When he tells me bluntly, 'If you're going to be like this, I may as well go out for one last drink,' my face stretches in surprise.

'Seriously, after all that's happened on this island, you're going out drinking?'

'Why not? It's all I've got left,' he mutters self-pityingly.

Anger surges inside me and it is several seconds before I can speak, but when I do my voice turns to thunder, 'People have died.'

'People die all the time,' he responds matter-of-factly, his words slicing right through me.

Wanting to punish him, I attack him with, 'And you'd know all about that after what happened to Bartosz's brother.'

He adopts an ugly expression, as though he is at breaking point, 'And you'd know all about stealing a kid from a dead man,' he sneers. 'You want to hope the police don't find out or you could be in serious trouble.'

'Are you threatening me?' I gasp fearfully, placing a trembling hand against my fluttering heart.

'All I'm saying is you should be nicer to your husband,' he sneers tellingly. Then, as his face returns to normal, he glances casually at his watch before saying in a conversational tone, 'I won't be late.'

I pretend to laugh as I crack a joke, 'I've heard that before,' to his departing back, but he doesn't respond.

Losing the phoney smile, I sink onto the incredibly soft, well-made bed and make a disgruntled sound in my throat. Nathan's jagged words have caused my heart to flip over and a string of vengeful thoughts to go off in my head. He clearly thinks he's got the upper hand. Does that mean he intends to blackmail me? Will my fear of losing my son force me to stay married to him? When Timothy passed away just forty-eight hours ago, I gave thanks to God since it meant one less person was preventing me from keeping my child. And now, the one person who I should be able to depend on — my very own husband — is the one standing in my way.

CHAPTER 59: ANGELIKA

I'm shaking like mad as I answer the door since I woke up late and am worried that I may have missed my flight. I was startled out of my drunken stupor by the loud and insistent rapping, but as soon as my eyes flickered wearily open, my thoughts instantly turned to Bartosz as they always do. I'm told his body will only be released once the inquest is over and that it will arrive home on a much later flight. I hate having to leave him behind but I will lose my mind if I have to spend one more day on this insufferable island. Because of the severe injuries he sustained, I haven't even been able to see his body, let alone have the chance to say goodbye or tell him how sorry I am for what I did. As for the scumbag who killed him, I hope Timothy rots in hell. Forever. Jonah too for what he did to my family and me. I have no regrets when it comes to those two.

After going days without showering I'm ashamed by the unmistakable smell of stale sweat coming off my body as I unlock the door. 'Just a minute,' I yell irritably, praying it's not too late for me to board the 12.30 p.m. flight to London via Dubai. Convinced that it's housekeeping at the door asking me to vacate my room, I'm shocked when I see Kadek on the doorstep, flanked by his two trusted uniformed officers who never speak.

Kadek looks at me icily before formally declaring, 'Mrs Dabrowksi, I have to inform you that you are under arrest for murder.'

I start at his tone, eyes flitting nervously between him and the police officers, before demanding, 'What are you talking about?'

'We will explain down at the station,' Kadek growls, jutting out his chin.

'Why should I go with you when I haven't done anything wrong?' I mumble nervously, lacking conviction . . . because I have done something wrong. Twice. *But he can't know that. Can he?*

'This isn't optional,' Kadek tells me in a firm voice, nodding furtively to his colleagues who immediately leap into action.

I'm not prepared for what happens next. While the first policeman restrains me, the other deftly slams a pair of cold, heavy handcuffs over my slender wrists. It happens so quickly that I'm taken aback.

'There's no need for that.' I argue stubbornly.

'This way,' Kadek orders briskly, turning his back on me and marching down the path, towards a waiting police car.

I am limp with fear as I am propelled forward. 'I've barely got any clothes on,' I stammer, appealing to them with panicked eyes.

'You are dressed in no less clothing than you would be at any other time of the day in this heat,' Kadek points out rationally.

'But how can I be under arrest for murder when you've already caught the killer?' I splutter, stalling for time. *I don't want to get in that car.*

Kadek is standing by the vehicle and is waiting for me to catch up. He says guardedly, as if he were sharing a secret, 'We hadn't expected a fifth murder to happen while our suspect was at the station under lock and key.'

As I feel his cold and detached gaze slide over me, I gulp nervously before asking, 'Did you say a fifth murder?'

'Indeed,' nods Kadek.

My eyes widen in terror as I stare at him questioningly. 'Who was it?'

'Come now, why pretend that you don't know exactly who I'm talking about,' he mutters, narrowing his eyes in an unfriendly fashion.

I literally stomp my foot and cry in a fit of frustration, 'I honestly have no idea who you are talking about.'

'You seem to be forgetting that you told me yourself that you wanted to kill him,' Kadek declares fiercely, attempting to catch me out.

Before I can reply, Kadek climbs into the front passenger seat and I'm bundled into the back of the vehicle. One of the cops is courteous enough to cover my bare limbs with a blanket. Wearing only an oversized T-shirt (one of Bartosz's), my exposed skin burns on the scorching leather seat.

I blink dazedly as I look around the car, as if unsure of how I got there. As it dawns on me who Kadek is talking about, my body tenses and I gasp incredulously, 'Do you mean Nathan?'

Kadek's voice is mocking as he repeats back to me my very own words which the sly bastard must have scribbled down in his notepad, 'Did you or did you not say when questioned, *the fucking liar. I'll kill him*?'

'In my defence, I said that in anger, when I realised Nathan lied about us spending the night together, leaving me without an alibi,' I protest vehemently. Then, as news of Nathan's death sinks in, my eyes fill with angry tears and I ask guiltily, as if it really were my fault, 'How did he die?'

'All in good time,' Kadek tuts disapprovingly, pausing to wave to the hotel reception staff as we drive past the white stone entrance. I keep my head low, not wanting to be seen. Until I see Sam and Connor, that is, getting into a waiting taxi. I try to bang on the window to get her attention, but the policeman prevents me. Sam doesn't have dark circles beneath her eyes as I do, and her cheeks are not pale and sunken like mine. For a newly bereaved widow, she looks more radiant than I've ever seen her.

Realising that not everything is as it seems, but unable yet to pinpoint exactly what is bothering me, my eyes suspiciously track her movements as I exclaim to Kadek, 'Sam will be able to tell you that I didn't do it.'

'On the contrary, Mrs Price was the one who told us about your visit to their hotel suite two nights ago, during which you made threats to her husband which made her worry for his life,' Kadek smugly informs me.

'I did no such thing,' I snap indignantly. 'I gave him a piece of my mind, that's all. He had it coming.'

Glancing back at me through the rearview mirror, Kadek's jaw twitches as he comments drily, 'In that case, why did the body have, *he had it coming*, stamped all over the torso?'

'I don't know,' I whimper tearfully. 'I just know that it's all lies, and I'm being framed. I never threatened Nathan, so it's his liar of a wife you should be talking to, not me.' By now Kadek is no longer listening. No one is.

I put my head in my hands and weep bitterly as I realise how badly I underestimated the woman I thought was my friend. And now, because of her, I could be found guilty of a murder I did not commit while escaping punishment for the two I did. How fucked up is that?

CHAPTER 60: SAMANTHA

One year later

I'm standing in our coastal-style kitchen that overlooks Poole harbour, lovingly preparing my son's packed lunch. The walls are plastered in colourful felt tip drawings of happy homes with happy faces and flower gardens. Connor is starting primary school today; therefore, I want to make sure he has a wholesome nutritious meal. Diced carrot, cucumber slices, a boiled egg, a pot of organic hummus, a handful of grapes and some wholewheat crackers are all packed into his "Little Mermaid" lunchbox. Then there's the glistening green apple on which I've drawn a heart. His adorable little face will light up when he sees that. These days, Connor is a different boy. Timothy and Jonah wouldn't recognise him. He is a well-rounded and popular child among his friends, and his awkwardness has all but vanished.

Naturally, it has been a challenging time, and considering everything we have been through, we are still in the process of healing. Thankfully, the adoption process will be completed in a few more months, which is something to celebrate at last. I was worried for a while that Timothy's father would file for custody but in the end, he recognised that the young-ster was content with me. I have no doubt that things would have turned out differently if Connor had been his biological grandchild. Since Connor currently has no other living rela-tives — that are known to the authorities, that is — I have been identified as the ideal candidate to adopt him because I am a reliable, solvent widow who can provide him with a beautiful home and endless love and attention. In addition, I have looked after him since his parents passed away tragically, and have worked as a nanny before, so I have experience with young children.

After inheriting Nathan's fortune along with the gated five-bedroom family home, yacht and numerous business assets, everything was sold and we moved to our elevated timber loft-style home, which is perched on a hill and has expansive views of the water. It features a lovely walled garden with its own vegetable plot, where I spend most afternoons pottering. Our open-plan living space is so much more me than Nathan's austere newbuild house was and, as a result, I've never been so content. In addition, we live close to several excellent schools, sandy beaches, shops and cafes.

I made sure Cora and her family were left financially secure, but I never let on that Nathan had discovered the chil-dren weren't his before he passed away. Had he not died when he did, she would have been made to suffer unimaginably. I will not pretend that I protected them out of selflessness; I had my own motivations for keeping it a secret. Even if he can't do anything about it from beyond the grave, Nathan would hate to learn that the company he fought so hard for had been sold off at the first opportunity or that his money was being used to raise a son who wasn't his.

I've heard that Angelika has filed another appeal with the Balinese authorities. Hopefully, when her case gets to court, she will be acquitted of the reduced charge of manslaugh-ter she is currently serving time for, so she can return to the UK to be with her beloved dogs. Although she betrayed our friendship by sleeping with my husband — and had to pay the price for it — I do not harbour resentment towards her. I even wish her well. I'm hoping she'll find it in her heart to do the same for me one day.

I find it surprising that her five-year sentence has held up so well considering that the prosecution was unable to produce any proof regarding the source of the illegal local spirit known as Balinese arak or the identity of the person who gave Nathan the fatal beverage. All that is known about how that fateful evening unfolded is that he was seen on the beach with a woman who insisted on him drinking the entire bottle. This led to him becoming inebriated and urinating and defecating on himself. Later, he was discovered dead and the incriminating words, "He had it coming" were stamped in bold black marker on his chest.

It was me, of course, not Angelika, who kneeled beside Nathan in the sand and watched him slowly drink himself to death. And it's true, he did *have it coming*, after what he did. Not only had Nathan threatened to report me to the police for kidnapping if I refused to comply with his demands, but his crime against Bartosz's younger brother will never be forgotten. The only thing I did wrong was to have a son that my husband was unaware of and have him adopted, but Nathan's uncontrollable rage caused the death of an innocent young man and he failed to tell me about it. I could never forgive him for that. Now that Jonah, Timothy and Nathan are no longer with us, nobody can prevent me from legally adopting the son that I gave birth to.

Ah, here he is now — my darling boy — standing in the doorframe and looking questioningly at me, as if wondering what his mum is thinking. Shaking off the dark recollections of the past, I greet him with a smile as he enters the room. In the soft lighting, his red hair moves like flames and he has a distinct toothpaste and citrus shampoo smell that follows him everywhere. I can't help but notice that his royal blue school cardigan matches his eyes.

'You look very handsome, Connor,' I say with admiration.

A grateful smile races across his lips. 'As handsome as my real dad?'

'Of course,' I reply, glancing over to the midnight-blue country dresser that has a treasured nautical seashell picture frame on it.

Connor allows me to kiss him very gently on the top of his head as I murmur into his ear, 'You remind me so much of him.'

When he scowls and complains, 'You'll mess up my hair for school,' I have to force myself to let him go, even though it goes against all of my maternal inclinations. He appears a little tense this morning, but that's to be anticipated. The first day of primary school is a milestone for both of us.

'How do you say his name again?' he asks earnestly, gazing intently at his dad's photo frame. I had previously revealed to him the identity of his true parents but cautioned him that this had to be kept under wraps for the time being. As a child accustomed to secrets, he seemed to accept this.

'Stanislaw,' I mumble softly as I close my eyes to chase away the painful memories that come to mind — of discovering that my boyfriend of six months, who was the love of my life, had disappeared — leaving me pregnant and on my own. I had no means of contacting him, other than his dead cell phone, and as he spent all of his time at mine I didn't even have an address for him. I had no way of knowing he had been killed in a road rage altercation so I did what I felt was the right thing for my son at the time and had him adopted since I was too young and broke to raise a child on my own. I spent years believing the man I loved had abandoned me only to find out years later, in a cruel twist of fate, that I was wrong.

Like I said, *Nathan had it coming . . . and karma can be a bitch.*

Connor is staring up at me through pale eyelashes as he struggles with the word, 'Stan . . . ish . . . laf,' often pronouncing it incorrectly. This is excruciating for me to hear, so to distract my son, I remove a stray hair from his cardigan and straighten his tie. When I offer him an irresistible deal, like maple syrup pancakes for breakfast, his expression brightens.

'Yes,' he exclaims, dancing joyfully, the promise of sugary treats making him completely forget about his father. If only it were that simple for me.

'Off you go and play for five minutes while I get it ready,' I grin and flap a hand at him. As he rushes off to explore his toybox, unearthing item after item, I grab a frying pan from the cupboard and am about to crack open the eggs when my phone vibrates against my leg.

I catch a glimpse of sailing boats bobbing about on the sea as I fish out my phone from my pocket. The sky is a faultless blue. The garden is a riot of colour, much like Connor's drawings that are stuck to the American fridge freezer. I have my son. Life is good. No, strike that . . . Life is amazing.

As I answer the call, I introduce myself as, 'Samantha Wood,' since I've gone back to using my maiden name.

A kind but professional voice enquires, 'Hello, Samantha. I'm calling from Barnardo's Children's Charity, and my name is Stella.'

'Oh, hello,' I respond warmly because throughout the years I have donated to the charity on numerous occasions, out of appreciation for the way they looked after me when I was going through the adoption process.

'How can I help?' I ask vaguely, keeping one eye on my five-year-old who is happily chattering away to himself.

'Are you the same Samantha Wood who used to live at Turlin Moor?'

I frown into the phone, mildly surprised, and say, 'I'm more than happy to make another, even more significant donation, this time around, but I'm afraid this isn't a very convenient moment.'

'I'm not calling about a donation,' Stella corrects me, in a brisk but apologetic tone. Before I can ask her what she is contacting me at eight in the morning for, she murmurs sadly, 'I'm afraid I have some bad news.'

Stumped, I mutter, 'Oh,' concluding that she must have dialled the wrong number as she can't possibly have any bad news to share with me.

'It's about your son,' she says cautiously.

Who I am looking at right now — I want to tell her — but I remain silent, eager to get the call over with so I can get back to my morning.

'There's no pleasant way of doing this over the phone,' she pauses again, and this time I want to scream at her to, "Get on with it", only to want to take my words back when she explains in the most compassionate way possible, 'I'm afraid I'm ringing to notify you that he has died.'

'What?' I cry out, shocked. 'That can't be right. You've obviously made a mistake,' I point out angrily, wanting more than anything to end the call.

'I wish that were true,' whimpers Stella. I can practically feel her squirming down the phone. 'However, I can assure you there is no mistake. Your son, Stanley James Wood, who was born at St Mary's Maternity Hospital in Poole and adopted as Arthur James Kenny, sadly passed away from leukaemia three days ago in hospital.'

This is followed by a long, awful silence, that I think is meant to give me time to process this information, and then Stella continues, this time in a more businesslike tone. 'As your adoption agency, we are not legally required to pass on this information, but Arthur's adoptive parents, Susan and Luke Kenny, wanted his biological parent to know.'

Numbly, I hang up the phone while the woman is still talking, and turn to stare at Connor, who has my red hair, my pale translucent skin and my glittering blue eyes — but, as it turns out, not my blood.

THE END

ACKNOWLEDGEMENTS

I visited the island of Bali in early 2024 armed with my trusty laptop, knowing I intended to set this book there. It really is paradise. I'd love to go back one day and explore the island further. As it is, I travelled extensively, first staying at busy, bustling Ubud, among the rice terraces. While visiting the sacred monkey forest I was attacked and bitten by a monkey (my fault entirely for accidentally standing on a baby monkey's tail) and decided to use this experience in the book. I still have the scar!

I then spent a few days glamping in Menjangan before moving on to Candidasa. My last destination was the white sandy beaches of Sanur, stopping at temples, waterfalls, twin lakes, and bathing in the holy springs on the way. The sunrise trek up Mount Batur was interesting, as like Sam in the book, I suffer from a fear of heights and was terrified I might fall.

The food though is just amazing, especially for vegans like me. The people, mostly Hindu and Buddhist, are kind-natured and heavily into karma. Every day they leave offerings for the Gods and tourists are advised not to tread on them or interfere with them as this is seen as disrespectful.

The dedication at the front of this novel refers to my beautiful sister Karen and wonderful brother-in-law Graham, who have been happily married for forty-six years. Writing about newlyweds and honeymoons meant I just couldn't resist celebrating their partnership. It goes without saying that I wish them many more years to come. Love you, big sis.

The idea for *The Honeymoon* was a slow reveal, but before I knew it the secrets were piling up, along with the bodies. Much of the content came as a surprise. It was as if the characters wrote it themselves. I've never written a book from three perspectives before, so at first, I was apprehensive but as the characters developed, so did my confidence. The couples in this book were not exactly squeaky clean, but as their creator, I felt some were more principled than others. I knew from the start that there could only be one survivor . . . Sam. But like the others, she too had to pay the price for her crimes. And what a price! I hope you enjoyed going along for the twisted ride with this cast of complicated characters.

I would like to say a massive thank you to everyone at Joffe Books for all their hard work in getting this story ready for publication. They have been an absolute pleasure to work with. Go Team Joffe. As always, special thanks go to Kate Lyall Grant, Joffe's publishing director.

If you are not from the UK, please excuse the English spelling. Oopsie- daisy, it's just the way we do things across the pond. Apologies also for any swearing but this is down to the characters and has nothing to do with me. Lol. The same goes for any blaspheming.

Now for the best bit where I get to thank my lovely readers for all their support, especially all the bloggers and reviewers. You know who you are!

Your loyalty and friendship mean everything. As do your reviews. ☺

THE JOFFE BOOKS STORY

We began in 2014 when Jasper agreed to publish his mum's much-rejected romance novel and it became a bestseller.

Since then we've grown into the largest independent publisher in the UK. We're extremely proud to publish some of the very best writers in the world, including Joy Ellis, Faith Martin, Caro Ramsay, Helen Forrester, Simon Brett and Robert Goddard. Everyone at Joffe Books loves reading and we never forget that it all begins with the magic of an author telling a story.

We are proud to publish talented first-time authors, as well as established writers whose books we love introducing to a new generation of readers.

We won Trade Publisher of the Year at the Independent Publishing Awards in 2023 and Best Publisher Award in 2024 at the People's Book Prize. We have been shortlisted for Independent Publisher of the Year at the British Book Awards for the last five years, and were shortlisted for the Diversity and Inclusivity Award at the 2022 Independent Publishing Awards. In 2023 we were shortlisted for Publisher of the Year at the RNA Industry Awards, and in 2024 we were shortlisted at the CWA Daggers for the Best Crime and Mystery Publisher.

We built this company with your help, and we love to hear from you, so please email us about absolutely anything bookish at feedback@joffebooks.com.

If you want to receive free books every Friday and hear about all our new releases, join our mailing list here: www.joffebooks.com/freebooks.

And when you tell your friends about us, just remember: it's pronounced Joffe as in coffee or toffee!